"WHAT'S THAT?" BENNIS SAID.

She was rising off her seat, leaning forward, her palms flat against the table and her arms straining to stretch just a little longer, just a little farther. The tone of her voice had been so shocked, Gregor found himself rising too, turning toward the cash register again, confused and alarmed.

The woman had moved away from the cash register, toward the center of the room. She was there now, alone, her head thrown back, the sound coming out of her throat a cross between a gurgle and a scream. Her chin had been stripped of skin and left raw and bloody. Something seemed to be eating into the front of her dress and the skin of her neck.

Gregor Demarkian felt as if he were being shot from a cannon.

"Dear sweet Jesus Christ," he said as he headed across the floor. "Lye."

QUOTH THE RAVEN

by
JANE HADDAM

BANTAM BOOKS
NEW YORK • TORONTO • LONDON • SYDNEY • AUCKLAND

QUOTH THE RAVEN
A Bantam Crime Line Book / October 1991

ISBN 0-553-29255-2

Published simultaneously in the United States and Canada

Bantam Books are published by Bantam Books, a division of Bantam
Doubleday Dell Publishing Group, Inc. Its trademark, consisting of
the words "Bantam Books" and the portrayal of a rooster, is
Registered in U.S. Patent and Trademark Office and in other
countries. Marca Registrada. Bantam Books, 666 Fifth Avenue, New
York, New York 10103.

PRINTED IN THE UNITED STATES OF AMERICA

RAD   0 9 8 7 6 5 4 3 2 1

This book is for

WILLIAM NICHOLAS DE ANDREA
(1926–1990)

who gave me the title.

Among other things.

QUOTH THE RAVEN

Prologue

Tuesday, October 29

Once upon a midnight dreary,
    while I pondered, weak and weary
Over many a quaint and curious
    volume of forgotten lore—

—E. A. Poe

The invitation to teach philosophy for one semester at Independence College came to Father Tibor Kasparian on the fifth of July. It came out of nowhere, with no advance warning. It descended into nowhere just as quickly, buried in that pile of papers and magazines Tibor thought of as his "things to do that will never get done." Most of the things in that pile were simple nuisances: copies of supermarket tabloids with stories about kidnappings by aliens in them, collected for a paper Tibor half intended to write on popular delusions; letters from women's groups in Armenian parishes across the country, asking him to speak on "living out your Christian faith in a Communist country." The alien kidnappings had begun to depress him. Too many people believed in them because they wanted to believe in them, because they found an irrational universe more appealing than the one the good God had actually made. The women's groups were simply impossible. Tibor had nothing against talking about what had happened to him—he did it all the time, with his best American friend, Gregor Demarkian— but he didn't know how to talk about it without telling the truth, and the truth had a lot of blood in it. He couldn't imagine delivering a sermon on the virtues of genital torture across a sea of melting ice cream, the *pièce de résistance* to a lunch of lemon veal.

The problem with the invitation to teach was somewhat more complicated. In a way, it was a miracle of biblical proportions, an affirmative answer to an impossible prayer. Teaching philosophy was what Tibor Kasparian had once set out to do, before he'd found both Christ and tyranny, before he'd begun to understand what the world was really like. Teaching philosophy was even what he'd been trained for, in the back rooms and root cellars of Yekevan, during that fragmented and dangerous process that substituted for the seminary in the worst days of Soviet rule. Unfortunately, teaching philosophy was also what had first gotten him into so much trouble.

He took the letter out of the mailbox, opened it on the spot, and read it. Then he went upstairs and put it on the pile. Then he came downstairs again and told himself the thing was safely in his study. He didn't have to answer it. He didn't have to see it again. He didn't have to tell anyone it had ever come. Only he knew—and his Anna, who was with God.

Two weeks later, in the middle of an argument about the Articles of Confederation, Tibor Kasparian sent Gregor Demarkian up to the study to find a book. The book was in a stack of books on a shelf behind the desk that held the pile. The letter from Independence College was still on the top of that pile, in spite of the fact that the pile had been added to a dozen times since the letter had come. Gregor Demarkian was by nature and profession a snoop.

Later, Tibor decided he had done it all on purpose. He had wanted to be saved from his fear. Most of all, he had wanted to be relieved of his guilt—the guilt that told him he should not accept this offer, because he and Anna had once plotted to come to America to find a place that would let him teach, because Anna had died in blood before they'd ever gotten started.

Gregor Demarkian came downstairs without the book, but with the letter, waving it in the air as if it were wet.

"You and I," he told Tibor, "are going to have to talk."

2

Now it was the twenty-ninth of October, just days before Halloween, and Tibor was sitting in the high-ceilinged, long-windowed office he had been assigned in Liberty Hall, trying to work out the particulars of a lecture he was supposed to give on the theological foundations of *The Federalist Papers* and their relationship to the Greek Schism. As it turned out, he had not been hired to teach philosophy in the ordinary sense, but to take part in something called an "interdisciplinary program." Like all the rest of the faculty in Liberty Hall—Donegal Steele, Alice Elkinson, Katherine Branch, Kenneth Crockett—he worked exclusively with students "pursuing a major" called The American Idea. He even liked it. American university jargon drove him crazy. American university structure bewildered him completely. Tibor didn't think he'd ever get used to "majors" and "core courses" and "remedial education." Still, this place, Independence College, was a good one. In the two months he had been here, he had been almost perfectly happy.

Except for one thing.

His desk was pushed up against one of the windows looking out of the back of the building, across Minuteman Field to the tall gray upthrust of mottled granite called King George's Scaffold. Back in the fall of 1776, the students at this college had decided to do two things to show their solidarity with the signers of the Declaration of Independence. First they had forced the faculty to change the college's name from Queen Anne's to Independence. (From what Tibor could figure out, force had not been strictly necessary.) Then they had burned the mad old king himself in effigy, against that outcrop of rock. They had gone on burning him every year since, on bonfires that got higher and higher, in effigies that got more and more wild. The effigy Tibor could see—a straw man with clothes from the Drama Department, a head made from a jack-o'-lantern, and a gold foil crown—sat on a gold-painted plywood throne that had been built on stilts so tall the throne's seat was two-thirds of the way up the Scaffold. Around those stilts, for the past month, students had been piling kindling and firewood. Three days ago, the pile had reached the effigy's feet. Today, it reached its knees. By full dark on Halloween—when one of the students would douse the pile with kerosene and throw a match on it, making the whole thing go up like an exploding oil well—the straw man would probably have firewood in his lap.

Tibor looked down at his papers again, then up and out the window again, and sighed. His door was open—he liked visitors—but it was four o'clock in the afternoon. There was nobody in the building but old Miss Maryanne Veer in the office, and Miss Veer wasn't likely to leave her post beside the chairman's desk just to have a talk with him. Tibor wondered if she would leave it once there was a chairman at the desk. The old chairman had been diagnosed with a particularly nasty form of cancer just before the start of the semester, and taken himself off to Houston. The program had been deadlocked over the choice of a new chairman ever since—but that was in the realm of what Tibor thought of as "academic politics," and he preferred to keep out of politics of any kind. He'd had enough of that in his former life.

What he could never get enough of, maybe because it had been nonexistent, even unthinkable, in his early life, were pets. That was what he was really doing here, so very late in the afternoon, when he had a perfectly good suite with a fireplace in Constitution House. Independence College was full of pets, and not just the dogs that faculty kept for company or the cats students kept in their rooms. There was a chipmunk who lived near Minuteman Field and came out to eat from the hands of the students lunching there. There was a family of deer so tame they would allow anyone who offered them salt to pet them. Mostly, there was Lenore, a great black raven who had turned up out of nowhere two years before, checked them all out, and decided to move in. She would fly into open windows—or tap on ones that were closed, asking to be let in—and eat whatever you fed her.

Tibor and Lenore had an understanding, a bargain entered into on the second or third day Tibor had been in this office. Lenore showed up every day except Sunday at four o'clock, and Tibor fed her crumbs from the pastries he brought up from Philadelphia every week after he'd gone down to say the Liturgy in Holy Trinity Church. Lida Arkmanian and Hannah Krekorian—and all the other good

ladies on Cavanaugh Street, grandmotherly or otherwise—
were thoroughly convinced that, in spite of a full college
dining program and a campus snack bar that operated
twenty-four hours a day, he had to be starving.

Tibor didn't wear a watch—every time he tried, the
watch in question went missing—but he could see the clock
face on Declaration Tower, and it said ten minutes after
four. He rapped his fingers against his desk and strained to
see as far across the field beyond his window as was
possible. For some reason, Lenore wasn't going to come to
him today, and that was worrisome.

What was even more worrisome was the fact that he
was sitting here, minute after minute, putting himself in
danger of being burst in on by the one faculty member
likely to turn up in this building at this time of day: the
Great Doctor Donegal Steele. The Great Doctor Donegal
Steele was the single fly in the otherwise perfect ointment
of Tibor Kasparian's happiness at Independence College.

Actually, the Great Doctor Donegal Steele was the
major fly in the ointment of the happiness of everybody
who had anything to do with Liberty Hall, but because that
knowledge was part of what Tibor called "academic politics," he didn't know it.

He only knew that the Great Doctor Donegal Steele
was an unalloyed, dyed-in-the-wool, world-class son of a
bitch.

3

To Miss Maryanne Veer, Donegal Steele was not a son
of a bitch—Miss Veer didn't even think in words like that;
they were vulgar and immodest, and never once in her
sixty-three years had she ever been tempted to either
sin—but a threat of apocalyptic importance, the trumpet
blast of an approaching Armageddon. Miss Maryanne Veer
had come to Independence College at the age of nineteen,
fresh from a year at the Katherine Gibbs secretarial school
in New York City. Except for the two-week educational
walking tours of European cities she took every July with

her friend Margaret Lorret, that year represented the only significant time Maryanne had ever spent outside this small Pennsylvania valley. First she had lived with her mother, then she had lived alone, then she had let Margaret join her in a small house she had bought at the edge of the campus with the money from her mother's life insurance policy. None of these changes seemed to her to be of the least importance. Miss Veer's life was a seamless garment. Houses came and went, friends and relatives came and went even faster, but The College went on forever. Ever since she had first wandered onto this campus at the age of six, a shy child with a ferocious passion for books being brought up among people who thought all reading was done by radicals and "queers," Miss Veer had known she was going to find her home in it.

Now she looked down at the piles of pink message slips spread out across her desk and sighed. Back then, it had never occurred to her to do the obvious and apply for admission. Half a dozen students in her own high-school graduating class had been taken on as commuters, all tuition paid by the Crockett Memorial Valley Scholarship Fund. Maybe it was the fact that those students had all been from the other side of town, where houses were neat and conscientiously painted and fathers were present and meticulously sober, that had made her believe, unconsciously, that she was not qualified to be among them. Maybe it was just that, in that time and in that place, "secretary" was the job most women were taught to aspire to. Either that, or "teacher." Miss Maryanne Veer had never suffered from the delusion that she had the talent to be a teacher.

Sometimes she wondered if she had the talent to be sixty-three years old. Maybe that was her problem. Under the old rules, she would have been forced to retire in just two years. Now she could stay on until she was seventy, and until the Great Doctor Donegal Steele turned up she had been looking forward to that. She had come to The Program—Miss Maryanne Veer always thought in titles and capital letters; The Program was her interior designation for The Interdisciplinary Major in The American Idea—at its inception, years ago. Since then, through a succession of weak-minded and weakly educated chairmen, she had pretty much run it on her own. She would go on running it on her own, too, as long as the Great Doctor Donegal Steele didn't get himself installed in the chairman's office.

She heard a squawk in her ear, and realized with some embarrassment that she still had the phone wedged up there, and that Margaret was still on the line. When Margaret started talking, she also started blithering. When Margaret started blithering, Maryanne tuned her out. It was a simple matter of self-defense. If Maryanne had listened to everything Margaret said, she'd have gone crazy in a week.

Once, back in 1975, when the college employee educational program was first started, Maryanne had taken a course in introductory psychology. Most of it she had considered criminal nonsense. Part of it she now had to admit the truth of. She and Margaret were the quintessential example of what that course had called The Female Couple: Margaret "feminine" and dependent to the point of ludicrousness; Maryanne herself rigid and rational to the point of caricature. The only thing the course had got wrong was the bit about sex. Miss Veer couldn't imagine having sex with Margaret. Miss Veer couldn't imagine having sex with anybody.

She adjusted the telephone receiver and said, "Margaret? I'm sorry, Margaret. I got distracted."

"Did you put me on hold?"

"Only mentally. I've got a desk full of message slips here."

"I know, dear. You're very busy. I ought to get off the line. But I think what I was saying had a lot of merit in it. Don't you?"

Because Maryanne hadn't heard a word Margaret had said beyond "hello," she grunted. Margaret would take the hint.

Margaret did. "I don't think you're giving enough weight to the seniority business, Maryanne. I really don't. After all, Dr. Steele has only been at the college since the start of the semester—"

"Dr. Steele came in as a full professor. Tenured. The administration likes him, Margaret."

"I know they do, dear, but—"

"And he wrote that book." Miss Veer made a face, and then wondered why she'd done it. There was nobody here to see her. "That book," she said slowly, "has sold six hundred thousand copies. In hardcover."

"*The Literacy Enigma.* Yes, Maryanne, I know. But you said yourself it wasn't very scholarly."

"It's famous," Miss Veer said patiently. "He's famous. Famous authors attract students. And with a dwindling student candidate population—"

"Yes, yes, Maryanne. I understand that. You explained it all yesterday. But I don't see how you can leave the seniority out of it. I mean, the college really doesn't know a thing about this man. And look at what's happened now. He's disappeared. He isn't reliable."

"He hasn't disappeared, Margaret."

"Well, what would you call it? He didn't show up for his ten o'clock class. You told me that yourself. And he hasn't shown up since. Have you tried calling him at home?"

"Of course I have."

"And was he there?"

"No, Margaret, he wasn't. If he had been, I wouldn't be fretting about these messages. But—"

"I think he's run off for the day with one of those students of his. You've told me again and again how awful he is about women. He's probably locked away in a motel room somewhere, doing—well, doing God knows what."

Miss Maryanne Veer sometimes read an off-campus, student-generated publication called *The Hedonist,* meant to be a contribution to "the alternative press." She corrected the grammar in it—which took a lot of work—but she also paid attention to the things it said. By now, although she would never have admitted it to anyone, she knew exactly what was implied by "God knows what."

Still.

She looked down at the message slips again and shook her head. The door to the office was open, as it always was.

Only the chairman's inner sanctum was kept private and shut. Anything she said could be heard outside in the hall—assuming there was anybody out there to listen to it.

Maryanne picked up the message slips she had written out to the Great Doctor Donegal Steele, looked through them, and found the three she wanted. They had come in at three-hour intervals over the course of the day, becoming increasingly hysterical. They were all from a girl named Chessey Flint.

That was the problem with Margaret's analysis of this little glitch in the life of the Great Doctor Donegal Steele. If he was going to be camped out in a motel room with anybody today, it was going to be with Chessey Flint. His only other interest at the moment was in Dr. Alice Elkinson, and that was entirely unrequited. Maryanne knew for sure.

She dumped the message slips back on the desk and said, "I have to get off the phone, Margaret. I still have a hundred things to do before I can come home."

"Of course," Margaret said. "You just get busy. We can talk about all this later."

"We'll talk about it over dinner."

"I'm making Yankee pot roast for dinner, dear. I know it's not your absolute favorite thing, but I had to do something with the meat. I just know it's not a good thing to leave meat for too long in a freezer."

The meat had been in the freezer for less than a week, and Maryanne hated Yankee pot roast. It didn't matter. Margaret had already hung up.

Maryanne hung up, too, and then sat for a while looking at those message slips. Then she got up and put them in the Great Doctor Donegal Steele's departmental mailbox.

At the back of her mind, a warning light was blinking on and off, telling her that something was very wrong here. Whatever else Dr. Donegal Steele might be, he was not the type to miss his classes or fail to show up for his appointments. He was not the kind to drop out of sight without phoning the office at least three times to make his presence felt. He was positively addicted to having an audience.

If it had been Ken Crockett or Alice Elkinson who had

started behaving like this, Miss Maryanne Veer would not have been worried.

As it was, she could think of only one thing: Wherever that slimy little fool had gone, she hoped to God he stayed there.

4

There was a phosphorescent cardboard skeleton hanging from the center of the archway between the foyer of Lexington House and its front utility hall, and Chessey Flint, coming out of the public phone room at the hall's front end, ran into it. She backed up, looked the skeleton up and down, and shook her head. She was a tall, solid girl in the best midwestern style, with honey blond hair that had been groomed to look fluid while never straying out of place. She had two tiny diamond studs fastened into her single-pierced ears and a twenty-four-carat gold heart-shaped locket on a twenty-four-carat gold chain around her neck. Her jeans were from Gloria Vanderbilt, and pressed. Her 100 percent cotton broadcloth, pink-and-white striped, stiff-collared shirt was from Brooks Brothers, but could not be buttoned down. Her sweater was from Marissa Christina. She looked as if she had already become the woman she had trained herself so long to be: the pretty wife of a solidly successful, upwardly mobile Battle Creek executive; the mistress of a modern ranch house with a steel-reinforced foundation and all the necessary appliances; the mother of two adored and adoring children, ages six and eight. There were people who would have called Chessey Flint a caricature, but she knew she was anything but. Her very-much-older sister had gone off to Wellesley and caught the Feminist Bug. The results had been just as disastrous as Chessey's mother had predicted they'd be. So far, Madeline had an MBA, four promotions, and two ex-husbands to her credit. As far as Chessey could see, Madeline led a life just a little less miserable than that of their oldest sister, Caroline, who had gone to Berkeley and been bitten by the Hippie Bug. Caroline lived alone in a three-room apartment in Santa Barbara with the child she had borne out of wedlock to who-knew-which of the scruffy young men she was constantly taking to her bed, and called home often for money. By the time she was eight years old, Chessey Flint had established the two great truths of her world: It was hard to get enough money to live nicely and it was harder still to put together a marriage that would stay with you and not leave you both poor and alone. From that time to this, she had been driven not by complacency, but by fear.

Now she brushed past the skeleton, walked into the foyer, and looked over the projects going on there. Lexington House was decorating for Halloween, getting ready for the open-house party they would give after the bonfire, preparing for their part in the parade that would wind through the campus in the early morning hours of All Saints' Day. Chessey was not only a genuinely nice girl, she was a good organizer. She would have made an excellent president for the kind of sorority more interested in who they could take in than who they could keep out. Because sororities, fraternities, and private clubs of every kind were barred from the Independence campus, she had become the unofficial head of Lexington House instead. It helped that Lexington House was the single dorm on campus assigned exclusively to women.

She stopped at a knot of girls sewing orange-and-black striped pumpkin costumes for the party servers, then at a knot making papier-mâché bats to hang over the front door. The first group was being led by a fat girl with too many pimples on her face, the second by an anemic-looking child who always looked just about ready to cry. At any other time, Chessey would have stopped next to both of them and trumpeted words of encouragement. She was very good about that kind of thing, and compulsive about it when she thought she saw a girl in need. Today, however, she couldn't seem to work up the energy.

She drifted through the foyer, smiling vaguely, and into the sitting room on the other side, which was crammed with people. Evie Westerman, her best friend, was stuffed into an ancient club chair in the far corner, sitting cross-legged and writing things down on a stack of papers that had to be a good inch thick. The stack of papers was attached to a brown wooden clipboard, because Evie never went anywhere without a brown wooden clipboard.

Chessey crossed the room, smiling at a few more people along the way, and sat herself down under Evie's feet. Evie put the clipboard down and stared at her.

"Well?" she said.

Chessey shrugged. The room was so crowded, there was so much danger of being overheard, that she didn't really want to talk about it. Unfortunately, with all this craziness going on for Halloween, she wasn't going to get another chance.

Chessey fingered her locket and said, "No luck. I've been trying and trying, all day, for both of them. They've . . . disappeared."

"Jack was supposed to go climbing this morning with Dr. Crockett," Evie said. "Maybe they're still climbing."

"After ten hours?" Chessey shook her head. "It's not the Himalayas out there, for God's sake, Evie. It's just a lot of rocks. And Jack isn't the one I'm worried about."

"No?"

"Jack has a lot of responsibilities," Chessey said vaguely. "He's head of the Bonfire Committee. He's President of the Student Council. The bonfire's less than forty-eight hours away. He could be anywhere."

"Right."

Chessey looked down at the fourth finger of her left hand, where, as yet, there was nothing. Only six weeks ago, she had confidently expected Jack Carroll to put something there at the beginning of the coming spring term. Most of the time, she still did expect it. Other times, she was uneasy. Things had gotten so strange lately.

Chessey looked back up at Evie and said, "The thing is, it doesn't make sense. Dr. Steele missing, I mean. He never does things like that."

"He's a maniac. Maniacs will do anything."

"I know, but he's not that kind of maniac. He's an egotist. He likes—performing. He gets the biggest charge out of standing up in class and talking silliness for an hour and making us all write it down as notes."

"Did he really say he'd mark down anyone he caught not taking notes?"

"First day of the course." Chessey made a face.

"If I were you, I'd have dropped that course, graduation or no graduation. If you're going to marry Jack, you don't have to graduate anyway."

"Jack hasn't even asked me."

"He will."

"And if he does ask me," Chessey plowed on, "what will I tell my children? That I was a college drop-out? How will I get them to finish their educations?"

"How are you going to explain to them that you flunked out of school? You know what's going to happen, Chessey. Come the end of the term, Steele is going to hand you an ultimatum. You're either going to give him your virginity on a silver platter, or you're going to fail that course."

"If he does that, I can go to the Faculty Senate about it."

"At which point, all you'll have to do is prove it." Evie looked exasperated. "Drop the course, Chessey. Make it up next fall at Michigan while Jack is doing law school. Even if you hold out in the end and let him fail you, he's doing you a lot of damage in the meantime."

"Jack doesn't believe any of that stuff."

"Everybody else does. You know that old cat in the office thinks you're spending your free time in half the rent-by-the-hour motels in eastern Pennsylvania."

"*Evie.*"

Evie shrugged. "If you're not going to listen to reason, I can't help you. And please try to remember it's not just my reason you're listening to. It's Jack's."

"I know." Chessey stood up. She had come to Evie to "talk it all out," fully expecting to be made to feel better. Instead, she felt worse. It hardly seemed fair. "I just wish I knew where they were," she said, "Jack and Dr. Steele both. I wish I knew what they were doing."

"Unless you know something I don't know, they're not

doing it together. Lighten up, Chessey. Go pat Susan Ledovic on the head. She's dying for your attention."

"Mmm," Chessey said. Evie had gone back to her clipboard, and Chessey could see Susan Ledovic, the fat girl with the pimples, ripping out a seam with the thread in her teeth. Evie was right. It was time to stop fretting over what she could do nothing about, and go back to being the Perfect College Coed instead.

What nagged at her, though, was that she did know something Evie didn't know. She knew that Jack had intended to see Dr. Steele today, and have it out once and for all.

5

Dr. Katherine Branch sometimes wondered what would have happened to her if she had been brought up in another time, or another country. When she was a child, she had read a roomful of books on Great Women Pioneers—Elizabeth Blackwell, Maria Mitchell, Elizabeth Cady Stanton, Marie Curie—but she had known immediately that she was nothing like them. Stuck in a situation that offered her any kind of real resistance, she would yield. By the time she was seven, she had yielded on a number of important issues, including Leggings, Lavelieres, and Sean Cassidy. If she found the strength to defy her hyperconventional, hypercritical, chillingly emotionless mother, it was only because she was desperate not to defy that small group of girls who represented Everything That Mattered at John F. Kennedy Memorial Elementary. Katherine Branch had always had a very fine eye for distinctions of status and a consuming passion of shame at the fact that she had been born worthy of belonging to none of the first-class categories offered for her inspection. She had figured out early that Women Didn't Count, and that all the things women did—nursing, teaching, raising a family—were irretrievably second-rate. She had figured out even earlier that, among women, being pretty was not enough, unless you had something else to back it up. Katherine had always been pretty enough, but the other things—wit, maybe, or that school-skewed form of intelligence that is so important in grades K–6—eluded her. She was a fairly attractive, moderately bright, nondescriptly pleasant child of the early sixties. From the day she started kindergarten to the day she graduated from high school, she was destined to fade into the woodwork.

At the moment, she looked like anything but part of the woodwork. Her red hair fell down over her back in a cascade of body-permed curls. Her bright orange sweater, chosen deliberately for shock and contrast, reached nearly to her knees, not quite hiding the black stretch pants she was wearing under it. Also under the sweater was a bright white, 100 percent cotton turtleneck, meant to save the skin of her chest from the scratch of ramie and wool. Ever since Katherine Branch had committed herself to wearing only natural fibers, she had had a great deal of trouble with chafing and rash.

She caught sight of her reflection in the side of her toaster, made a face at it, and walked on past, to that small stretch of her cramped kitchen counter where she kept the instant coffee. Behind her, at the tiny round table, Vivi Wollman was sitting over a plate of Betty Crocker carrot cake and staring out the square kitchen window at the quad. Vivi Wollman was Katherine's best friend at Independence College and the only other person who really hated the fuss that got made around her about Halloween. Vivi had even been an ally in Katherine's one attempt to put a stop to it all, that year that Katherine had called the Pennsylvania EPA and reported the bonfire as a "pollution hazard." Unfortunately, that foray into common sense and political correctness hadn't turned out the way Katherine expected. The bonfire was so famous, people simply couldn't think rationally about it. The Governor had issued a proclamation blocking the EPA's attempt to shut the bonfire down, the state legislature had passed a special law to allow Independence College to go on making bonfires until the final blast of Gabriel's trumpet, and someone had sneaked her name out of the EPA's files and given it to the press. It was a good thing she'd already had tenure, because if she hadn't she would never have gotten it. For the next year, with the exception of Vivi, not a single person spoke to her—except to call her a bitch.

Katherine got the jar of instant coffee, took a couple of spoons out of the rack next to the sink, and headed back to the table. Because there was no way to avoid looking out the window at the quad, she was faced for a few seconds with a sight that grated on her nerves: dozens of students, dressed up in ridiculous costumes, milling around among the greenery and playing seduction games. Katherine wondered if Alice Elkinson was out there, showing off her engagement ring, acting like a teenager instead of a woman old enough to know the score. Then she sat down.

"Crap," she said, to the air rather than to Vivi. "I'm so rattled I can't think straight. Do you have a cigarette?"

Vivi reached into her pocket and brought out a pack of Marlboro menthols. She was a small woman, dark and attractive enough except for the fact that she was oddly lumpy. A decade of weight-training and macrobiotic diets had twisted her out of shape. She got a blue Bic lighter from her other pocket and lit Katherine's cigarette.

"I think you're jumping the gun," she said. "I mean, I think you're panicking before you have to. After all, nothing has happened yet."

"A lot has happened," Katherine said. "This time last year, there was a Women's Studies Department. This time this year, there isn't."

Vivi brushed this away. "That was our fault, not some plot on the part of the administration. We didn't go about it right. At Berkeley—"

"This is *not* Berkeley."

"I know it's not Berkeley," Vivi said patiently. "My point is, if you're going to keep a department like Women's Studies alive these days, you've got to have the numbers. You've got to have your classrooms full. The way to do that is with sex and spirituality—you know, self-actualization courses. Instead, we had all that stuff about women's historiography and the sociology of housework in the Middle Ages, all this linear-logic, male-dominated crap—"

"*Vivi.*" Katherine took a great drag on her cigarette,

blew smoke into the air, and sighed. Sometimes, talking to Vivi gave her a headache. "The Faculty Senate would never have put up with the kind of thing you're talking about. They barely put up with my witchcraft course and you know it. They're so hyped on academic rigor."

"They're so hyped on male supremacy," Vivi corrected. "We should have sidestepped them, Katherine. We should have offered a course like 'Images of Women in the Art of the Renaissance' and then done what we wanted with it. Talked about birth control in the sixteenth century. Run some consciousness-raising sessions. The word would have gotten around after a while."

"Mary Gillman tried that two years ago," Katherine pointed out. "She got fired."

Vivi got that long-suffering look on her face, usually reserved for men. "Mary Gillman got fired because that stupid girl accused her of sexual harassment, and then the parents threatened to sue. That isn't the point. The point is, I don't see how all this ties in with Donegal Steele."

Katherine looked at the tip of her cigarette, a red coal burning into the filter. She took the saucer out from under her cup and stubbed the butt out in it. "All right," she said, "let's do this as a sequence. Have you read Steele's book?"

"Oh, yes."

"Then you must know he isn't a friend of ours. He thinks all the minority studies departments ought to be run off campus on a rail—I'm sorry. I'm making a mess of this. Anyway, he isn't likely to be a big supporter of what we want to do."

"What we *have* to do," Vivi corrected.

"We'll get to that later. The fact is, the administration didn't even think about hiring him until old Yevers got sick, then they went crazy and offered him a ton of money and practically dragged him out here by the heels—don't you ever wonder why he agreed to come?"

"Why shouldn't he?"

"Why should he be bothered?" Katherine said. "He's famous, after all. His book is a best-seller. He has all the money he wants. What are we except an obscure little liberal arts college in an even more obscure part of Pennsylvania?"

Vivi considered this. "We've got the best rated undergraduate major in American Studies in the country. Donegal Steele is a professor of American history."

"He could have been a professor of history at Yale. Or at Harvard, for God's sake—they'll hire anything at Harvard as long as it gets its name in the newspapers. But Vivi, there's one thing he couldn't have gotten, at Harvard or at Yale or anywhere else but here."

"What?"

"Power."

Vivi Wollman threw up her hands. "For God's sake, Katherine, will you listen to yourself? You've gone totally paranoid. Power to do what? You just said yourself this was nothing but an obscure liberal arts college—"

"First the administration forces him down the throats of all the rest of us as Chairman of the Program. Then they boot him upstairs as Dean of Studies. Then he gets to make policy."

"So what?"

Katherine got another cigarette out of Vivi's pack and lit up herself. She felt dizzy, the way she always did when she got scared. The air in front of her eyes looked like patterned mayonnaise.

"Vivi," she said, "listen to me. Tenure is all very well and good, but all it does is ensure that you don't get fired for cause without a hearing. Did you know that?"

Vivi looked confused.

"Back in the seventies," Katherine went on, "when the student population was down and the colleges started losing money and had to cut back on staff, there was a case that went before the AAUP arbitration board. Some small college in Ohio or somewhere cut a third of its faculty jobs and pink-slipped a lot of tenured people as well as nontenured ones. And the AAUP—"

"Had a shit fit," Vivi said confidently.

"Not exactly." Katherine took a deep breath, her hundredth of the morning, her millionth since she'd first worked all this out—and that had been less than four days ago. "The AAUP decided that colleges had to be free to cut departments they could no longer afford to run, and cutting departments makes no sense without firing professors, tenured or not. Vivi, you and I are professors without a department."

Vivi Wollman blanched. "Oh," she said. "*Oh.*"

"Exactly. If Donegal Steele gets what he wants—and he wants the highest administrative post he can lay hands on, trust me, I know the bastard—if he gets what he wants we're both going to be out on our asses in less than a year. And you know what the job market is like."

"But—"

"But nothing." Katherine stood up, grabbed her cup and saucer, and threw them in the sink. The sink was full of dishes she never got around to doing and brightly colored sponges that seemed to appear out of nowhere. She picked up one of the sponges and tore it in half.

"It makes no sense for Donegal Steele to be here if the administration didn't promise him at least a couple of significant promotions. It makes no sense for the administration to promise him a couple of significant promotions if their first concern isn't getting rid of us. We're being ambushed, Vivi. We're being power-lunched right out of existence. If we don't do something to stop it fast, we're going to be up the brown creek without so much as a canoe."

"Oh, *Katherine.*"

Katherine wasn't listening. She had torn the sponge into shreds, and the ache in her head had turned into a ferocious pounding that felt like a jackhammer slamming against the walls of a decompression chamber.

"Oh, Christ," she said, "I wish that nasty two-bit son-of-a-whore was dead."

6

For Ken Crockett, the problem with Dr. Katherine Branch was not that she was a woman, or a feminist, but that she made so much out of being a witch. He knew nobody believed that, but it was true. Even her name was a signal, the name of a woman who had been hanged for witchcraft in Puritan New England—not at Salem, but somewhere else. Ken didn't remember the particulars. Like everyone else at Independence College, he had been treated to Katherine's standard lecture on witchcraft in colonial America. Also like everyone else at Independence College, he hadn't retained the details. Salem was just the tip of the iceberg. Five hundred people were hung as witches in New England between the founding of Plymouth Colony and the American Revolution. Whatever. Alice Elkinson, who knew more about American history than anyone Ken had ever met, said that Katherine's research was not only lousy, but positively creative—but Ken didn't care about that. He did care about his suspicion that Katherine Branch was not Katherine Branch's real name. Unfortunately, he had never been able to prove it.

For Ken Crockett, the problem with Dr. Donegal Steele was entirely different. Ken would have had a hard time putting it into words he was willing to allow anyone else to hear. He had a hard time putting it into words he was willing to allow himself to hear. That was why he kept Steele's book, *The Literacy Enigma*, out on the coffee table in his living room. Seeing it there that way focused him.

At the moment, *The Literacy Enigma* was covered with strips of black and orange crepe paper. The antique breakfront on the other side of the room, which had belonged to Ken's mother, was covered with cardboard masks. The blue-and-green Persian rug Ken had bought in New York was covered with mud. The mess was making the small woman sitting in Ken's mother's blue-patterned wing chair look terribly uncomfortable, and Ken felt very guilty about that. The little woman was named Mrs. Winston Barradyne, and she had been of great help to Ken over the past fifteen years. Mrs. Winston Barradyne was the President—for life, Ken sometimes thought—of the Belleville, Pennsylvania, Historical Society.

"The problem," Mrs. Winston Barradyne was saying, sipping at the cup of tea Ken had brought her while Ken paced around the room, wondering what he dared pick up, with Halloween only two days away and students rushing in and out to get what they needed to go on with their decorating, "is that I don't know what the man *wants*. It's the way I told you on the phone yesterday morning. We're not exactly the National Aeronautics and Space Administration—"

"Meaning you don't have any secrets," Ken said.

"Exactly. Everything we do have is right out there in the files for anyone to see, in the original or on microfiche, depending on the state of the documents. We've always encouraged professors from the college to do their research with us. We've always encouraged scholarly interest in the history of the valley."

"You certainly encouraged mine."

Mrs. Winston Barradyne waved this away. "You're local. I remember how dedicated your mother was to the Historical Society. It's in your genes. But this man—"

"Dr. Donegal Steele," Ken said.

Mrs. Winston Barradyne nodded vaguely, turning her head from left to right to take in the room behind Ken's back. She always did this, and it always made Ken uncomfortable. What was back there, on the breakfront, was the collection of photographs Ken had brought from home after his mother had died. Most of the photographs were of her, stuck into silver frames, showing a progression from her days at Oldfields to the beginning of her last illness. Some of them were of the house where not only Ken, but his mother, his grandmother, and his great-grandmother had all grown up. The house was now on the National Historical Register and in limbo. No decision could be made about what to do with it until the intricacies of Ken's mother's will were cleared up. Ken always felt that Mrs. Winston Barradyne lusted after those pictures, the way he always thought she lusted after his house. President of the Historical Society or not, she lived in a brand-new ranch house in Belleville's only subdivision. Her husband insisted on it.

Ken picked up his hiking boots from the patch of indoor-outdoor carpet he kept for them near the door and held them in his hands, blocking the woman's view of the breakfront. Now she had nothing to look at but the picture of the college hiking club he kept on the coffee table next to Donegal Steele's book.

"This man," Mrs. Winston Barradyne said, "made me very uncomfortable. He seemed to be insinuating something."

"He always does."

"He treated our entire interview as a kind of—clandestine tryst, I suppose you'd have to say. As if we were a pair of counterspies."

"I wouldn't worry too much about that," Ken said. "He's a very strange man."

"I am perfectly aware of the fact that he's a very strange man." Mrs. Winston Barradyne picked up the picture of the hiking club. There were a dozen people in it. Ken was probably the only one she recognized. She put it down again. "Have you read Bernard Oldenston's books on the American Revolution?"

"Of course."

"There's a lot of that sort of thing going on now," she said. "Debunking. Digging up nasty personal scandals of national heroes. Making careers and reputations by blackening the names of the people who founded this country. It's not just the Revolution, either. Have you read Oldenston's book on Abraham Lincoln?"

"No."

"All about how Lincoln was supposed to have hated black people and thought they were stupid," Mrs. Winston Barradyne said. "I wrote Oldenston a letter after I read it, asking what possible difference it could make, even if it were true. It wasn't what Lincoln thought that matters. It was what he did. That's how I feel about Dr. Bernard Oldenston, too. I don't care a fig for what his motives are. What his actions are is reprehensible."

"Donegal Steele is no Bernard Oldenston," Ken said.

"I know. But—" Mrs. Winston Barradyne rubbed at the tweed skirt of her suit. "I was thinking, after the talk I had with him yesterday, that he might be trying to turn himself into a Bernard Oldenston. You see what I mean. Dr. Steele has written this book." She looked down at the book and frowned. "The book has sold a great many copies. Now what?"

"Now," Ken said, "he does his damnedest to make sure that he gets installed as Head of the Program."

"You ought to be installed as Head of the Program."

"Actually, Dr. Elkinson ought to be installed as Head of the Program, but that's neither here nor there. I've been through all the files you've got, Mrs. Barradyne. Even if Donegal Steele is looking for someone's reputation to destroy, he won't find the ammunition to do it with over at the Historical Society. I know for a fact there's nothing like that there."

"You're not worried about what he might be up to?"

"No, of course not."

"You're much too easygoing," Mrs. Winston Barradyne said. "You were like that even as a child. I remember how Lucy used to fret over you, always letting other children take your lunches and never hitting back."

"Funny," Ken said, "in the army, they used to tell me I was a regular savage."

"Oh, the *army*." Mrs. Winston Barradyne stood up. "You *are* much too easygoing, Kenneth, no matter what you like to think. I know you're comfortable the way you are, but you ought to have higher ambitions for yourself. You're a very accomplished young man. You shouldn't let this— this fake take away your chance of promotion."

"I don't need a promotion, Mrs. Barradyne. I've got tenure. And it's like I said. If I had to vote for a new Head of the Program, I'd—"

"Choose Dr. Elkinson," Mrs. Barradyne finished for him. "Yes, I know. I happen to think Dr. Elkinson has more sense than that, though. I don't think she wants to be Head of an academic department her husband is working in."

"I'm not her husband yet."

"But you're going to be," Mrs. Barradyne said. She had moved all the way to the door, walking carefully over the mud and between the scraps of crepe paper. She still looked worried. "I think you ought to sit down and give it some serious thought," she said. "He really was very strange when he came to see me, and he got stranger after he looked through the files. I didn't like the man, Kenneth, and I don't think you should like him either."

"I don't."

"I think you should do something about it for once."

Mrs. Winston Barradyne twisted the knob, and opened the door, and stepped out into the hall. Like Ken's apartment, it was full of crepe paper and cardboard masks.

"Really, Kenneth," she said, "the man is up to no good. I've had two fine, upstanding husbands, and I know shenanigans when I see them."

Then she pulled the door shut and made herself disappear.

On the other side of the room, the window began to bounce and jangle and sing. Ken turned around and found Lenore, pecking at the glass, asking to be let in.

He didn't think he had ever been so frightened in his life.

7

"The real problem with the people around here," Dr. Alice Elkinson said to Dr. Lynn Granger, "isn't that they play academic politics. I took my doctorate at Berkeley. Trust me, I know academic politics. The problem with the people around here is that they're so damn *Federalist* about it."

"That's better than being so damn Marxist about it," Lynn Granger said. She was standing on a chair, trying to be absolutely still, while Alice pinned up the hem of her white muslin ghost's shroud. Alice was in a very bad mood. Originally, she had wanted the women faculty at Constitution House to dress up as witches, but Katherine Branch had had a total fit about it in the Faculty Senate, and that had had to be shelved. The ghosts' shrouds weren't nearly as good, being practically genderless. Alice Elkinson had always been very much at peace with herself about being female. Unlike many of the women she had known in her life, especially in graduate school, she had never for a minute thought less of herself because she was a woman.

She had certainly never wanted to be a man. The idea of walking around in one of these white tents, when she had a body that belonged on the cover of *Cosmopolitan* magazine, made her positively furious.

On the other hand, she did not have a dress style that belonged on the cover of *Cosmopolitan* magazine. At the moment, she was dressed in her customary jeans, turtleneck, and tunic sweater—what she wore whenever she was not actually in class. Students used to seeing Dr. Alice Elkinson walking back and forth in front of a blackboard in three-inch heels and a Diane Chambers dress were always a little startled the first time they showed up for office hours. Alice had a tendency to meet her students while seated cross-legged on top of her desk in Liberty Hall. What with one thing and another—the thick cloud of honey blond hair that was perfectly natural; the finely etched bones of her Raphael face; the fact that she was only thirty-two, already tenured, and the country's leading authority on original intent in the United States Constitution—Alice was something of a legend on the Independence College campus. She was also the only person in the history of the institution who had been granted tenure in under five years.

Now she stabbed the last pin in Lynn Granger's hem and said, "Get that thing off and we'll sew it. It's dowdy as hell, but I don't see what we can do about it at this late date."

"I don't see what we can do about anything." Lynn stepped off the chair and pulled the shroud over her head. "I know you're frustrated, Alice, but I don't understand why you put up with it. You could go anywhere. Why stay here?"

"Why not? Look, I've been all those places you're so depressed you couldn't get a job at. Even if it wasn't for the politics—I don't mean the academic politics, I mean all that crap about being politically correct—what would I have there that I don't have here? The right to tell people at cocktail parties that I teach at Harvard?"

"It would be nice," Lynn Granger said.

"It would be crap. I got my B.A. at Harvard. I ended

up graduating in three years because I couldn't stand the place."

"I got my B.A. at Southern Connecticut State," Lynn Granger said dryly. "I ended up graduating in five years because I flunked my math requirement twice."

"You just got a late start in academics, Lynn. You shouldn't judge yourself on the things you did while you were undergoing adolescent paralysis."

"A lot of people don't seem to go through adolescent paralysis."

"If they don't go through it as adolescents, they go crazy when they're forty."

"Like Donegal Steele?" Lynn said.

Alice Elkinson had put the shroud down on the sewing machine and slid the hem of it carefully under the needle. Now she looked up, caught Lynn Granger's eye, and burst out laughing.

"Oh, Lord," she said. "Donegal Steele."

"Don't you mind it?" Lynn asked her. "The man comes in here, spends all his time trying to take over your life, runs around bad-mouthing you to the administration, puts his hand up your skirt twice a day—"

"Donegal Steele is a lot older than forty."

The sewing machine was making a very odd noise. Alice had turned it on without thinking about it, and now the shroud's hem was caught in the bobbin thread and bunching up. She switched the machine off automatically and began to unravel the mess. The truth was, she did mind about Donegal Steele, she minded very badly, but not in any way she could explain to Lynn Granger. Lynn was a brand-new faculty member, just arrived on campus this term. She had an equally brand-new doctorate under her arm, from Michigan State. Alice didn't think she had ever met anyone who had actually completed a doctorate who was as self-conscious, excruciatingly insecure as Lynn. Alice could have understood it if Lynn's insecurities had centered on her appearance, which was bulgy and a little sad. Lynn's insecurities centered on her intelligence, and that made no sense to Alice at all. A doctorate, even from Michigan State, was a doctorate. Most people didn't have one.

The shroud's hem was unraveled. Alice put it back under the needle.

"What I mind," she said, "isn't so much what Steele's doing to me—I can take care of me. What I mind is what he's doing to Ken."

"What he's doing to Ken is what he's doing to everyone else," Lynn said. "I heard him in the Beer Cellar the other night, ranting and raving about what an unutterable fool Dr. Carraway was. Dr. Carraway was sitting in a booth in the corner with three of his students."

"Well, that's Donegal Steele, all right. But that isn't what I'm worried about. Ken can handle that. It's all this nonsense about being Head of Program."

"Do you think they'd really make Donegal Steele Head of Program?"

"I haven't the faintest idea. But Steele's always pushing it at Ken, you know, hammering away at it. Ken's given his life to this college, for God's sake."

"Ken's not as good an historian as you."

"I think you're wrong, but that's not the point. There's more to being Head of Program than being a good historian. No matter what you think, I'd be a thoroughly lousy Head. Some fool would come into my office, spill his neuroses all over my desk, and I'd decapitate him."

"Decapitate Donegal Steele."

"I've been thinking about biting him hard enough to tear flesh the next time he pinches my ass. Do me a favor, will you? Go out on the porch and get me the hand bleach. This thing seems to be turning grey."

"Hand bleach," Lynn repeated dubiously.

"It's the one in the white bucket."

Lynn tromped off through the kitchen. A moment later, Alice heard her open the back door and go out on the "porch," which was really a balcony. That was when she began to get a little nervous. She kept a lot of things out on that porch. She never worried about them, because nobody ever went there but herself. With the way Lynn felt about her, it would only be natural if Lynn went looking through things she shouldn't touch.

Alice got up off the sewing machine stool, walked

through the kitchen, and came to a halt at the open back door. Lynn was standing in the middle of the porch holding the white plastic bucket of hand bleach. She was frowning down at the other buckets, all blue and all painted over in red with skulls and crossbones.

"Are the skulls and crossbones real?" she asked Alice. "Are those trick-or-treat buckets, or what?"

"No," Alice said. "They're not trick-or-treat buckets."

"What are they?"

Alice rubbed the side of her face with her hand. She didn't like having those buckets on her porch. She didn't like having them anywhere in her life. It bothered the hell out of her that she needed what was in them.

Lynn was still standing out there in the wind, head tilted, curious. Alice cleared her throat.

"What's in them," she said, "is lye."

"Lye," Lynn said in wonderment. "Where did you ever get lye? I didn't think anybody used it anymore."

"They use it in Drāno," Alice said, hesitating. And then, because she'd been dying to tell somebody, she said, "I got it from Donegal Steele."

8

No cars, faculty or otherwise, were allowed onto the campus of Independence College. Members of the college who had cars had to park them in a lot high on a hill to the back of King's Scaffold. Most of the faculty kept cars and complained about the inconvenience. Most students didn't bother to keep cars. Jack Carroll did—a heavily used, religiously cared for, Volkswagen Beetle convertible— because he had a job at the Sunoco station in Belleville three days a week. Freshman year, he had tried getting there by bus. There was excellent bus service to Belleville, paid for by the college, for just such people as Jack Carroll, who had to work. Jack, however, liked to work late for the overtime, and he felt stupid working as a mechanic and not having a car of his own. He'd brought the Beetle up from home at the beginning of his sophomore year and kept it in the lot ever since. Sometimes, he thought about it enough to be grateful that Independence College was as isolated as it was. The Beetle was an antique. Kept at a city school, it would have been dead meat.

Now he shook his head at the tangle of wires under the Beetle's hood, drew his head back into the air, and motioned to Ted Barrows, who had come up to help him, to follow him into the shed. The shed was really a shop, fully equipped. Anyone who knew how to fix his car himself could use the tools in there, or get a friend who knew to use them. Anyone who had to call a garage in Belleville could be assured that it wouldn't need to be towed anywhere for anything less than a junking. It was a small concession on the part of the college, but it was an expensive one. Before he'd made up his mind to go to law school, Jack had thought hard and long about owning his own body shop. Then he'd checked into the costs of equipping one, and decided law school would be cheaper.

Over on King's Scaffold, students dressed up as Frankenstein and Batman were dropping logs down the face against the side of the effigy. Jack was keeping his fingers crossed that they were doing it right. If they weren't, he was going to have to go over there and straighten it out. Sometimes he thought he was nuts. His college education was being pieced together by four scholarships, two loans, and thirty hours a week in a grease pit. His law school education was going to be just as crushed. He didn't have time to be President of Students, which he was. He just couldn't seem to stop himself.

He let himself into the shed and headed for the soldering bench. Someone had been there before him, God only knew when, and left the solderer lying out. The solderer wasn't clean, either. None of these academic types seemed to have the least respect for good tools.

Jack sat down and started to clean up. Ted Barrows came in from outside and stood beside him. Ted was from a very rich family on the Main Line, and he found the things Jack did with metals fascinating.

"So you see," Ted said, continuing the conversation they had started outside, "the whole campus is in an uproar. I mean, the guy's totally disappeared. Just totally. Freddie Murchison says somebody finally went and offed him."

"I think a hell of a hangover finally went and caught up with him," Jack said. "Just look at this crap. I can't believe people do this to tools."

Ted pulled at his scraggly little mustache, the one he'd been trying to grow for three years now. Jack had counted the hairs in it once. There were eight.

"You know," Ted said, "I was in Liberty Hall? The old lady was on the phone to the other old lady and what she was saying was that Steele and Chessey—"

"I know where Chessey is," Jack said.

"Well, I know you know. But let's face it, Jack, he's got practically the whole rest of the college thinking—"

"I *know* what he's got them thinking. For Christ's sake, Ted. What do you think I'm looking for the asshole for?"

"I know you're supposed to be looking for him," Ted said patiently, "what I'm trying to tell you is, the joke around campus right now is that you found him."

"I wish I had."

"Found him and stuffed his teeth down his throat and that's why—"

Jack put the solderer down on the bench. His head hurt. It always did when he had to talk about Donegal Steele, especially about Donegal Steele and what he was doing to Chessey. For Jack Carroll, Chessey Flint was a kind of miracle. She had everything the girls who wouldn't go out with him in high school had had, except the attitude. The girls who wouldn't go out with him in high school had looked at his clothes, and at the tiny house his family had lived in, and at the used car that his father had to drive, and made up their minds right away: Jack Carroll wasn't the kind of boy who was going anywhere. Chessey had looked at all the same things their freshman year, and decided Jack Carroll was the kind of boy who *was*. Add to that Chessey's virginity—which Jack saw less as a miracle than as a crazy, wildly extravagant form of heroism—and the fact that Chessey Flint was in love with him often made Jack Carroll feel as if God had appointed him king of the world. It also went a long way to explaining why he did as much as he did. Without Chessey to show off for, Jack would probably have left extracurricular activities strictly alone.

He plugged the solderer into the wall socket to heat it up—the only way to get hardened solder off the tip—and said, "Look, I saw Steele last night, in the Beer Cellar. He was drinking himself silly, popping beers."

"Popping beers in the Cellar? How did he get away with that?"

"He's the Great Doctor Donegal Steele." Jack shrugged. "It's like that little guy says. Father Tibor Kasparian. Him. The Great Doctor Donegal Steele."

"I don't have Father Kasparian for anything," Ted said. "Everybody tells me he's good."

The solderer was hotter than an electric range burner on high. Jack shook it a little, but the solder wasn't soft enough yet.

"Steele was punching his holes in the bottom of his cans with an ice pick," Jack said. "He must have got it from the bar. Then he'd stand up on a table, tilt his head back, pull the tab—"

"And a can of beer would go down his throat in thirty seconds. I know how to pop beers, Jack."

"I wasn't trying to tell you how to pop beers. I was trying to tell you Steele wasn't making a secret of it. He was standing on tables, for God's sake."

"So?"

"So," Jack said. The solder was finally off. Jack unplugged the solderer. "I was in there with Stevie and Chuck, in the back, and we heard him. He said he was warming up for a challenge."

"A beer can challenge?"

"That's what it sounded like. Christ, Ted, he must have popped five cans of beer while we watched him. Can you imagine what happened to him if he went off and took a challenge?"

"Maybe he cracked up his car somewhere," Ted said. "Maybe he's in a smash somewhere at the side of the road."

"If he was, we'd have heard about it. There aren't that many roads, and the cops around here don't have anything else to do. Don't be an ass. He passed out someplace, that's all. He's probably just coming to."

"With a head the size of a watermelon."

"Trite, but undoubtedly accurate. I just wish I knew who he had the challenge with. I'd just love to get that son of a bitch in a corner when he couldn't fight back. *Chessey* can't fight back."

"I always think what you ought to do is kick him in the head with those climbing shoes of yours," Ted said. "Those cleats would go right through his skull to his brain."

"Right." The solderer was clean. Jack got up and started looking through the boxes on the shelf above his head for something he could use for a speedometer cable.

The problem, as Jack saw it, was this: You could take the boy out of the grease pit, but not the grease pit out of the boy. Most of the time he was an ordinary college kid, polite, civilized, neat. Some of the time, what came up out of the core of him looked a lot more like his brother Dan. His brother Dan had committed his life to stomping butt from the time he reached six feet—when he was twelve—to the time he'd smashed his Ford Falcon into a concrete abutment out on Route 94. He'd had a passion for violence that was like something out of a Freddie movie, and all his friends had had it, too. So did all the guys Jack knew down at the Sunoco station, if they were young enough.

When Jack Carroll's brother had smashed his Ford Falcon into that concrete abutment, he had not only killed himself, but his girlfriend, his best friend, and the twenty-dollar-an-hour whore his best friend had picked up for celebratory purposes in Allentown.

Sometimes, when Jack thought about Donegal Steele, what he saw was Steele's body in that Falcon, crushed and crumpled and covered with blood.

Now he draped the cable he needed over his shoulder and headed for the shed's door.

"Come on," he told Ted Barrows. "Let's not talk about Donegal Steele."

9

At quarter to six, Father Tibor Kasparian gave up. Lenore *had* shown up at his window, finally, but she hadn't stayed long. The raven had been edgy and inconsolable, pecking at his fingers when he tried to give her food. He had gotten her to eat a little pile of pine nuts covered with honey. After that, she hadn't wanted anything. It made Tibor depressed.

A lot of things made Tibor depressed. Once Lenore was gone, his mind drifted back to Donegal Steele. That always made him feel tight, as if he'd been roped around the chest and was now being squeezed. He kept getting a picture of the worst thing he had ever seen Steele do, the definitive act that had defined the Great Doctor's character for him for all time. It had happened at the opening convocation at the beginning of the college year. The faculty had been assembled on stage facing the student body, standing while the school song was sung, and Donegal Steele had raised his arm, swung it sideways, put it down the front of the robe of a young woman in the Department of English, and squeezed. Just like that. In front of hundreds of people. Students. Faculty. God only knew who else. It had all happened so fast, and so decisively, nothing had come of it. When it was over, no one could think of what to do. And the look on Steele's face—Tibor got itchy even thinking about it. The look on Steele's face had had no triumph in it at all. It had been sly and self-satisfied, as if he did that kind of thing all the time, and in much more sensitive circumstances—and as if the fact that he always got away with it signed and sealed the truth of what he had always believed women were.

Meat.

Tibor sighed, and then looked up to see that the clock tower was showing six thirty. He started to stack his books into a pile, starting with the Castleford history of the anti-Federalist papers and ending with the magazine he carried everywhere these last few weeks, the one with the story of the

Long Island murders and Gregor Demarkian's picture in it. Seeing Gregor's face always made him feel better. If he'd had his way, Gregor would have moved up here with him, and brought some of the others: Bennis Hannaford, Donna Moradanyan, Lida Arkmanian. The names from home rolled through Tibor's mind and made him feel pleasantly melancholy. True sadness was either a curse or an opportunity. It could destroy you or make you into a saint. This kind of sadness was a luxury.

He had a green canvas book bag to carry his things in, just like the students did. He put his books inside it and started to put the magazine in there as well. Then he stopped and opened the magazine up again. "America's Premier Private Sleuth Nabs Another One," the subhead said. The picture underneath it made Gregor look half-furious and half-terrified. Tibor smiled a little, closed the magazine, and tucked it in the book bag.

Poor Gregor. He'd always hated publicity, and now he had it all the time. What was he going to do when they wanted to make a TV movie about his life? Tibor was sure someone would want to make a TV movie about Gregor Demarkian's life. That was the sort of thing people did in America.

He went down the empty corridor to the front stairs, then down the front stairs to the wide foyer that led out onto the path to the quad. The bushes that crowded the sides of the great stone building were covered with crepe paper and bats. The paths were covered with students in costume. Tibor wondered what was going on back in Philadelphia, on Cavanaugh Street. He liked all this enthusiasm about Halloween, but it felt a little wrong to him, undernourished somehow, without children. He passed a boy dressed up as the Incredible Hulk and a girl dressed up as Little Red Riding Hood and smiled and nodded to them both. He couldn't tell who they were under all the makeup, but he thought he might as well be pleasant.

At the place where the path curved to join the quad proper, Tibor could see the stretch of Minuteman Field again and the effigy against King's Scaffold. The Scaffold was swarming with people and the pile of logs was higher than ever, but there were neither logs nor kindling in the effigy's lap. Maybe the students had decided they didn't want anything to block their view of good King George in flames.

Tibor turned into the quad and walked slowly toward Constitution House, through the crowds, through the gossamer spiderwebs, through the ambushes of plastic bats and sateen ghosts and rubber balloon jack-o'-lanterns. Someone in one of the quad dorms was playing music on a stereo system through his windows. Tibor recognized the piece as something called "Monster Mash," which both Donna Moradanyan and Bennis Hannaford liked.

"Hey, Father," a boy in a Count Dracula suit said, "you got your costume ready? You coming to the bonfire dressed as Lucifer with a tail?"

"I'm coming to the bonfire dressed as myself," Tibor told him, wishing he knew who the boy was. "I'm too old and too tired to go running around pretending to be the Devil."

"What about your friend, the great detective? Is *he* going to come in costume?"

"I don't think so," Tibor said, and blushed.

"I hope he talks about blood a lot in his lecture," the boy said. "It would be absolutely rad."

Tibor didn't know what it meant to be "absolutely rad," but he didn't have a chance to ask. Everybody on the quad seemed to be dancing to the "Monster Mash" song. A girl in a space helmet and electric pink tights chugged up and nabbed his boy, and they both disappeared.

It was, Tibor thought, just as well. He still felt a little guilty about what he had pulled on Gregor, asking him up here at first just to the Halloween party, to keep him company, and then dumping this lecture on him. Tibor had no idea how Gregor felt about lectures, but he could guess.

The book bag was hurting his shoulder, so he readjusted it. Then he got started again on his way to his temporary home. When he got to the center of the quad he looked up reflexively and saw Lenore above his head, circling and circling, her caws drowned out by the pounding bass of the music around him. Lenore was nearly tame.

She never went circling through the air like that, agitated and angry.

There was something else that was strange, and he didn't like it either. He hadn't seen the Great Doctor Donegal Steele all day. He thought he ought to consider it a blessing—Donegal Steele was probably the first man Tibor had honestly hated since he left the Soviet Union—but he couldn't. There was something so fundamentally wrong about it, it made his flesh crawl.

Lenore and Donegal Steele.

Tibor turned down the path that led to the front door of Constitution House. It would be all right, he told himself, because Gregor was coming. In just two days, Gregor would be on campus and everything would be fine.

When Tibor had Gregor with him, everything always was.

Part One

Wednesday, October 30

While I nodded, nearly napping,
    suddenly there came a tapping,
As of someone gently rapping,
    rapping at my chamber door.

—E. A. Poe

One

1

Like every man who has ever been part of an American police force during the month of October, Gregor Demarkian was ambivalent about Halloween. In principle, he tended to like the idea: a holiday for children, stripped of its religious baggage decades ago, dedicated absolutely to silliness and sweets. On Cavanaugh Street, both the silliness and the sweets were particularly in evidence, because the adults insisted on getting in on the act—not cynically, as the adults had in so many of the cities Gregor had lived in over the course of his career, but with a childlike lack of psychological complication Gregor found astounding. There was Howard Kashinian, the perennial juvenile delinquent of Gregor's grammar-school class and now President and Chief Executive Officer of one of the largest stock brokerages in Philadelphia, standing out on the corner of Cavanaugh and Muswell streets, dressed as a clown. Howard had a brand-new, never used, industrial-size plastic garbage can beside him, filled with Halloween candy that he passed out to anyone who asked. Lots of people asked, too. It was Wednesday, October 30, and the children were out of school in favor of a teachers' meeting. Some of them had put on paper masks and gone to stand around Howard. Some of them had come barefaced, in their inevitable jeans and sweaters. All of them seemed to have brought their mothers. The mothers stood on the fringes of the crowd and munched away on sugar pumpkins and candy corn. Then there was Lida Kazanjian Arkmanian, the Most Beautiful Armenian Girl of Gregor's adolescence, now grandmother to a dozen small children and mistress of an enormous town house at number 48. What Lida was doing was what Lida was always doing these days, cooking. So was Lida's best friend from high school and best friend still on Cavanaugh Street, Hannah Oumoudian Krekorian. There was supposed to be a party in the basement of the church for the smallest children on Halloween night, and Lida and Hannah intended to be ready. Finally, there was old George Tekemanian, aged eighty-six, occupant of the ground-floor floor-through apartment in Gregor's building. The party in the church basement might be for small children, but old George was getting ready for it, too. He was teaching himself to bob for apples. In principle, there was no reason for Gregor to be uneasy about Halloween on Cavanaugh Street. In principle, Cavanaugh Street was an Eden where the serpent had been headed off at the pass.

In practice, standing at the check-out counter in Ohanian's Middle Eastern Food Store while young Mary Ohanian rang up package after package of honey cakes, what Gregor felt was a sense of impending doom. It was a state of mind so melodramatic, it made him uncomfortable all by itself. Surely there was nothing doomlike about Ohanian's. There was a handkerchief ghost hanging from the back of the cash register, but it had a sheepish grin on its cloth face, as if it was embarrassed to be a spook. There was a jack-o'-lantern on the counter, but it was smiling sappily, a harbinger of gushing sentimentality, not of violence and death. It was the same with all the decorations the Ohanians—and everybody else on Cavanaugh Street—had put up. The skeletons looked ashamed to be naked. The witches had the faces of fairy godmothers. The bats were so cuddly cute they might as well have been puppies. There was a vast array of Halloween gear for sale in card shops and drugstores across America, some of it so realistically bloody and meticulously evil it made Gregor, a twenty-year veteran of the Federal Bureau of Investigation, cringe. The people of Cavanaugh Street had chosen only those things that could have fit just as comfortably in a Christmas display.

On her side of the counter, Mary Ohanian was counting up the honey cakes for the second time, a frown crease wrinkled into her forehead, the tip of a front tooth biting into her bottom lip. Mary was a small girl, not yet sixteen and not particularly pretty, but compactly built and con-genitally pleasant. Gregor had gone all through grammar and high school with her father, her mother, and all three of her uncles.

"When Miss Hannaford called, she said you were to get two dozen of these, Mr. Demarkian. You only have twenty-two."

"I know. That's all there were on the shelf."

"We've got some more in the back. I'll get them. I don't think you ought to give Miss Hannaford anything less than she was asking for."

"More would be all right?"

"For Miss Hannaford?" Mary smiled slightly. "Yes, I think more would be all right. Let me get the other two, anyway. It won't take me a minute."

Mary disappeared through the curtain into the back, and Gregor found himself biting back a smile. "Miss Hannaford" was Bennis Day Hannaford, a woman he had met during the conduct of the case he still thought of as his first extracurricular murder. Through a complicated series of made friendships and personal dislocations, she had started to spend a lot of time on Cavanaugh Street, and now spent almost all her time here. To the people who knew her well, she was just Bennis, Bennis the Menace as Father Tibor Kasparian sometimes put it, a young woman with enormous energy, monumental enthusiasm, outrageous generosity, and a limitless capacity for work—but a crazy person, definitely, whose safety had to be guarded as carefully as an idiot child's. To the people who did not know her, and especially to adolescent girls like Mary Ohanian, Bennis was a kind of goddess: not only WASP and Protes-tant, but rich, beautiful, and connected to every famous old money name on the Philadelphia Main Line. Gregor sometimes wondered what people like Mary Ohanian would think if they knew that Bennis woke up every morning of her life, looked in her mirror, and told herself she was getting fat.

Mary Ohanian emerged from the back with two more

packages of honey cakes in her hand and put them on the counter.

"There," she said. "I think you have everything. I wrote it all down."

"So did Bennis," Gregor said, holding up the list she had sent him out with. "Bennis thinks I'd forget to tie my shoelaces if somebody didn't remind me."

"Well," Mary said seriously, "maybe you would, Mr. Demarkian. You do get a little—um—distracted."

"I never get that distracted."

"My father says that when you and he were in high school you came in one day with no shoes on at all. And it was February. He said you were studying for some kind of test and you forgot."

It was true. It had been his senior year, in those days before SATs and routinely rationalized college admissions procedures, and he had been working overtime to get an A in Latin. Without that A in Latin, he had been absolutely sure the University of Pennsylvania would not have him.

Maybe it wasn't only Bennis whose safety had to be guarded as carefully as an idiot child's.

Mary Ohanian had put his honey cakes in a bag, along with the other things Bennis had sent him out to get: three big round loaves of bread; four jars of apple preserves; six small bottles of ground spices; two lemons; a thick brick of halvah. She had used a separate bag for the non-Armenian food, as if she were taking pains to incarnate a not-very-subtle cultural difference. In that bag were Lay's potato chips, Cheese Waffies, barbecue-flavored Pringles, pizza-flavored Combos, Chicken-in-a-Bisket crackers, and God only knew what else. Gregor wondered what it was Bennis thought they needed all this stuff for. Back in his apartment, where she was doing the last of the packing up before they left for Independence College, there were already seven oversize picnic baskets stuffed with food.

Mary rang the last of the mess up on the cash register and said, "It comes to a hundred and two ninety-five. If you don't have that much, you could come back with it after Halloween. Daddy and Mother wouldn't mind."

"I have it," Gregor said. "I stopped at the bank

machine on my way up. I knew it was going to be expensive."

"Do you think Father Tibor eats this kind of food because he was deprived in the Soviet Union? I mean, it's not very healthy."

"I don't think Father Tibor is worried about being healthy."

"I don't, either. It's strange, isn't it, Mr. Demarkian. It's like a whole different way of looking at the world. It's like Father Tibor thinks getting old is something you can't do anything about, and dying is going to happen to you no matter what."

"You don't think dying is going to happen to you no matter what?"

Mary Ohanian looked confused. "Well," she said, "I don't think you ought to think about it that way. I don't think that's healthy."

Gregor had a sudden urge to tell her there was nothing healthier in the world than thinking about "it" that way, that there was no other way on earth to make a life for yourself that made any sense—but he didn't. She was very young, and he knew where the urge was coming from. He was still riding the wave of his ambivalence, and nothing—not even the ludicrousness of Father Tibor Kasparian's taste in food—was going to talk him into a more salutary frame of mind. He got his right arm around the heavy bag, the one full of Armenian food, and his left around the light one.

"If you see Mrs. Arkmanian," he said, "tell her we're leaving at ten o'clock. If she comes in after ten, tell her we'll be up at Independence by eleven thirty."

"Do you want to leave a number she can reach you at?"

"She has Father Tibor's number. Have a good Halloween, Mary."

"Oh, I will," Mary said. "I'm going to dress up as Cinderella, in my sister Evelyn's prom dress from two years ago. I love that dress. It makes me feel pretty enough to have Michael Keaton fall in love with me."

It makes me feel pretty enough to have Michael Keaton fall in love with me.

Right.

There was a fine curtain of gossamer spiderwebs across the top of the store's door. Gregor ducked his head going under it, holding the bags close to his chest, and went out onto Cavanaugh Street, to the carnival that was just a vaguely ethnic version of a state fair. Down on the corner of Cavanaugh and Muswell, Howard Kashinian was doing a handstand, wobbly, threatening to fall over. Two blocks north of that, the Ararat restaurant had replaced its customary sidewalk display—a phalanx of Armenian national flags—with a huge jack-o'-lantern leaf bag stuffed solid. Even his own building was decorated for the season, although in such an incongruous way that the sight of his own front door had begun to make Gregor a little dizzy. Donna Moradanyan, his upstairs neighbor, had covered that door with orange-and-black crepe paper—tied into bows.

The bag full of junk food began to slip. Gregor jostled around until he got it positioned solidly into the curve of his arm again. Then he turned south and made himself walk briskly and purposively in the direction of home.

2

The problem, he decided later, as he climbed the marble steps to that crazily covered door, was in his history. It was nice to pretend that Halloween was nothing but a holiday for children, that nothing went on under the cover of it but the benign fantasies of little boys who wanted to grow up to be superheroes. It was even nice when grown-up people, who ought to know better, worked overtime to make sure their children got a cozy, unthreatening picture of the dead of night. It was not so nice when the grown-up people began to believe their own propaganda. Gregor Demarkian had not only spent twenty years of his life in the FBI. He had spent ten of those twenty years—the whole second half of his career, from the day the states of Washington and Oregon had requested federal help in catching a killer called "Ted" to the day his wife Elizabeth, ill with cancer, had entered her final crisis—

chasing serial murderers. He knew far too much about the things people did to each other and more than far too much about Halloween. Halloween was, as a colleague of his had once said, the night of the werewolf. For 364 days out of every year, things went along more or less as they could be expected to go along. Even the Green River Killers, the Ted Bundys, the Sons of Sam, had their routines. On the 365th day, all hell broke loose. The rabbity serial killer you had been tracing for six months suddenly took his knife and cut fifteen people in half an hour. The teenage boy who had always seemed only to want to look like James Dean suddenly decided to ram himself and six of his friends off the edge of lovers' lane. The nicest little old lady in the neighborhood suddenly made up her mind to put cyanide into the caramel apples she passed out to the children who came to her door. *Suddenly* was definitely the best word for Halloween. *Unexpectedly* was the second-best one.

Gregor managed to find the keyhole under all the crepe paper, tried his key, and found it wouldn't work: the door was already unlocked. He let himself into the vestibule in a rising state of exasperation. None of the doors on Cavanaugh Street were locked these days. Lida and Hannah and all the rest of those silly women were much too concerned that the small children who came to their doors wouldn't be able to reach the doorknobs. They intended to keep their doors not only unlocked, but open, all Halloween night. What kind of a world did they think they were living in? Cavanaugh Street was a prosperous neighborhood, ten blocks of miraculous self-styled urban renewal— but it was surrounded by nastiness. Even if all they did was pass through the neighborhoods on their periphery while safely ensconced in the backseats of cabs, they ought to know that.

He got to the third floor, saw that his own door was standing open, and barged in.

"Bennis?" he said. "Bennis, come out here for a minute. I want to talk to you."

"Bennis is in the bathroom," Donna Moradanyan said, emerging from the kitchen in a cloud of fair wispy hair and flour. Donna Moradanyan looked less Armenian-American than anyone Gregor had ever met, but she was definitely Armenian-American. Not only both her parents, but all four of her grandparents, all eight of her great-grandparents, and all umpteen-thousand of her other ancestors were of Armenian extraction. Exactly how she had come out looking like a virginal Swedish exercise nut, Gregor didn't know.

"We're almost all packed," she said now, taking the heavier of the two bags out of Gregor's right arm, "so if you want to add something we haven't counted on, I don't know what we'll do. And the kitchen's a mess. Tommy got into the flour when I wasn't looking, and it's all over the place."

So that was what the flour was about, Gregor thought. Tommy was Donna Moradanyan's infant son, just now going on six months old and threatening to become seriously mobile.

"I don't want to add anything to what you're packing," Gregor said. "I'm not crazy. I just want—"

"—to ream us out about the doors," Bennis finished for him.

Gregor turned around to see her emerging from the living room, which led to a little hall at the back with the bedroom and bathroom off it. She had her great cloud of trademark Hannaford black hair pinned haphazardly to the top of her head, the tails of her flannel shirt hanging out, and nothing but knee socks on her feet. She looked impossibly beautiful and impossibly disorganized. She was, in reality, both.

"I have," Gregor said, "a perfect right to ream you out about the doors. I know I seem to be talking to thin air on this subject, but whether it has dawned on either of you or not—and on Lida, and on Hannah, and on Sheila Kashinian and all the rest of them—this is not a Hollywood movie set in the thirties. This is Philadelphia in the nineties. Not three blocks from this apartment there's a crack house that operates twenty-four hours a day and gets raided once a week. You leave the doors on this street standing open and unlocked all Halloween night, and somebody is going to get killed."

"Well," Bennis said, "I hope you're wrong, because

there's nothing I can do about it. Every time I try to tell Lida what you tell me, she pats me on the head and says, 'Yes, dear, and now, that boy who took you out last week, is he responsible?' "

Donna smiled. "Lida wants to fix Bennis up with Hannah Krekorian's son Johnny. He just got divorced."

"But it's okay," Bennis said, "because he got divorced from a non-Armenian girl who wasn't even Greek Orthodox or anything, and any food with a spice in it gave her indigestion, and Hannah and Lida couldn't stand her."

"I have to get back to Tommy," Donna said. "He's probably breaking plates by now."

Donna whirled and went back through the kitchen door, cooing out mother-sounds in advance. Bennis turned to Gregor and shrugged.

"Look," she said, "I know how you feel about the doors. I don't even think you're wrong. But there really isn't anything I can do about it. They treat me like a pet."

"Do you mind that, Bennis?"

"No." Bennis paced around his foyer, stopping to look at his badly framed pen-and-ink drawing of the signing of the Declaration of Independence, stopping again to look at the vase of wilted flowers on the small occasional table. It wasn't much, but it beat the way the foyer had looked for the first six months after he bought this apartment—meaning empty.

She came to rest in the exact center of the foyer floor, looked at the ceiling, looked at her feet, and said,

"Gregor? Can I ask you something?"

"Ask away."

"Well. Okay. Um. Look, it's been, what, two months since my mother died?"

"About ten weeks."

"You always did have a better sense of time than I have. Anyway, the house belongs to Yale University now, and they're getting antsy. I've got to find a new place to live."

"You know how I feel about that, Bennis. I thought you should have found a new place to live last New Year's."

"Yes. Well. I had obligations. Gregor, I don't know if you've realized it, but the second-floor apartment in this building is for sale."

"Ah," Gregor said.

"Oh, for God's sake, don't say 'ah.' " Bennis threw up her hands. "Look, I don't want to impose on you, all right? I don't want to push things where they shouldn't go. It's just that Donna and I have been talking, you know, and I spend half my time here anyway, and we were thinking it might be the perfect solution. The apartment isn't even very expensive."

"You're the only person I know who could describe a quarter of a million dollars as 'not very expensive.' "

"I make a lot of money. Gregor, would you mind? I absolutely promise not to cook for you any more than I already do—"

"That's a threat."

"—and if I'm seeing some man, I'll go to his place—"

"I'd rather have you bring him here. You tend to date psychopaths."

"—and if I'm working later than two o'clock in the morning, I'll put a towel under the typewriter so you can't hear it and I won't wake up old George downstairs—"

"Worry about old George, not about me. I'd be relieved to hear you were back at work."

"—and all that sort of thing," Bennis finished up. "Would you mind, Gregor? Would it bother you?"

"No," Gregor said. "But Bennis, this is a fine time to tell me."

"A fine time? Why?"

"Because you closed on that apartment yesterday. I ran into Stephen Telemakian last night and he told me all about it."

Bennis took her cigarettes slowly, carefully, deliberately out of her shirt pocket, extracted one from the pack, lit up, and blew a stream of smoke at the foyer ceiling.

"Never try to surprise a detective," she told him solemnly. "All it does is get you kicked in the ass."

3

Half an hour later, they were standing out on the curb, loading picnic baskets into Donna Moradanyan's van while Donna stood by with Tommy in her arms, looking wistful. The sun was still shining brightly and there wasn't a cloud in the sky, but the day had grown sharply colder. Bennis had tucked her shirt back into her jeans and put on a pair of L. L. Bean's Maine Hunting Shoes.

"I wish you were coming with us," she was saying to Donna. "I know it would have been problematic with Tommy along, but Father Tibor loves Tommy. We could have found a way to make do."

"Lida has me signed up to tell fortunes at eight o'clock tomorrow night. It's all right, Bennis. I've got all that work to do on my portfolio. Besides, if I'm not here, who will sign for your furniture?"

"Old George?"

"He'd send it all back and get his grandson Martin to buy you a set of new."

"I need a set of new." Bennis climbed into the van, counted to seven twice—checking out the picnic baskets, Gregor thought—and climbed out again. "Remember, if Mitzy Hansen from Doubleday calls, you want fifteen hundred for cover art and no less. Don't worry about what's-his-name from Random House. They always pay all right for artists."

"Okay."

"What about you, Gregor? You ready to go?"

Gregor was definitely ready to go. Cavanaugh Street was beginning to get to him. Howard Kashinian had given up handstands for a prancing little vaudeville act that was positively surreal. Little Susan Lekmejian, aged six, was hopping up and down on the bottom step in front of her parents' town house, dressed as a potato plant. Any minute now, somebody was going to decide to tie himself to the top of a tall tree and swing through the air like Peter Pan.

Bennis slammed the side door of the van shut. Gregor

climbed into the front passenger seat and hooked himself into his seat belt. Donna Moradanyan caught Bennis by the sleeve and said, "Don't forget about the downshift. It sticks."

"I won't forget."

"And don't drive faster than fifty-five."

Bennis didn't answer that one. She climbed into the driver's seat, fastened her seat belt out of deference to Gregor, and put the van in gear.

"You know," she said, "there's been something else I've been meaning to ask you. About Father Tibor."

"What about Father Tibor?"

"Well, is he all right? Is something seriously wrong with him all of a sudden or something?"

"Of course not," Gregor said, surprised. "Why would you think there would be?"

"It's just all these changes, that's all. We were supposed to go up there tomorrow morning, and then he calls you up in the middle of last night and wants us up there today—"

"It wasn't the middle of the night, Bennis. It was about six thirty."

"Whatever. It isn't like him. When Tibor makes a plan, he usually sticks to it."

The van was easing out into the sparse traffic on Cavanaugh Street, rolling south toward a red light, and Gregor thought: That's true. It isn't like Tibor. The problem was, it hadn't been not like Tibor, either. It hadn't been hysterical, or overwrought, or insistent. It had been—sort of small and sad.

"I think," he said carefully, "that Tibor is a little homesick. You've read about the fuss they make out of Halloween in that place. I don't think he knows how to deal with it."

"Hannah Krekorian told me that some priest who was here when you were all children said that Halloween was a Protestant plot to turn good Armenian Christians into Devil worshipers."

"I don't think Tibor would go that far. I think he just feels out of place and out of step."

"Out of place and out of step," Bennis repeated. "Oh, well. That's practically a definition of the man, isn't it?"

Actually, Gregor didn't think it was, but he didn't have time to protest. As soon as the light turned green, Bennis shifted into first and slammed her foot on the gas.

Two

1

Father Tibor Kasparian was waiting for them in the parking lot at the back of King's Scaffold when they drove up, standing hatless, coatless, and sweaterless in the stiff chill wind that had been flowing ever since they first entered the Allegheny Mountains. Maybe it was the Appalachians. Gregor could never get the geography of this part of Pennsylvania straight. In his childhood he had perceived it as a wilderness, a natural fortress that protected hillbillies and leftovers from the old west. Thinking about the fact that Philadelphia, a civilized city, was propped up from the south by places like this had made him lose his sense of linear time. Many years later he had come back and discovered what he should have expected to discover: that this might be the northern tip of the hill country, that hillbillies there might be, but that most of the territory was occupied by what everyplace else was occupied by. Small, neat ranch houses built of clapboard and stone, small collections of false-fronted stores antiqued with specialty vinyl siding, brick and redstone post offices and town halls—it wasn't suburbia exactly, because there wasn't enough of anything in any one place, but the aesthetic was in harmony with Levittown and Shaker Heights. Every once in a while Gregor caught a glimpse of something modern in cedar and glass and knew just what it was. The back-to-the-landers had their outposts here, offering up their Ivy League educations on the altar of politically correct environmentalism.

Seeing Tibor, Gregor's first reaction was fret and frustration. Dressed in nothing warmer than his day robes, the priest had to be freezing. Then Bennis jerked the van to a stop, pulled the Walkman headphones off her head—she had been listening to Joni Mitchell tapes all through the drive up, not talking to him—and cut the engine. Gregor found himself feeling suddenly grateful. He was grateful that the van had stopped. Bennis's preferred speed in road vehicles was somewhere around ninety-five, and she hadn't made much concession to the twisting mountainside roads they had had to travel to get here. He was grateful, too, for Tibor. Left on his own, he couldn't have found a college anywhere in this landscape. There was certainly no sign of one.

Bennis had detached her seat belt and, instead of getting out of the van, gone into the back where the picnic baskets were. Gregor detached his own seat belt, opened his door, and climbed out onto the tarmac.

"Tibor?" he said.

Tibor had been staring at a small shack at the back of the parking lot, near the drive where they had come in. Now he nodded to it, as if he'd been talking to it, and turned his head away.

"Krekor," he said. He looked at the van and frowned. "You did not drive yourself, all the way down here from Philadelphia?"

"Bennis is in the back with the food. And it's funny, but I keep thinking of us as coming *up* here from Philadelphia."

"You have been traveling south, Krekor."

"I know. But we've also been traveling up."

Over at the van, the side door slid open and Bennis Hannaford jumped out, holding one of the picnic baskets in her arms and staggering under its weight.

"We're never going to get all this stuff where we've got to go," she said, "not unless that's a lot closer than I think it is. Hello, Father. Is there a college less than a mile from here, or should I have brought my hiking shoes?"

"*Tcha*," Tibor said. "Your hiking shoes would have been appropriate, because so many of the people here hike. And climb mountains. And jog. It is very remarkable, Bennis, this is such a place of peace, such a place of rest, and nobody ever stops moving."

"Right." Bennis put the picnic basket back on the floor of the van and walked over to them. If it hadn't been for the way she moved, they might have taken her for a college student herself. She had none of the slackness of skin, none of the distortions of body, that time and gravity visit on most people by the age of thirty-five. It was her sophistication and apparent self-confidence that was off, both too strongly settled and too deeply felt to belong to an adolescent.

She drew up to them, shoved her hands in her pockets and asked, "*Is* there a college around here somewhere? Is there anything?"

"Over there," Tibor said solemnly, pointing away from the shack across a long flat expanse of ground that seemed to go nowhere. "What do you see?"

"Something orange," Bennis said doubtfully.

"A pumpkin," Gregor said.

"A jack-o'-lantern," Tibor corrected them. "You see it from the back, so you can't tell it has been carved. That is the top of King's Scaffold there, King's and the jack-o'-lantern is the head of mad King George. You know that they burn every year the effigy of King George?"

"I've heard of it," Bennis said, doubtful again.

Gregor *tsk*ed at her with impatience. "It's famous," he told her. "At least, it's famous in the state. There was some fuss a few years ago, the state Environmental Protection Agency tried to shut it down, the Governor practically had to call out the state militia."

"Dr. Katherine Branch," Father Tibor said.

"Who's Dr. Katherine Branch?" Gregor asked him.

"The lady who started the fuss. She is a professor in the program in which I teach, Krekor, a very strange lady. She says she is the reincarnation of a witch."

"Well," Bennis said, "that's perfect for Halloween."

"For Halloween, Bennis, yes, but she does not confine her silliness to Halloween. If it is silliness. She is not a woman I like very much. There is another woman, Dr. Alice Elkinson, and her I do like very much. And a man. Kenneth Crockett."

"Doctor?" Gregor asked.

"Oh, yes, Krekor. Here they are all doctors, except me, and I have what they call, what they call—"

"An equivalent," Bennis said.

"Yes, Bennis, that is right. An equivalent. How they can possibly think I have an equivalent, considering how I studied, I do not know. Perhaps they think stubbornness under torture is educational. But it is as I said. Here they have only doctors, even in the most minor of teaching positions, which I think is a mistake. A doctorate is a degree for research. Here we do very little research. We teach."

"You write," Bennis pointed out.

"Yes, Bennis, I write. I write so much these days, I think I have diarrhea of the pen, to change an expression a student of mine explained to me the other day. I like my students, Krekor. They are very—enthusiastic. Very energetic. Uneducated to a point that is criminal, you understand, and in complete ignorance of history, but we do what we can about that."

"Right now I think we ought to do what we can about these picnic baskets," Bennis said. "Hannah and Lida packed them this morning, and they weigh a ton. We've got to get them to your room somehow, Tibor. I couldn't just bring them back to Philadelphia."

The three of them turned to look back at the van. Its side door was still open. The picnic basket Bennis had carried forward still sat on the carpeted floor just inside the door. A new wind was rising, even stiffer and chillier than the last, ruffling their hair and their clothes and the loose asphalt shingles on the roof of the shack.

"It's hard to believe we're only an hour and a half from Philadelphia," Gregor said, and meant it. It was hard to believe they were still in the state of Pennsylvania.

Tibor brushed the palms of his hands against the sides of his robes, his customary gesture for getting on with it. "We will go down onto the campus," he said. "We will leave the picnic baskets and ask some of the boys to come for them after lunch. The boys will not mind, Bennis. They are true Americans. Very obliging."

"Is that what we are?"

"Yes, Bennis. That is what you are. Also very tolerant,

very open-minded, very friendly, and very lazy. Especially
intellectually lazy. *Tcha*. Such fine minds my students have
and all they want to think about is *Batman, The Movie*. We
will go now, Bennis, yes?"

"Yes," Bennis said.

Gregor watched her walk across the tarmac to the van
and slam the sliding side door shut, her hair whipping
around her face in the wind and her jacket nearly falling off
her shoulders. She was securing the sliders when he tapped
Tibor on the shoulder and pointed across the parking lot at
the shack.

"What's that?" he asked.

"That is a shop for fixing cars," Tibor told him. And
then he grinned. "In Armenia, Krekor, when the Soviets
came in—in my grandmother's time this is—we had much
trouble with a program that was to make us all comrades. In
the end, the intelligentsia retreated into their offices and
the mechanics into their garages and nothing was changed.
Well, Krekor, here is capitalism for you. Here we have the
cars for all the faculty. The Jeep over there is the car of a
member of my Program, Dr. Crockett. They say maybe he
would be the next Head. He has not a large reputation, but
he is very local. But there, that black Mercedes, that
belongs to a philosopher. A philosopher, Gregor, not a
famous one, but still a philosopher. And like every other
intellectual here, he fixes his own car!"

2

Up in the parking lot, it had been impossible for
Gregor Demarkian to imagine that a full college
campus—or a full measure of anything else artificial and
civilized—was anywhere close. Once Tibor had led them
down the narrow winding path that ended at Minuteman
Field, it became impossible to imagine that the campus of
Independence College could ever end. It wasn't that the
physical plant was so very big. Gregor had been a student
at Harvard and a participant at conferences at Yale, Chicago, Johns Hopkins, and Georgetown. All those places had

larger and more impressive collections of architecture, more inclusive and more diverse student bodies. Maybe the problem was that all those places were also set down in the middle of cities, so that they came to seem like just one more kink in an already tortuously convoluted urban landscape. Set down by itself, surrounded by nothing visible but trees and hills, Independence College defined itself—and its self-definition was distinctly eighteenth century. The redstone buildings were all Georgian and Federal in design. Even the ones whose shiny newness of material and lack of ivy indicated they must have been recently constructed maintained the artistic sensibility of 1778. Then there were the paths that had been threaded through the lawns from the door of one building to another, straight paths in straight lines, testimonies of symmetry to the triumph of reason. Lawns were lush but closely mown, hedges boxed and closely clipped. The statue of a Minuteman stood at the center of the largest quadrangle, at the place where all the quadrangle's paths met. It had been cast in bronze and allowed to weather to green. Seen from halfway down the path from the parking lot, Gregor thought it radiated the confidence of self-control.

The campus had been built on what must have been the only piece of solidly flat land in this part of Pennsylvania, and at the moment it was crowded with students. Students in mummy costumes, students in Frankenstein costumes, students made up to look like undefined victims of bloody violence—in no time at all, Gregor began to feel shell-shocked by how many of them there were, and by how many of them seemed fascinated with death and gore. Obviously, Gregor thought, this must have been going on for some time. Tibor, usually the most squeamish of men, wasn't fazed by it at all. Gregor caught a look at Bennis Hannaford and saw she wasn't fazed by it, either. Maybe all those horror movies she watched with Donna Moradanyan had made her immune. Gregor refused to believe she had been inoculated by seeing her own sister dead on the floor.

When they got to the very bottom of the path, Tibor turned slightly sideways, and waved his arms in the air.

"There. There it is. King's Scaffold and old King George. What do you think?"

Gregor didn't know what to think. The Scaffold was impressive all by itself, a massive outcrop of rock jutting straight up from the ground, at least as high as a three-story building and maybe higher. The bonfire, though, was the kicker. It didn't make a bit of difference that it was unlit. Hundreds of logs climbed up the rock face of the Scaffold, decorated here and there by bits of paper and cloth. At the top, regally seated on a plywood throne, was a straw-stuffed dummy that looked too much like a man. Only the jack-o'-lantern head made it possible for Gregor to look at it without cringing.

"Good Lord," Bennis said. "That's very realistic, isn't it?"

"The pile has gone too high for you to see its hands," Tibor told her. "You can see them if you try. They give it all away."

"I'm glad something gives it away," Gregor said.

"Just a minute, Krekor. It is that boy there in the bat suit that we need. I will be back."

Tibor darted into the crowd. Gregor returned his attention to the effigy, dodging visual interference from costumed revelers beneficent and malign: an Alice in Wonderland, a Devil with pitchfork and horns, a Little Red Riding Hood, a walking zombie from *Night of the Living Dead*. Everybody seemed to be carrying crepe paper streamers and confetti. Everybody seemed to be dancing to music that existed only inside their heads. Gregor kept having to beat back the nauseating suspicion that they all had the *same* music inside their heads. Finally he got momentarily clear of the crowd and caught a clear look at what he wanted: the effigy's hands, white gloves badly stuffed with straw, much too small for anyone but a child.

"Tibor was right," he said to Bennis Hannaford, who was standing just behind him. "Once you see the hands, the illusion's broken. The hands are so wrong, you start to see what's wrong with the rest of it."

"That's nice," Bennis said. "I'm too damned short to see the hands."

"Take my word for it. It's not just the hands. The shoulders are two different sizes. The arms have lumps in all the wrong places. There isn't any neck."

"There isn't a shred of mental stability on this entire college campus."

Gregor had often thought there wasn't a shred of mental stability on any college campus—but this wasn't the time to bring it up, and Tibor was coming back. Coming with Tibor was a man—given his enormous size and muscularity, Gregor refused to call him a boy—in head-to-toe black, his hair and face and neck encased in a mask-hood, his arms and shoulders attached to a broad cape that looked like wings when he moved. Gregor looked at Bennis and Bennis looked back.

Tibor hopped to a stop in front of them—Tibor always hopped when he was excited—and pulled on the edge of the man's cape.

"Bennis, Krekor," he said. "This is Mr. Jack Carroll. Mr. Carroll is a student of mine."

The man in the cape hesitated, then reached up and pulled the hood off his head. Now that he could see his face, Gregor had to give Tibor his description—this was a boy, although not as boyish a boy as most of the others around him. If Gregor had been sizing up Jack Carroll for a possible job in the FBI, he would have said: very bright, very poor, working his way through.

Jack Carroll had the black hair and blue eyes and fair skin of a certain brand of Irishman. When he shook Gregor's hand, his grip was as strong as a steelworker's.

"Mr. Demarkian." He took Bennis's hand. "Miss—"

"Hannaford," Bennis said faintly.

Gregor shot her a look that said: *This boy is ten years younger than you at least. Make sense.*

Tibor was still prancing up and down, antsy. "Well," he said. "Krekor, Bennis. Mr. Carroll has agreed to help us, you see. He will go to the van and get the picnic baskets—"

"If you don't mind," Jack Carroll said, "I'll send Freddie and Max to get the picnic baskets. You know Freddie, Father. He's the one who wrote the paper comparing James Madison to Chingachgook."

"*Tcha*," Tibor said. "This Freddie, he is a nice boy, but he is here because he has no other place to be. Yes, Mr. Carroll. Freddie and Max, this is fine. Listen to me, Krekor. When I like their work, I know to call them by their last names. When I don't—" Tibor shrugged.

"I'd do it myself, but I'm supposed to be organizing a torchlight parade that goes off tonight. The witch's parade, Father. You remember about that. It was Dr. Branch's idea."

"Mr. Carroll has a problem with Dr. Branch," Tibor said.

"Everybody has a problem with Dr. Branch," Jack Carroll said. He turned around to look up at the effigy and the students who surrounded it. Two tall ladders had been placed on either side of the pile of logs, but they weren't tall enough. The students who stood on top of them, being passed logs like the end men in a bucket brigade, were tossing heavy pieces of wood into the air. Sometimes the pieces of wood landed on the pile and stayed there. Sometimes they bounced off and rolled down into the crowd. "That's getting dangerous," Jack Carroll said. "I'll have to tell Mike to start loading from the top."

"It's very impressive," Bennis told him.

"Yeah. Well. Like I said, I'll go get Freddie and Max, they'll get the stuff out of your van and bring it to Father Tibor's room. Are you staying in Constitution House?"

"Mr. Demarkian is staying in the guest suite in Constitution House," Tibor said, "Miss Hannaford is staying in the guest suite in Liberty House."

"Miss Hannaford is staying on your floor," Bennis said, "or Gregor's."

"Miss Hannaford is a law unto herself," Gregor said.

Jack Carroll wasn't listening. His attention had wandered from the effigy. He was staring into the crowd with an expression that was half-puzzled and half on the verge of angry. Gregor stared into the crowd with him, but saw nothing he would have called unusual, under the circumstances. There was a young girl dressed as a harlequin. There was a boy dressed up as Scrooge. There was somebody else, sex indeterminate, in an elephant suit. No fake blood, no fake wounds, no imaginary mutilations. It was all positively benign.

"Mr. Carroll?"

Jack Carroll came to, blinked twice, and shook his head. "I'm sorry. I've had a lot to do. I'm afraid I'm a little tired."

"Mr. Carroll is President of Students," Tibor said.

Bennis smiled at him. "You must be exhausted."

Jack Carroll pulled the black hood back over his head, smoothed it down, and fastened it at his neck—with Velcro.

"Glad to have met you," he told them, shaking hands all around again, even with Tibor, as if he had learned his etiquette in a peculiarly rigid dancing school. "I'll get on to Freddie and Max right away. You'll have your baskets in under an hour. I promise."

He strode away, the picture of a Hollywood superhero, except for a slight hitch in his gait. Gregor thought he could read that hitch, because he'd suffered from it once or twice himself. It was the walk of a man trying to control a steadily rising but doomed to be frustrated fury.

Something tugged at his sleeve. Gregor looked down to see Tibor trying to pull him along the path, in the direction of the college buildings.

"We must go now, Krekor, or we will miss lunch. It is important. At lunch, you will meet everybody I want you to meet."

"At lunch, I intend to meet lunch," Bennis said. "I'm starving."

3

Five minutes later, going up the steps of Constitution House with Tibor in the lead, they ran into a tall, blond woman with a face like a *Vogue* cover girl's and a pair of jeans that had seen better days in 1968. The woman was paying no attention to them, or to much of anything else. Constitution House was a faculty residence, but it had been decorated as thoroughly and exuberantly as any of the student dorms. White plastic glow-in-the-dark skeletons had been hung around the rim of the great double doors like fringe on a gypsy curtain. The edges of each of the steps were occupied by gigantic pumpkins cut into jack-o'-lanterns of every possible expression. Gregor saw one with a sheepish smile on its face and another that looked about to go cannibal. Fine white threads, knotted into webs, hung in the open doorway. Clusters of Indian corn, red and orange and yellow and black and brown, were tied to every window but one on the second floor.

Halfway down the steps, the blond woman stopped, turned, and looked up at the second floor. She shook her head, impatiently but almost imperceptibly. Then she turned around again and saw Tibor.

"Father," she said.

"Dr. Elkinson." Tibor was smiling. "Dr. Elkinson, these are friends of mine, Gregor Demarkian and Bennis Hannaford."

Dr. Elkinson bowed in Gregor's direction. The gesture looked perfectly natural. "Mr. Demarkian," she said. "I've heard a great deal about you. All my students are very anxious to hear your lecture."

"They may be something other than anxious after they do hear it."

"It isn't until tomorrow night, isn't it? You're here early."

"He is here because of me," Tibor said. "I was getting lonely in all of this. I am not used to it."

Gregor thought Dr. Elkinson was going to ask just what it was Tibor wasn't used to, but she didn't. She merely adjusted the waistband of her jeans and brushed at her hair. Neither gesture seemed to accomplish anything. She didn't seem to expect them to.

"I was looking for Ken," she said abruptly. "Have you seen him around, Father? We were supposed to meet for lunch and he seems to have gone missing."

"I haven't seen anybody around today," Tibor said, "except Jack Carroll. That I know of. Possibly, if Dr. Crockett is in costume . . ."

"Ken wouldn't be in costume." Dr. Elkinson made a face. "Never mind. He went rock-climbing this morning, and I thought he might have stranded himself up on Hillman's Rock or forgotten about the time. But if you've seen Jack Carroll, Father—"

"Just a few minutes ago," Tibor said helpfully.

"Yes, well. If Jack's back, then Ken must be back, too. They always go together. I'll try the office."

"He is perhaps working on a paper and too involved to know that he is hungry."

"Of course." Dr. Elkinson nodded to Gregor and to Bennis. "It was nice meeting you both. If you're going to be on campus for two days, I hope we'll run into each other again." Then she turned on her heel, walked the rest of the way down the steps, and disappeared into the crowd on the quad.

Gregor had forgotten about the wind. Walking across campus, he had been shielded from it by the bodies of the students and the solid sides of the buildings. Now it ruffled his hair and chilled his scalp, making him feel feverish.

"Pretty woman," Bennis said.

"Also very intelligent," Tibor told her. "The most intelligent in the Program. A very good degree from Berkeley and she received it at only twenty-four. Three books published before she was thirty and very scholarly. I have read them. And then tenure here, very fast, the youngest person ever given tenure in the history of the college. She is a formidable woman, Dr. Elkinson."

Gregor grunted. "I'm beginning to think there isn't a single person on this campus who isn't upset about something. Did you notice that?"

"No," Bennis said.

"I noticed it," Tibor said. "It is true, Krekor, we are all upset about something. I do not think we are necessarily all upset about the *same* something."

"I wouldn't expect you were. It's just that this sort of thing gets so damned tiring."

Gregor had put down his small suitcase while they'd been talking to Dr. Elkinson. He didn't remember doing it, but there it was, next to his feet, instead of in his hand. He picked it up again and began to climb the rest of the steps to the door of Constitution House, wishing that whoever was playing that music in the quad wouldn't play it so very loud.

"It's bad enough," he said, "to be worried to death about giving a lecture, without having to try to figure out what's on everybody else's mind at the same time."

"You don't have to figure out what's on everybody else's mind," Bennis told him. "I mean, for goodness sake, there hasn't been a murder."

Still far down at the bottom of the steps, away from the door, Father Tibor Kasparian coughed.

Three

1

It was twenty minutes to twelve, and by the rigid schedule she had set for herself on the first day she came to work for the Program, Miss Maryanne Veer was late for lunch. In fact, she was late for more than lunch. She had made it a rule never to leave anything on her desk when she left the office, even to go to the bathroom, unless there was another secretary in attendance to watch over it. Her desk was still covered with the detritus of a very long and annoying end-of-October day. This was the last week students could drop courses without penalty. She had half a dozen computer drop cards and their accompanying handwritten explanations—what Miss Maryanne Veer thought of as essays on "Why I Couldn't Stand Professor X For One More Minute"—laid out in a line just above her pen holder. This was also the week when the midterm grades were supposed to be in, to be collated and sent along to the students' academic advisers. Technically, grades weren't due in until Friday, but she had most of them already, in a tall stack at the middle of her green felt blotter. Then there were the pink message slips that needed to be passed out to the faculty mailboxes, the course descriptions that needed to be packaged up and sent along to the Dean's office, the syllabi and book lists that needed to be filed, the proposals for next term's All College Seminars that needed to go to typing. Halloween might be a midterm holiday for the faculty and students of Independence College. For the secretaries and assistants, it was the very definition of a living Hell. Everything had a deadline, and the deadline was always the first of November. Everything was a matter

of life or death, and—like the phone that sat next to the
electric chair in all those ancient Jimmy Cagney movies—
reprieve would either come by the close of All Saints' Day
or it might as well not come at all. Miss Maryanne Veer
picked up the blue cardboard folder she was using to
organize the New Publications Reports and sighed. The
New Publications Reports had to be typed in triplicate and
then distributed, one copy to the Dean, one copy to the
Academic Standards Review Board, one copy to her files.
She wanted to take a match out and burn the whole silly
self-delusive thing.

Instead, she got up, went to her essential files cabinet,
and opened the drawer for faculty schedules. She got
Dr. Donegal Steele's out and looked at it for the fortieth
time since eight o'clock. There was a tradition at Independence College of leaving Wednesday afternoons free of
classes, theoretically to give students a solid block of time
for study. In reality, the tradition was maintained because it
gave faculty a solid block of time to write. Like a lot of other
senior professors with clout—and it bothered Miss Maryanne Veer no end that this man should have clout, when
he'd only been at the college since the start of the
term—Dr. Donegal Steele had contrived to have no classes
on Wednesday at all. There was no reason for her to expect
him to be in his office, or even on campus. There was no
reason for her to expect him to put in an appearance in front
of her desk, just to tell her that he wasn't really lost.

Except, of course, that there was.

Miss Veer checked the schedule again—History of
American Education, Tuesdays and Thursdays at ten; Religion in the New England Common School, Mondays and
Fridays at twelve; Senior Seminar on the History of
Ideological Attacks on the Western Canon, Mondays at
five—then shoved the file back into place, angry at herself.
If she had a real charge to lay at the door of Dr. Donegal
Steele, it would be this: that he made her act in such
uncharacteristic ways. Miss Maryanne Veer was not a
ditherer. She had never aspired to being a ditherer. It was
the pride of her life that she had always been able to make
up her mind about what she wanted, make up her mind

about what to do about it, and then go do it. Now, just because a man she loathed had been out of her sight a little over thirty-five hours, she was behaving like a veteran bimbo.

She had slammed the file drawer shut and gone back to her desk, determined to clear her paperwork and free herself for lunch, when Vivi Wollman came through the outer office door. Miss Maryanne Veer didn't like Vivi Wollman much—partly because Vivi was the protégée of Dr. Katherine Branch, partly because she was so infuriatingly pathetic. Miss Maryanne Veer had been homely all her life. She knew what that required of a woman, if the woman was the least interested in not making herself ridiculous. She had learned early not to fawn, not to flirt, and not to hope. It had left her with only Margaret for company in her old age—which would have been inevitable in any case—but it had also left her with her self-respect. In Miss Maryanne Veer's eyes, Vivi Wollman had no self-respect. For all the hysterical inflammatory talk about total feminism and learning to live your life without men, Vivi was a bundle of vulnerabilities and weaknesses, a walking open sore of fantasies unfulfilled. Miss Maryanne Veer didn't like Dr. Katherine Branch much, either, but she didn't have any of this to hold against her. Whatever it was Dr. Katherine Branch needed to fill the gap in her life, it didn't have anything to do with men. In Miss Maryanne Veer's eyes, that made it all the worse that Dr. Branch would take on someone like Dr. Wollman.

Dr. Wollman.

Miss Maryanne Veer folded her hands on top of her desk—on top of the stack of midterm grade reports really—and said, "Yes?"

There was a sprightly little jack-o'-lantern sitting on the counter that divided the outer office from the inner pen where Miss Maryanne Veer worked. Vivi Wollman picked up the lid of it, put it back on again, picked it up again. There was a votive candle in there that Miss Maryanne Veer had lit this morning when she first came in to work. Every time Vivi took the lid off the jack-o'-lantern, the candle's flame sent up streams of heat that made the air above it look jellied. Vivi didn't seem to notice.

Vivi put the lid back on one more time and said, "Well. Yes. Here I am."

"Yes?" Miss Maryanne Veer said again.

"With my New Publications Report," Vivi said helpfully and a little desperately. "You left a note in my mailbox yesterday. About its being late."

"Oh," Miss Maryanne Veer said. "Yes."

Any other faculty member would have come through the swinging door into the pen and stood at Miss Maryanne Veer's desk, but Vivi was easily intimidated and Miss Maryanne Veer had gotten into the habit of intimidating her. She watched impassively as Vivi, still on her side of the official divide, searched frantically through the pockets of her tattered baseball jacket and came up with a crumpled piece of paper. Then she rose majestically from her desk and approached the counter, the secretary of the Queen ready to accept a petition that was likely to be denied.

"I know it's a mess," Vivi Wollman was saying, "but I did type it, just like you asked me to. I've got such a heavy schedule these days, I just can't seem to get around to the administrative details. I know the administrative details are important, Miss Veer, but the thing is—"

Miss Maryanne Veer had unfolded the piece of paper and was looking down at it. "*RiverWomb: The Feminist Review of Literature*," she read. "*GoddessRite*."

"*GoddessRite* is actually a very good journal." Vivi was defensive. "It's published at Harvard. You ought to look into things like that, Miss Veer. It could change your whole perspective."

"I like my perspective the way it is."

"Well. Yes. Maybe you do. But you've got to admit, Miss Veer, if it wasn't for rampant sexism, you'd be Head of this Program yourself."

You'd be Head of this Program yourself. Miss Maryanne Veer refolded Vivi Wollman's New Publications Report, took it back to her desk, and sat down. She didn't know what was worse, that Vivi had been sincere, or that in her sincerity she had actually thought she was paying

Miss Veer a compliment. Miss Maryanne Veer didn't think she would ever understand the sensibilities of modern young women. They were so consummately irrational.

She opened the blue cardboard folder, put the New Publications Report inside—and then thought of something. Poor specimen though she might be, Vivi Wollman was a faculty member. Unlike Miss Maryanne Veer, she lived on campus.

"Dr. Wollman?"

Miss Maryanne Veer had expected the little chit to be halfway down the hall by now, but she wasn't. Vivi was still leaning against the counter, waiting for Miss Maryanne Veer to do the Good Lord only knew what.

"Yes?" Vivi said.

Miss Maryanne Veer put her best effort into not letting out the granddaddy of all sighs. "Dr. Wollman," she said again, "you live in Constitution House, don't you?"

"Yes, Miss Veer. Of course I do. Most of the people who teach in the Program do."

"Have you happened to see Dr. Donegal Steele around at all in the past two days?"

"Dr. *Steele*?"

"Yes, of course, Dr. Steele. I've been unable to get in touch with him."

"Well, Miss Veer, I don't usually see Dr. Steele, if you know what I mean. I mean, he and I aren't exactly *simpatico*."

"No, of course you're not. I thought you might have seen him in the hallways, in passing. Or in the college dining hall, for dinner last night or breakfast this morning."

"I wasn't at dinner last night," Vivi said, "I had a meeting of the Intercampus Council on Sexism in Philadelphia."

"What about breakfast this morning?"

Vivi Wollman blushed. "Well, Miss Veer, you see, I don't tend to be too alert at breakfast. I don't notice much of anything except my *New York Times*."

"No," Miss Maryanne Veer said. "Of course not."

"Is it really all that important that you get in touch with him?" Vivi asked. "I mean, I know he has to be around somewhere, he always is, but it's been really relaxing not having him just swoop down from nowhere without warning. I was kind of hoping he'd decided to bug out until after Halloween. You know, to avoid the fuss."

"If Dr. Steele was going to do that, he'd have left word with me."

"Well, maybe." Vivi Wollman was doubtful. "But you know, Miss Veer, maybe not. And he's a senior professor. If he wants to take off on his own, what can you do about it?"

The student drop cards at the top of the desk had become disarranged, the way papers on desks always become disarranged, for no discernable reason. Miss Mary-anne Veer pulled them toward her, and made two piles of them: cards proper to one side, explanation sheets to the other. She was not, after all, a ditherer. She was certainly not the kind of ditherer Vivi Wollman was. She knew what it was she had to do next. She only had to work up the courage to do it.

She deposited the drop cards and explanation sheets into the long center drawer of her desk and said,

"I can do what I ought to do, Dr. Wollman. I can go to lunch, and come back, and if I haven't seen or heard from Dr. Steele by then, I can call the police and report him missing."

2

In spite of what Dr. Alice Elkinson thought, Dr. Kenneth Crockett didn't always go rock-climbing with Jack Carroll. Sometimes he went on his own, which was what he had done this morning. He knew he shouldn't. The first thing he taught the new people who joined the Climbing Club was never to go up anything you needed pitons for on your own. Even Sir Edmund Hilary had gotten into trouble on climbs. Everybody did. Everybody got tired. Everybody got sick. Everybody got stupid once in a while. It was the iron law of human nature, the flip side of Socrates's old *know thyself*. Never trust yourself. That was the ticket.

Now it was ten minutes to twelve, and he was back,

tired and sweaty, sitting on the porch of the log house that served as the Climbing Club's in-season headquarters. What was below him wasn't a climb but a walk. The slope was too gentle to feel like anything else to anyone but the most out of shape of amateurs. What was around him was silence. "In season" for the Climbing Club meant the spring, or maybe the very early fall. This late in October, the temperatures were too low and the threat of rain too constant. That was why he was stuck with Jack if he wanted a companion. Jack Carroll was the only other person he knew at Independence College willing to go up Hillman's Rock at six o'clock in the morning and in a temperature of twelve degrees.

Ken Crockett adjusted his behind on the hard seat of the rocker, shifted the cellular phone to a more comfortable place on his shoulder, and stretched out his legs. He always carried a cellular phone in his backpack when he climbed, even though he knew there were places in these mountains where a cellular phone wouldn't work. It was a precaution. He always called Dr. Alice Elkinson as soon as he got back to the log house, to make sure she didn't worry. Now she was jabbering away in his ear like an agitated bird.

"I don't know, Ken," she was saying, "if you really had to climb this morning, you could have asked me. I climb."

"I know you climb. You hate to climb in the cold."

"I'd rather climb in the cold than have you lying up there with a broken leg and no one to send for help."

"I'm fine, Alice. It's you who doesn't sound fine."

"Maybe you should have asked Katherine Branch," she said. "Then she'd have been up there bothering you, instead of down here bothering me."

"What was our Kathie bothering you about this time?"

"Something Maryanne Veer said to Vivi Wollman. About calling the police and reporting Dr. Steele missing. It seems he really has dropped off the face of the earth."

"Lucky for us."

"Good riddance to bad rubbish, my mother would have said. Oh, Ken. Let's not talk about it. Vivi was totally hysterical, God only knows why, and Katherine came bursting into my room ranting about Nazi storm troopers and I don't know what else. Vivi probably has a bag of marijuana stashed under her mattress."

"Borrow some," Ken said. "They say it's very good for sex."

"We already have everything we need for good sex."

Ken shifted the phone on his shoulder again—it was amazing how hard it was to find a place to rest it that stayed bearable for more than a few minutes—and smiled. It was true. He and Alice did already have everything they needed for good sex, and he found that a little surprising. Alice was not exactly an emotionally forthcoming woman. She gave good public appearance, and fine party, but when he'd first met her he'd thought she was cold. Maybe it was just that, having always been reasonably well-heeled and reasonably attractive, he'd gotten far too used to women falling in his lap.

He leaned over and started to untie his hiking boots, which he really shouldn't have been wearing on the porch anyway. The cleats dug holes in the soft pinewood.

"So tell me," he said, "what else have you done with your day? I came up before breakfast. The place could have blown to pieces for all I know."

"The place hasn't blown to pieces. Somebody in my Civil War class rigged my desk so that every time I leaned on it, it screamed. That was fun. I think it had something to do with microchips. Oh, and I ran into Father Tibor and that friend of his, the one who's giving the lecture."

"Gregor Demarkian?"

"That's the one."

"What was he like?"

What came across the wire was the sound equivalent of a shrug, except that it wasn't a sound, exactly. It was more like a sudden contraction of auricular space.

"I don't know what to tell you," Alice said. "He's tall. A little too heavy. Looks like he's in his fifties."

"Intelligent?"

"It would be hard to say. He didn't look stupid. He didn't look like the man who caught the Fall River Knifeman, either."

"I think the point about him is less who he caught than

the system he set up to catch him. Them. You know what I mean. I was on the committee that reviewed the proposal for the talk. We ended up with all this stuff in our file about 'internal consistency.' "

"What's that?"

"A method for catching murderers. Serial or otherwise."

"I wish he'd devise a method for catching practical jokers. It wasn't just the screaming desk, Ken, it's been the whole day. And Halloween isn't until tomorrow. You know that tree out in front of Liberty Hall, the one with the hole in the side of it?"

"Sure."

"If you lean up against it in the right place, it yells 'boo.' "

"Yell 'boo' back," Ken said, laughing. Then he sat up straight. His boots were off. His feet felt cold even in their thick climbing socks. He stood up and stretched the kinks out of his back. "Why don't you hang in there for about fifteen more minutes and I'll be down to take you in to lunch. That way, if Katherine tries to nail you, I'll be there to fight her off."

"I don't know where Katherine's gone. She went stomping out of here, saying she knew exactly what to do about the arrival of the police state. Or words to that effect. I expect to find her boiling eye of newt and toe of frog in the middle of the quad. Are you sure you're all right?"

"I'm fine, Alice. I love you."

"You sound depressed," Alice said. "Never mind. I love you, too. Hurry back."

"I will."

The phone went to dial tone in his ear. Ken reached around with his left thumb and shut the power off.

It was funny, but it was true: Alice always seemed to be half-right about him. He wasn't depressed, exactly. He was sort of floaty, the way he got when there was too much in his life he had to deal with immediately and not enough information coming in about how he ought to act. He went to the edge of the porch and looked down into the trees, into nothing, into a place where there was neither Halloween nor Donegal Steele. Ken didn't mind Halloween much—after all these years not merely at Independence College, but in Belleville, he had learned to live with it—but Steele had been on his mind for days. There didn't seem to be any way to get him off.

If he had had to put a name to it, he would have said that Alice was just too innocent. She didn't understand why Maryanne Veer was upset at Steele's absence, or why Katherine Branch and Vivi Wollman were upset at the prospect of a visit from the police. He, on the other hand, understood both these things far too well.

The very idea of them made his blood run cold.

3

It was noon by the time Jack Carroll and Chessey Flint came downstairs from Chessey's room, and by then the living room of Lexington House was full of students in heightened states of exasperation. It was at times like these that Chessey realized how little different college was from high school. What was supposed to be happening here was a snake dance, across the quad to the dining hall. It went off every year. In theory, anyone at Lexington House could have got it going at any time at all. What was holding it up was the rigid economy of campus status. Among the classes, seniors were more important than anyone else. Among the seniors, Chessey and Jack were more important than anyone else. The categories were so thoroughly ingrained and so deeply felt, they were paralyzing. These were grown men and women here in the living room of Lexington House, twenty-one and twenty-two year olds who were supposed to leave campus in less than eight months to go out and conquer the world. They were hanging around on sofas and love seats, waiting for the Most Popular Girl and the Most Popular Boy to lead them in a bunny hop.

She was not, Chessey knew, being fair. She was much too rattled to be fair. In the face of what the last few minutes had proved to her to be true—that Jack had changed; that he had changed toward her specifically; that he had changed toward her sexually most of all—all this stuff, these crepe paper streamers and plastic ghoulies and satin costume masks that squirted blood and water at the touch of a string, seemed like so much lunatic nonsense. They had read Poe's *Masque of the Red Death* last year in her Nineteenth-Century American Lit course, and suddenly Chessey thought that that was what this was like, a not very benign exercise in group torture. Usually, when she came down from her time with Jack, she felt high. There was something exhilarating about not quite having sex, about letting him touch her when she knew the completion would be postponed. At the moment, she just felt terribly wrong, as if she had done something inexcusable.

As if, in her virginity, she had become imprisoned in the pointless and inane.

Chessey was looking through the crowd for Evie Westerman, hard to find with so many girls dressed identically in satin pumpkin costumes. Jack touched her on the shoulder and she jumped.

"Are you all right?" Jack said.

"I'm fine."

"You don't look fine."

You're the one who doesn't look fine, Chessey thought. She didn't say it. She was too frightened to say it. Instead, she went on looking for Evie and said while she was doing it, "Why don't you get the dance started on your own? I want to talk to Evie for a minute."

"Evie's over there by the punch bowl. I think she's got it spiked."

Evie was most definitely over there by the punch bowl—and she probably had got it spiked. She had her mask on top of her head instead of over her face and her gloves tucked into the neckline of her pumpkin dress.

"Go talk to Evie and I'll wait for you," Jack said.

"It might take too long." The last thing Chessey wanted was Jack waiting for her. "Go ahead, all right, please? I'll catch up to you at lunch."

"Chessey, if I've done something—"

"You haven't done anything." It was true. It wasn't

what he was doing. It was what he'd stopped being. "Go ahead, all right? I have a lot to talk to Evie about and I don't want to feel—rushed."

"Rushed," Jack repeated.

"I'll see you at lunch," Chessey told him. Then she plunged into the crowd, moving against the current, in the direction of Evie.

When she got to the punch bowl, the crowd was moving out the door, led by Jack, and Evie was pouring herself another drink. The punch was spiked. It was much paler than it ought to have been, and that meant vodka. Chessey Flint almost never drank, literally never at noon, but she took a cup of it anyway.

"Come to the ladies' room," she told Evie. "We have to talk."

If she had waited around to see the expression on Evie's face, she would have known she was about to hear a lot of things she didn't want to hear. As it was, she was in the hall leading to the ladies' room before the last words were out of her mouth, and leaning, panting, against one of the marble sinks by the time Evie made her way in. By then, Evie looked the way she always looked, except a little more skeptical.

"Love on a mattress hasn't done you much good today," Evie said. "What's the matter, Jack get a little out of control?"

"No."

"No," Evie assented. "Jack wouldn't."

There was a bar of Camay soap in each of the brass soap dishes attached to each of the marble sinks along the wall. Chessey picked up the bar closest to her and started to wash the makeup off her face. That way she had her back to Evie and her eyes closed so she couldn't see her own face in the mirror.

"Listen," she said. "I think he's starting to believe it."

"Believe what?"

"All those things Dr. Steele said about me. All those rumors he put out about the things we did together. Except that we didn't do them. We really didn't."

"I know you didn't. Jack knows you didn't."

"No, he doesn't. He's changed, Evie. Just in the last two days, he's changed. Do you know what I think happened?"

"No."

"I think he found Dr. Steele yesterday, even if he says he didn't. I think they had a talk and I think Dr. Steele— convinced him."

"Well, there's an answer to that, isn't there, Chess? You just let Jack sleep with you, and when you bleed all over the sheets, he'll know he was wrong."

"*Evie.*"

"Oh, Chess, for God's sake, what do you want me to say? You're being such a goddamned jerk."

The water was backing up in the sink, making a small puddle filmy with soap. Chessey held her hands under the clean cold water from the tap, making them wet, making them wrinkle. Then she splashed water onto her face and turned the tap off.

"Does he talk to you?" she asked Evie. "Does he tell you things—about us?"

"Jack?" Evie shook her head. "Jack doesn't talk to anybody. Not even to Dr. Crockett. Not about you."

"Then how can you possibly know I'm being a jerk?"

"Common sense," Evie Westerman said piously. Then, Chessey thought, she must have seen the effect she'd had. She made a small moue of self-disgust and reached under her costume for her cigarettes.

"Chess, listen to me. Jack didn't see Dr. Steele yesterday. Nobody did. Nobody's seen him today, either. I got it from Mandy Cavanaugh. She went over to Liberty Hall to drop a course and she heard Miss Veer talking about it."

"Talking about what?" Chessey asked, confused.

"Talking about how Dr. Steele has disappeared." Evie was impatient. "According to Mandy, he hasn't just disappeared, he discorporated. No one's been able to find him. Miss Veer was talking about calling in the police."

To Chessey, this was not just confusing, this was incomprehensible. "Calling in the police about what?" she demanded. "What's Dr. Steele supposed to have done?"

"It's not what Dr. Steele is supposed to have done, it's what somebody maybe did to him. I mean, let's face it, Chess, senior professors don't just fall off the face of the earth without telling anybody about it. Dr. Steele did."

"So?"

"So maybe he's had an accident. Maybe he was mugged. Maybe a lot of things. But if Jack talked to him yesterday, it would have to have been on campus, wouldn't it?"

"I guess so," Chessey said. "Jack didn't work yesterday. He went for a climb, but that was with Dr. Crockett."

"There. Dr. Crockett would not go on a climb with Jack and Dr. Steele together, or with Dr. Steele at all. I don't even think Dr. Steele climbs."

"I still don't get it."

"If Dr. Steele was on campus yesterday," Evie said carefully, "somebody besides Jack would have seen him. He would have made his ten o'clock class. He would have met his office hours. Hell, he would have had to eat. Somebody would have seen him."

"And nobody did," Chessey said slowly.

Evie looked into her cup of punch, made another moue of disgust at it, and poured it down the sink next to the one Chessey was standing at. Chessey took a paper towel out of the dispenser on the wall and dried her hands with it.

"Evie, you know, I'm not making this up. Jack has changed. Just in the last couple of days."

"Oh, Jack's changed all right."

"I don't see what else it can have anything to do with, if it isn't that he talked to Dr. Steele."

"Can't you?"

"No."

"I think I'm going to go catch that snake dance and have some punch."

Chessey dropped her paper towel into the wastebasket and turned around. Evie was leaning against the rim of one of the sinks, staring at her in a sad, almost affectionate way—and that made Chessey even more frightened than she had been, up in her room this morning with Jack.

"Evie," she said tentatively.

But Evie was shaking her head. "Never mind, infant. It'll all come out in the wash, one way or the other."

"That's what I'm afraid of."

"Look on the bright side," Evie said. "Maybe the Great Doctor Donegal Steele is dead."

Four

1

Father Tibor Kasparian liked to arrange his life in habits. Schedules were beyond him. Simple things—like the hour every Sunday he had to be in Holy Trinity Church to pray the Liturgy, or the half hour he had to be in Liberty Hall to give his class—he could manage. More complicated things ran afoul of his one true passion, the reading and study of books. Gregor thought he must have run up against it more than once in his life, that panicky moment when he realized it had been days since he ate, or talked to another person, or even left his house for a few moments to buy a newspaper at the corner store. Back on Cavanaugh Street, Tibor had turned the rectory of Holy Trinity Church into a kind of book warehouse, with paperbacks and hardcovers, works of classical philosophy and the novels of Mickey Spillane, stacked haphazardly one on top of the other on every available surface. Gregor was amused to find that he had managed to do the same thing to his two large rooms in Constitution House—and in only a few weeks. The front room, meant to be the living room and fitted out with a couch, two wing chairs, and a glass-topped coffee table, was lined with heavy volumes in dull green dust covers and paperbacks in garish red and silver. The couch was covered with periodicals, both academic and tabloid. The wing chairs held what looked like complete collections of *The Philadelphia Inquirer* and *The New York Times* from the day Tibor had moved in to the present. Only the coffee table was clear of literate debris, maybe because Tibor distrusted the strength of glass. Gregor wondered where all this stuff had come from. He had moved Tibor into these rooms himself, with Bennis and Donna for company, in the very same van in which he and Bennis had come up today. He knew what they'd brought with them, and it wasn't all this. Nor could he blame the collection on the small additions Tibor might have been able to make to it from his stash back in Philadelphia, going back and forth every Sunday to meet his duties at the church. For those, Tibor came and went by bus. He wasn't a strong man. He wouldn't have been able to carry much.

Gregor took the stack of *Philadelphia Inquirer*s off the seat of the wing chair closest to the window, discovered a copy of Judith Krantz's *I'll Take Manhattan* buried in their folds, and dumped the whole mess on the floor. Where did Tibor get these things? As far as Gregor knew, there wasn't much of anything anywhere in the vicinity of Independence College—no large towns, no malls. Did the college book-store sell *I'll Take Manhattan* and—Gregor spied it across the room, sitting on top of the first volume of Thomas Aquinas's *Summa*—Danielle Steele's *Daddy*?

Bennis sat down on the floor, cross-legged, and picked up a copy of *The Illustrated Guide to the Films of Roger Corman*. It was a ridiculously thick, outrageously oversize paperback with a picture of a decapitated woman on its cover.

"Well," she said, "it's relaxing, in a way. Not to have to look at Halloween decorations all the time."

"But I have Halloween decorations," Tibor said. "I have a jack-o'-lantern on the window ledge, right outside the window."

"That's not the same as what's going on in the quad," Bennis said.

"What is this place?" Gregor asked. "Are you supposed to be a faculty adviser in a dorm? Are we surrounded by students?"

"No, no," Tibor said. "This is a house for faculty only. It is a part of the philosophy here, Krekor, which I find very strange. The faculty here are supposed to be open to the students—available, that is the word. Not like in Europe, where we were supposed to be gods. We are supposed to be here so the students can knock on our doors and ask us questions."

"Do they?" Bennis asked.

Tibor shrugged. "Some of them do and some of them don't. That young man I introduced you to, Jack Carroll, he comes sometimes just to keep me company. He brings wine and the girl he is in love with, a nice girl but not of his seriousness. That is all right, I think. It is enough to have one serious person in a marriage. We talk about everything but what goes on in the class he has with me, and the girl—Chessey, her name is; have you ever heard a name like Chessey?—the girl sneaks into my cooking alcove and cleans my pots."

"I wouldn't think faculty would want to live on campus in a place like this," Gregor said. "A cooking alcove is fine for you, Tibor. You ought to be discouraged from cooking in any case. But with a family—" Gregor shrugged.

"The ones with families don't live here," Tibor said. "The ones without are required to. It has its advantages, Krekor. It does not cost any money and we are given green cards to take to the dining hall, so that our meals cost almost no money, too. And the library is right across the quad, only a few steps away."

"What about the people from your department?" Bennis said. "Do any of them live here?"

"It is not a department," Tibor chided, "it is a Program. You must remember that while you are here. To say otherwise will get everyone very upset. And yes, Bennis. They do live here. All the permanent senior members and myself. Which is stranger than you realize."

"Why?"

"Because this is not the only faculty house, Bennis. There are two more. I talked to Dr. Elkinson just after I came here and she said she thought the administration had done it on purpose, to try to get us to act as a unit. As a 'team,' she said. But—" Tibor shrugged.

"But, what?" Gregor said.

Tibor sighed. "Here," he said. "Look. There are in this building four floors, the ground and the three above. The ground floor has four apartments and the foyer. The other three floors have five apartments each. On the fourth floor, there are Dr. Elkinson and Dr. Branch, and also some faculty from other Programs and other Departments. But of us, Dr. Elkinson and Dr. Branch."

"All right," Gregor said. "The only thing I can think of is that you didn't seem to like Dr. Branch."

"I don't like her, Krekor, but that is not the point. Did you know the building is built on a courtyard?"

"No."

"Well, Krekor, it is. It is a big block with a hollow middle, and four staircases, one in each corner—"

"Oh," Bennis said, "I see. You really only get to know the people who live on your staircase, and the people who live on the other staircases you never even see. In the building, I mean. And Dr. Elkinson and Dr. Branch live on different staircases."

"Exactly," Tibor said. "Dr. Elkinson lives on the north staircase. Dr. Branch lives on the east staircase. Then, on the third floor, there is Dr. Kenneth Crockett. He lives on the south staircase."

"Don't tell me," Gregor said. "You live here on the second floor on the west staircase."

"Yes, Krekor, but then the analogy breaks down. I am not the only one of us who lives on the second floor and on the west staircase."

"Who else is there?" Bennis asked.

Tibor composed his face into a solemn mask and said, "The Great Doctor Donegal Steele."

Gregor's mind had caught on the word "analogy" and snagged there. There was no analogy involved, and he couldn't get over the bizarreness of it. Tibor's English was always halting and sometimes incoherent. He'd lived in too many places under too many linguistic dispensations to be entirely comfortable anymore even in his mother tongue. But wrong—no. Tibor never got it wrong. He was much too careful for that.

It was Bennis who picked up on it, maybe because she was the one who was really listening.

"Donegal Steele. Isn't he the one who wrote *The Literacy Enigma*?"

"Yes," Tibor said. "He did write that."

"Good Lord. I had no idea he taught at Independence College. In fact, I'm sure I saw somewhere that he was at Berkeley."

"He was at Berkeley. Then, at the beginning of this term, he came here."

"As a visiting professor?"

"No, Bennis. As a permanent appointment, with tenure and without a probationary period. This would not be unusual in Europe, but Dr. Elkinson tells me it is very unusual here."

"Yes," Bennis said, "it is."

"And then there are all the rumors about the money," Tibor said. "I try not to listen to rumors, you know how I am, but this rumor is in so many places, it is impossible not to hear. There are people who say the college is paying him in excess of one hundred thousand dollars a year."

"A college this size?" Bennis was shocked. "But that's absurd."

"It may not be true," Tibor said.

Bennis blew a raspberry. "If it is true, I'd say the college got held up. I mean, *The Literacy Enigma* was a hardcover best-seller for forty weeks. The man has to be a millionaire by now. He can't need the money."

"I'd say that all depends on what you mean by *need*," Gregor said. "In my experience, people can think of reasons to *need* as much money as there is. And more."

"Yes," Tibor said sadly. "I have heard that, too, Krekor. I think it is true."

While they had been talking, Tibor had sat down on the couch, wedging his small compact body in between the literary Leaning Towers of Pisa, resting one arm on *The Truth about Lorin Jones* and the other on Thomas More's *Utopia*. Now Gregor watched him get up and pace abstractedly to the window, his hands clasped behind his back in the classically stereotypical pose of a schoolmaster. He stopped when he got to the window and looked out on the quad. Then he leaned forward and pulled up the sash.

"Here," he said, "here is something much more pleasant to talk about." He formed his lips into a fish-circle and brought up a noise from the back of his throat, loud and raucous, that made Gregor jump.

"Here," Tibor said again. "Here she is, Krekor, as I have told you. Lenore."

What came through the open window was the largest raven Gregor had ever seen, so black and glossy its beak looked almost canary yellow. It hopped onto Tibor's arm and then began to climb up his shoulder, moving carefully, as if it knew its talons could hurt and it was taking care not to hurt Tibor. It came to rest on Tibor's shoulder.

"You look like Edgar Allan Poe," Bennis said.

Tibor had been hunting around in his pockets. He came up with something small and round, put it in the center of his palm, and offered it to Lenore. The bird looked at it for a moment and then ate it.

"Hamburger," Tibor said. "I feed her pastry, sometimes, but it is not right. Ravens are carnivores."

"You carry hamburger around in your pockets for a bird?" Bennis said.

"I change it every day."

Gregor thought the more proper question to ask in this case would have been: Why would anyone want to cultivate the friendship of something that looked so much like a harbinger of death? He wouldn't have asked it, because he knew it was just one more manifestation of his skewed feelings about Halloween. As it turned out, he wouldn't have had a chance to ask it even if he'd wanted to.

"Say 'hello' to Gregor and Bennis," Tibor commanded the bird.

Lenore hopped off Tibor's shoulder, flew into the room, and came to rest on the back of the empty wing chair. She stared first at Gregor, then at Bennis, then at Tibor. Then she opened her mouth and let out the most blood-curdling scream Gregor had ever heard.

"I don't understand," Tibor said, "what's that?"

Lenore jumped onto Tibor's hand and said very clearly: "Bastard. Bastard, bastard, bastard."

2

"The real problem with Mattengill's analysis of the sociocultural parameters of evidentiary psychosis," the man ahead of them in line was saying, "is that it doesn't take into account the essential functions of spatiotemporality."

The college dining hall was a cafeteria—inevitable, Gregor would have realized, if he'd thought about it—and Tibor was leading their way down the line past the plates of Swedish meatballs and roast beef au jus. Beyond the line was a large, unusually graceful room, high ceilinged and marble floored, furnished with sturdy Shaker tables and high-backed chairs. Gregor had been under the impression that every college in the country had given up that sort of thing in favor of painted steel and laminated wood. The line itself, though, was the epitome of the twentieth-century American college dining hall aesthetic. It had stacks of rectangular plastic trays with rounded corners. It had heavy stainless steel tableware devoid of any ornament. It had a long tray-rest made of stainless steel tubes. Most of all, it had food: starchy, gelatinous, and colorless. It was food that promised fervently to be bland.

Tibor had loaded up his tray without really thinking about what he was going to eat. Tibor never thought about what he ate. Bennis had taken a wilted-looking chef's salad that seemed to be blanketed by indeterminate cheese. Gregor, remembering all those picnic baskets in the back of the van, had settled for a doughnut and a cup of coffee. He knew he wasn't going to starve. There were two dozen honey cakes on the way. Now they were approaching the cash register, Tibor with his green card out. The man who had been talking about spatiotemporality was just paying up.

"I don't know what was wrong with Lenore," Tibor was saying. "She never did anything like that before. She says 'Hello.' She says 'Good-bye.' She says 'Good luck.' To Dr. Branch she says 'You have a nice ass.' I think

Dr. Crockett taught her to do that. She does not scream like a banshee in its death throes."

"If she says all those things, she's a he," Gregor said. "Female ravens can't be taught to imitate talk."

"That's a sexist thing to say," Bennis said.

Gregor gave her a withering look. "Sexist or not, that's nature. Here, I'll do another sexist thing. I'll buy your lunch."

Tibor had already passed beyond the cash register, waving his green card and smiling vaguely at the student who was manning it. He was walking briskly through the large room toward a table next to one of the tall windows. Watching him, Gregor realized he had been wrong to think, as he had at first, that the dining hall had not been decorated like the rest of the campus for Halloween. The decorations were there, but the room was so large and well proportioned it swallowed them. Every table had a tiny jack-o'-lantern in the middle of it, candlelit from within. Every column had a bouquet of Indian corn tied to the center of it. It all looked superfluous.

"Six ninety-five," the student at the cash register said.

Gregor gave her a ten, took his change, and motioned Bennis to follow him to Tibor's table. She had been listening to the conversation behind her—something about the intergenerational reenactments of mythic gravities that Gregor hadn't really heard—and Gregor wasn't sure she'd seen where Tibor had gone.

"Over there by the windows," Gregor told her, as they passed between two students who were, blessedly as far as Gregor was concerned, talking about the latest *Star Wars* movie. "He's been joined by a man who looks like a cover model for one of your L. L. Bean catalogs."

The man not only looked like the model for the cover of one of Bennis's L. L. Bean catalogs, he behaved the way Gregor had always suspected those men would behave. As soon as Gregor and Bennis reached the table, he leapt to his feet. Then he reached out, took Bennis's tray, and put it down for her. Gregor's tray was already on the table, so he didn't bother with that. He simply put out his hand, smiled heartily, and said,

"How do you do, Mr. Demarkian. I'm Dr. Kenneth Crockett."

Father Tibor Kasparian never leapt to his feet for anyone, although he'd done it once or twice from sheer excitement. He stared at Dr. Kenneth Crockett for a moment in utter astonishment, then waved Dr. Crockett, Gregor, and anyone else who might be in the vicinity into their seats.

"This is Miss Bennis Hannaford," Tibor said. "Miss Hannaford is a member of my parish."

Gregor nearly choked on his coffee. Had Bennis told everyone on earth, except him, that she was buying that apartment?

"We have been talking," Tibor was going on, "about Lenore. Have you seen Lenore today, Dr. Crockett?"

"Call me Ken," Dr. Crockett said. It sounded automatic, as if he'd gotten used to telling Tibor this same thing over and over again. "I've seen Lenore a couple of times. I've been wondering if she's ill."

"She sounded like she was strangling when we met her," Bennis said.

"I haven't heard her talk. I was up at the cabin today—we have a rock-climbing club here; the club keeps a log cabin up near Hillman's Rock—anyway, she was out there, circling around this morning. I've never known her to circle as much as she has the last few days."

"The last two," Tibor corrected. "She was all right the day before yesterday. I had her in my office, eating out of my hand, and she was talking away just as usual."

"Maybe the circling has something to do with sex," Bennis said. "Maybe she's getting ready to mate or looking for a mate or something like that."

Gregor found it absolutely astounding, how Bennis could manage to bring sex into any conversation. It was a trait he had come to decide was universal in her generation of women, and he didn't like it. He took a bite out of his doughnut, which was stale. He took a sip of his coffee, which was nearly as bad as the stuff Tibor made at home. Then he pushed the whole mess away from him and said, "In the first place, as I was telling you before, if it talks, it's a him, not a her. In the second place, ravens don't mate in the fall and they don't mate by circling, either. They circle when they're coming in for a kill."

"Is that so?" Dr. Kenneth Crockett looked bemused. "In that case, I suppose we'll have to find Lenore a bird psychologist. What she seems to be circling in to kill these days is Constitution House."

"I thought you said you saw her circling a cabin in the woods somewhere," Gregor pointed out.

"She wasn't actually circling the cabin," Dr. Crockett corrected. "She was just up over Hillman's Rock circling. But the last couple of days, what she's been doing most often is circling over Constitution House. Even Father Tibor's noticed it."

"That is true, Krekor. I have noticed it. She goes up into the air and around and around our house."

"She never comes down?" Gregor asked, realizing at the last minute that he had done it himself, called the raven "her." "He never swoops or lights on anything anywhere?"

"He never swoops," Dr. Crockett said.

"Of course she lights on things, Krekor," Tibor said. "She came into my apartment not half an hour ago. You saw her yourself."

"He wasn't lighting to kill. He was just coming in to see what he could find."

"Well, there it is, then, Krekor. The behavior does not make sense. It doesn't matter if Lenore is a him or a her. It only matters that she is not well."

The ebb and flow of contradictory pronouns was beginning to make Gregor dizzy. Accuracy mattered to him. He could never understand why it didn't matter to everyone else. He looked at Dr. Kenneth Crockett with some curiosity. Here was a man, a Ph.D. and a scholar, a man whom Tibor had pronounced himself in favor of—and yet there was something about him that Gregor didn't like. It all seemed jerry-rigged somehow—his personality, his conversation, even his clothes. It was as if Crockett had woken up one morning and decided on the man he was going to be, and then gone out and become that man, but only from the outside. The core of him was someplace else, some*thing* else. It didn't fit with the rest of him, and it chafed.

Gregor shifted a little in his chair—why was he forever the victim of uncomfortable chairs?—and said, "You know, there is one possible explanation for the kind of circling you've been talking about. He may have been spotting."

"Spotting?" Dr. Crockett asked.

"Carrion," Gregor said. "Ravens aren't vultures, of course. They kill their own meat. But any carnivorous bird will spot carrion, if there's enough of it."

Father Tibor blanched, "What do you mean, Krekor, if there's enough of it?"

"I mean if the kill is big enough, of course. It would have to be a very substantial kill, I'd think, in the case of a bird like Lenore. He's well fed without having to work too hard for it."

"I don't understand why she bothers to work for it at all," Bennis said. "All she has to do to get fed is show up at Father Tibor's window. Why should she knock herself out chasing small animals?"

"Instinct," Gregor said. "Community responsibility. In case you didn't know it, birds are fairly communal animals, even if they don't live in herds. If Lenore is spotting carrion, then he's not just spotting carrion for himself. He's spotting it for any of his fellow ravens who happen to be able to see him."

"Krekor, Lenore has no fellow ravens. Lenore is the only raven anyone has ever seen in this part of Pennsylvania."

"Excuse me," Dr. Kenneth Crockett said. "That's Alice. We were supposed to meet and we kept missing each other."

He was already on his feet, looking away from them, his legs bent slightly at the knees, getting ready to move him quickly. From his initial politeness, Gregor would have expected handshakes, rituals, trivialities—but that initial politeness had been stripped away. Dr. Kenneth Crockett didn't seem to care about anything but getting across the room to Alice—or maybe, Gregor thought, away from them.

"Excuse me," Dr. Crockett said again. Then he spun around and hurried off, into the crowd.

Bennis got out her cigarettes and lit up. "Good grief," she said. "Who's Alice?"

"Dr. Elkinson," Father Tibor said. "We met her when we were going into Constitution House. She's over there, by the cash register."

Someone else was there, by the cash register, in deep conversation with Dr. Elkinson—an older woman with an iron permanent and a face of steel and ice who reminded Gregor far too much of the most terrifying Sunday school teacher he had ever had. The older woman seemed to have nothing on her tray but a cup of tea, as if she were made of metal inside and didn't need human food. Dr. Elkinson's tray was much more reassuring: a hamburger, a little cardboard boat full of french fries, and a garishly colored old-fashioned tin can that said Belleville Lemon and Lime All Natural Soda.

"Who's she talking to?" Gregor asked. "Is that the infamous Dr. Branch?"

"No, Krekor, that is not Dr. Branch. That is Miss Maryanne Veer. She is the secretary for our office."

"I think I'll stay out of your office," Bennis said.

Gregor dragged his attention away from Dr. Elkinson, Dr. Crockett, and Miss Maryanne Veer, and found himself face-to-face with a very worried Father Tibor. He felt almost instantly guilty. He had meant to rattle Dr. Crockett and see what came of it. He hadn't meant to put Father Tibor Kasparian off his food.

"Tibor," he said, "don't get so upset. I was just presenting a possibility. I don't have any real—"

"What's that?" Bennis said.

Bennis was an immobile sitter. She got comfortable where she wanted to be and stayed there. Now she was rising off her seat, leaning forward, her palms flat against the table and her arms straining to stretch just a little longer, just a little farther. The tone of her voice had been so shocked, Gregor found himself rising too, turning toward the cash register again, confused and alarmed.

He had every reason to be alarmed. What he saw,

when he finally got himself into position, was a tragedy out of a cheap horror movie. Miss Maryanne Veer had moved away from the cash register, toward the center of the room. She was there now, alone, her head thrown back, the sound coming out of her throat a cross between a gurgle and a scream. Her chin had been stripped of skin and left raw and bloody. Something seemed to be eating into the front of her dress and the skin on her neck. At her feet, where her teacup had fallen and shattered, a puddle of brown and green was having no effect on the floor at all.

Gregor Demarkian felt as if he were being shot from a cannon.

"Dear sweet Jesus Christ," he said, and he headed across the floor. "Lye."

Five

1

It should have been simple—in fact, in the beginning, it was simple. There is nothing on earth like a poisoning with lye. Gregor could have recited the indications from memory, just the way he had learned them in his second month of Bureau training at Quantico: the stripping away of the skin that looked worse than it was but not nearly as bad as it would get; the gagging heaves that turned to choked strangling and brought up no vomit; the short-term invia-bility of all the nonhuman surfaces. Miss Maryanne Veer's dress must have been made of silk. Silk was one of the few materials lye would eat through on contact, except for human skin. Or animal skin, Gregor thought irrelevantly. The effect would be the same on most animals as it was on human beings. He could remember a case, years ago, from when he was new in the Bureau and assigned to kidnapping detail. A small girl had been snatched from the playground of her expensive private grammar school in Beverly Hills and taken high up into Coldwater Canyon and killed. Her mother, half-insane with grief and self-recrimination, had been unable to stand the sound of the girl's tiny kitten mewling disconsolately through the house. She had taken the kitten and locked it in the back pantry. Then she had gone on with her life and forgotten all about it—unsurprising, because her life at that point had consisted of a bottle of Stolichnaya before breakfast and whatever she'd had to drink afterward to get herself unconscious for the rest of the day. The kitten had remained locked in the back pantry for three days without food, kept alive only because a small leak in the roof made a puddle of water on the pantry floor. Then the kitten had gotten too hungry to care about anything else and had gone looking for something open and chewable. It had found an open tin of drain cleaner that had been made mostly of lye.

Gregor Demarkian was not a physically active man. When he read the detective novels Bennis sometimes gave him, he preferred the ones about Nero Wolfe and Hercule Poirot, men who solved the problems of the world from the safety of their living rooms, who sat and thought instead of ran and shot. Because he had been determined to join some sort of police force when he was young—he couldn't remember why now—it was a good thing the Bureau had existed. He couldn't imagine himself, even at twenty-five, chasing across the landscape with his gun drawn. He couldn't imagine himself directing human traffic in an emergency, either—but now, he knew, that was what he had to do.

For what seemed like minutes after Miss Maryanne Veer dropped her teacup and began to gag, nobody spoke and nobody moved. Miss Veer was the radial point in a large empty circle, central and spotlit. The only sound in the room was the low-grade hissing Gregor knew came from the puddle at Miss Veer's feet, lye mixed with water, activated. Then Dr. Alice Elkinson threw back her head and began to scream.

"Dear God," Bennis Hannaford said, "will somebody please shut her *up*?"

"Never mind about shutting her up," Gregor said. What he had been afraid of was beginning to happen. Miss Maryanne Veer had fallen to the floor, and the rest of them were converging on her, throwing themselves at her. There were things that needed to be done and done quickly, and a roadblock of bodies was going up that could become impossible to penetrate at any moment. Gregor grabbed Tibor by the shoulders and spun him around, so that he was facing the cafeteria line and the door out. "Go," he said. "Call 911. Ask for an ambulance and the police. Tell them we've got an attempted murder by lye."

If Tibor had been thinking clearly, he would have protested. There was no way to know, now, whether what they had was an attempted murder, an attempted suicide, or some kind of gruesome accident. Because Tibor was thinking no more clearly than any of the people now clotting up the center of the room, he took off at a brisk trot without asking questions. Gregor turned to Bennis and said, "Go get some milk. Lots of milk. As much as you can carry. Bring it to me when I get in over there and then go back and get some more."

"Milk?"

"Don't ask stupid questions, Bennis. Just go."

Bennis went. The clot in the center of the room was pulsing, sending up waves of sound that weren't words and weren't music but had something in common with both. Dr. Elkinson had stopped screaming and begun crying hysterically instead. She kept altering sobs with wails, sobs with wails, so that she sounded like a defective police siren.

"We've got to make her vomit," someone in the crowd was saying. "We've got to force her to bring the poison up out of her system."

Gregor pushed through two young girls, students, whose skin was tinged with the whitish-green of incipient nausea. As he forced himself through the second layer and into the still empty but smaller circle of the center, he saw one of the girls turn away and bend over. He wedged himself into the open space next to Miss Maryanne Veer's body and dropped to his knees.

"For God's sake," he said, "whatever we do here, what we can't do is let her vomit."

"Who's that?" someone in the crowd said.

Bennis pushed through, her arms full of those small waxed-cardboard cartons of milk that seem to be sold only in school cafeterias. She had at least thirty of them. She dumped them on the floor next to Gregor and stood up again, looking a little wild.

"Is that what you wanted?"

"More," Gregor said.

"More?"

"Just in case."

Bennis whipped around and ran off again. Gregor looked up and tried desperately to judge the character behind the faces he saw. Dr. Elkinson was in no shape to help anyone with anything. She had fallen out of the crowd and collapsed into a chair. Gregor could see the top of her head, bent and shuddering, between the shoulders of a student dressed as Leonardo the Ninja Turtle and the shoulders of another student dressed as Snow White. That was part of the problem, the way all the students were dressed. The face Gregor most wanted to see was that of Tibor's friend, Jack Carroll. He remembered that the boy had been dressed as a bat, complete with hood, but there were two bats in the crowd, both complete with hoods. Gregor hadn't paid enough attention to the way the rest of the boy had looked to be able to determine if either of these bats was the one he wanted. He didn't want to call out the boy's name, either—although at that moment he couldn't have said why. There was just something about it that felt damned wrong, maybe even dangerous for the boy, and Gregor had to go with that. He didn't have the time or the inclination to work it all out.

"I know who that is," someone in the crowd said. "That's the man who's giving the lecture about crime."

Gregor examined the faces before him, the ones he knew and the ones he didn't know. The ones he knew were few in number and not always attached to names. There was Dr. Elkinson in her chair, yes, but there was also the pretty, blond, athletic girl hanging on to one of the bats. She was dressed as a pumpkin and her face was streaked with tears. Gregor had seen her on the quad when Tibor had been leading them to the dining hall for lunch. She had been part of a whole line of girls dressed as pumpkins, and she hadn't looked happy even then. Gregor mentally rejected her services out of hand—not only was she too upset, she wasn't strong enough—and went back to his search. Finally, he came to rest on Dr. Kenneth Crockett, upset, even horrified, and hanging back as far as he dared, but blessedly still in control of himself.

"You," Gregor said, "Dr. Crockett. Come here please. I need some help."

"Me?" Kenneth Crockett said.

"I have more of them," Bennis said, stumbling into the

open space and dumping another load of milk next to Gregor's knees. "More?"

"No. Go find out what's happened to Tibor. I sent him to the phone."

"Right," Bennis said. She took off again.

Gregor motioned Dr. Crockett in toward the writhing body. This time, he came, slowly but steadily, as if he were forcing himself to move.

"What I need you to do," Gregor told him, "is to get her mouth open and your finger on her tongue, so that she can't swallow it or block the progress of the milk. She'll have third-degree burns in her mouth and we'll get to them, but we have to get to the esophagus first. Lye is a corrosive. It will eat right through her windpipe if we let it, and if it does she won't be able to breathe, not now and not later, no matter what anybody does for her."

"Lye," Ken Crockett hissed. "Oh, my God."

Gregor took one of the cartons of milk, ripped it open, and poured it on Miss Maryanne Veer's chin and chest. It wouldn't be much help, but it would be some. He didn't want to look at that pulped, untreated skin a moment longer. He motioned to Ken Crockett and the other man leaned forward, got his thumbs around Miss Maryanne Veer's teeth, and pulled.

"Dear God," Ken Crockett said. "She's fighting me."

Gregor got another carton of milk open, took aim, and poured the contents straight down Miss Maryanne Veer's throat.

"She's not fighting you on purpose," he said. "From the state of her pupils, I'd say she was barely conscious. But she will try to clamp down. It's sheer instinct. The lye came in that way. The body is trying to keep it out."

"I don't blame her," Ken Crockett said.

Gregor opened another carton, took aim again, poured again. "You were standing near her when it happened. Do you remember what she was carrying on her tray? What besides tea or coffee or whatever was in the cup?"

"I remember the tea. She always had tea."

"The lye couldn't have been in the tea. Tea is full of tannic acid. Lye is an alkali. Even if the tea was weak—

even if the tannic acid wasn't strong enough to neutralize
the alkali, and it probably wouldn't have been, it isn't that
strong an acid to begin with when it's derived from tea
leaves—anyway, tannic acid or no tannic acid, most of the
available forms of lye foam when they come in contact with
water."

"What do you mean, 'most of the available forms'?"

Another carton, another aim, another pour. Dr. Crockett was holding Miss Maryanne Veer's mouth wide open
and her head tilted back toward the light. Gregor could see
well into her throat. The skin there was raw and unforgiving. He grabbed another carton and opened it.

"Drain cleaners," he said. "Almost all of those have
sodium hydroxide. So do the acids in some batteries—"

"Sodium hydroxide is lye?" Ken Crockett said.

"That's right. In the days before packaged cleaning
products, people used to keep it, almost pure, in buckets,
for washing out latrines and that kind of thing. But these
days almost nobody—"

"I know somebody who does." It was the girl in the
pumpkin dress, pushing forward in the crowd. "I don't
mean somebody. I mean someplace. I've seen it."

"Seen what?" Ken Crockett demanded. "Chessey,
what are you talking about?"

"The Climbing Club," Chessey said desperately. "The
cabin up on Hillman's Rock. There are outhouses up there
and there's a bucket just outside of them and it's marked
'lye.' "

Gregor opened another carton, took aim again, poured
again—the process was beginning to feel like assemblyline
work, and just as futile. He thought: *So this is the Chessey
that Tibor was talking about; there couldn't be two girls
named Chessey on a small campus like this one*. Then he
grabbed another carton and started all over again.

"Even if what we had here was pure sodium hydroxide," he said firmly, "it still would have at least fizzed when
it came in contact with water. The best way to feed
somebody lye—"

"*Feed* somebody?"

Gregor had no idea who had said it. Part of him was

concentrating on Miss Maryanne Veer. Part of him was delivering this absurd lecture on sodium hydroxide. The rest of him was thinking that the bat the girl Chessey had been hanging on to must have been Jack Carroll. She was supposed to be Jack Carroll's girlfriend. "—or for someone to take it accidentally," he went on, "is for the lye to be delivered dry. For best effectiveness, it should be delivered dry and washed down with some kind of nonacidic liquid, done fast, so that the victim wouldn't notice until it was too late."

"Oh, God," somebody else said.

Carton, aim, pour. He was getting a headache, straining to see into that throat. "If the lye had been in her tea, she would have seen it foam. She wouldn't have drunk it. There had to be something else. A sandwich. A piece of cake. Something."

"There isn't any lye up at the cabin on Hillman's Rock," Ken Crockett said. "There never has been while I've been with the Climbing Club. The cabin was remodeled for plumbing years ago."

"We're beginning to make some progress," Gregor told him. "I want to do a wash of the mouth. When I tell you, release the tongue so I can get some milk under it."

Ken Crockett braced forward, ready. Gregor reached for yet another carton of milk, thinking as he did that the seriously adrenalated part of this crisis was over. From now on it would be steady, a routine, holding the fort until the medical people arrived and could get a tube down Miss Veer's throat to ensure that the air passage stayed open. He got the carton open and poured it in with a swirling, circular motion that reminded him—it was horrible, but he couldn't help it; the metaphor was there and it wouldn't leave him alone—of the way you were supposed to pour heavy-duty cleaners into toilet bowls. He tossed the empty carton on the floor and reached for another one, wishing that Bennis and Tibor would come back and tell him that help was on the way.

He was just reaching for carton number three, destination the mouth, when all hell broke loose.

2

At first, it was impossible to know what was going on. Gregor was in the process of pouring even more milk into Miss Maryanne Veer's mouth. He couldn't turn around or look up or do anything else to pinpoint the cause of the disturbance. He didn't dare. Dr. Kenneth Crockett was looking up, and the expression on his face was shock. Gregor tried to tell himself that the noise he was hearing was the arrival of the ambulance men—who else could be coming in force at a time like this?—but there was no way to sustain the illusion, even with his back to the source of the commotion. What he was hearing was not the barked commands of an emergency medical squad, but the wavering distortion of a Gregorian chant.

"Jesus screaming Christ," Ken Crockett said, and then rose, involuntarily, to his feet, letting Miss Maryanne Veer's face drop out of his hands and the back of her head hit the floor with a thud. "Jesus screaming Christ, what do these idiots think they're doing?"

"Dr. Crockett," Gregor said. "Get back here. Get back here now."

Dr. Crockett was walking away, unhearing. Gregor was giving serious consideration to screaming out loud when one of the bats dropped into the doctor's place, grabbed Miss Maryanne Veer's mouth, and yanked it open.

"Jack Carroll," the bat said.

"I thought so," Gregor told him.

Behind Gregor's back, the chant had grown louder, strident. He'd had enough Latin in school to know it wasn't Latin he was hearing. It was nonsense, but angry nonsense, and it was getting louder.

Suddenly, Bennis dropped down beside him, holding a carton of milk in her hand.

"Get up," she said. "I'll do this for a while. Somebody's got to get those people out of here."

"Where's Tibor?" Gregor demanded. "Where's the ambulance?"

"The ambulance and the police are on the way. I talked to the sheriff of the county myself and explained the whole thing. You shouldn't have sent Tibor, Gregor, he's in shock."

"I had to send Tibor. He was the only one I could trust who knew where the phones were."

"Right. Let me do this. Turn around and see what's going on. And get that Crockett person and calm him down. Oh, for God's sake. I can't believe this."

She shoved him unceremoniously out of the way, positioned herself right in front of Miss Maryanne Veer's mouth, and shot the carton of milk down it as he had been doing at the beginning. Obviously, she hadn't been watching him over the past three or four minutes. She didn't realize he had switched from the throat to the mouth. It didn't matter. The throat was the important thing anyway. It was time somebody got back to it.

Gregor stood up, turned around, and stopped. For endless minutes it seemed as if he could enumerate everything he saw, but make no sense of it. There was a small knot of women standing in a circle at the end of the room near the cash register, blocking all passage in or out except by window. They were all dressed in identical black—black tights, black ballet slippers, black leotards, black gloves. Their faces were painted in mock harlequin design, black on one side and white on the other, with a symbol Gregor vaguely remembered as being an ancient sign of the Devil plastered under each of their right eyes. The one in the center was taller than the rest and had hair so red it seemed to burn. It was long and teased out around her face like radioactive cotton candy. She stepped out a little into the room, threw her arms out, threw her head back, and screeched.

"*Ad hoverum sancterum dessit cray,*" she said, and sounded like she was praying. "*Quemmor stempanos knevit.*"

Tibor was standing almost in front of her, frozen. Gregor lurched through the crowd toward him, grabbed him by the arm, and pulled him back.

"Tibor," he said, "what's going on here? Who is that woman?"

Tibor shook his head violently, as if to clear it of hallucinations—and Gregor didn't blame him.

"Branch," Tibor said in a croak. "That is Dr. Branch."

"Who? The redheaded woman? That's Dr. Katherine Branch?"

"That is what I said, Krekor, yes."

"For God's sake. What does she think she's—"

"I told you, Krekor, I told you." Tibor was suddenly agitated. "She says she is a witch. She thinks she is a witch. She's doing her witch's things that she says they did in New England before the Revolution except that they didn't." He grabbed Gregor, pulled him close, and began to whisper urgently in his ear. "Krekor, I think she takes belladonna and puts it on her wrists to make her—to make her—like a drug, Krekor, I am losing my English and you don't understand Armenian. Like a drug, Krekor. I have seen her in class. She does this often."

"Listen," Gregor said. "Can you hear that?"

It was hard to hear anything. The women in black weren't the problem. Now that Dr. Katherine Branch had finished her prayer, or whatever it had been, they were absolutely silent. They had moved out into the room and begun to dance, slowly and deliberately, in a circle. It occurred to Gregor that they were probably the calmest people in the dining hall. It was the crowd that was getting hysterical and loud. The crowd might be used to Dr. Katherine Branch's antics, but it wasn't used to Miss Maryanne Veer keeling over after a little light snack of lye. They were all wound up. They were all starving for a release. Now the release was here and they had begun to send up small ripples of reaction.

"It's a siren," Tibor said suddenly. "I hear it, Krekor. It's a siren."

"It's a siren," Gregor agreed. "Do you see Dr. Crockett?"

"No."

"We've got to find some way to let the ambulance men in here, and the police, too. Everybody's surging up to the front and cutting off the access. Isn't there any other way in and out of this room?"

"The windows open, Krekor, for fire escapes."

"That's fine for fire escapes. The medical people would have a hell of a time getting their equipment through that way."

"Look, Krekor, they are all lying down on the floor."

They were indeed all lying down on the floor. Gregor didn't find it hard to credit Tibor's comment about belladonna. That, at least, would have been an authentic touch from the world of New England witchcraft. Tibor had told him about it once. So many men and women had confessed to consorting with the Devil and flying on broomsticks because they thought they had consorted with the Devil and flown on broomsticks. Belladonna was a poison. Like so many other poisons—strychnine, foxglove, airplane glue— you got high on it by flirting with a fatal dose. A miscalculation could kill you. A perfect calculation could make you feel like you were floating through air. They had done it, those old witches, in the covens of Massachusetts and Connecticut. Gregor was sure Dr. Katherine Branch and her friends were doing it now.

Whoever her friends were.

Did it matter?

"What we are going to do," he told Tibor, "is go in, and get them, and pull them out of the way. Just grab their arms and pull."

"Krekor, I am not a strong man—"

"Neither am I, Tibor. It won't matter. They're potted on something, if not belladonna then something else. Not a stimulant. It won't be difficult. Just grab their arms and pull—"

"The crowd is going to riot, Krekor."

"Not if we're fast enough."

They weren't fast enough. Gregor had barely reached the first of the bodies on the floor when a roar went up behind him. He turned instinctively and saw Dr. Kenneth Crockett standing on a table, looking almost literally like the wrath of God.

"Katherine," Dr. Crockett screamed. "Katherine, you world class bitch, you get up off of there!"

"Damn," somebody else said.

Something flew up out of the air from the back of the room in a long graceful arc and smashed into the floor next to Katherine Branch's head. It took a moment for Gregor to recognize it as one of the jack-o'-lanterns that had been out on the tables for decoration. It was a while after that before he realized that the candle inside it was still lit, and by then another one had come, and another, until it began to feel like it was raining pumpkins.

Up at the other end of the cafeteria line, at the doors that led to the foyer and the front of the building, the medical people had arrived. Gregor could see what looked like hundreds of them crowding in beside the Swedish meatballs and the roast beef au jus.

"What the *hell*," one of the men back there said. And then a low, twangy voice cut in from deep in the ranks and said, "Let me through. Just let me come on through."

If the crowd heard the men at the door, or even noticed they were there, they gave no indication of it. They seemed to have run out of pumpkins. What was raining down now was an eclectic collection of Indian corn, cardboard masks, crepe paper, and ball-point pens. The debris hit the bodies on the floor and bounced off of them without making any impression Gregor could see. Dr. Katherine Branch and her friends—six of them, Gregor counted, obsessively, six of them—lay absolutely still and absolutely silent, as if they were dead.

Down in the cafeteria line the twangy voice was droning on and on, on and on. "Let me come on through. Let me come on through. Let me come on through." Gregor strained to see who it belonged to and caught only the movement of men in firemen's uniforms and medical whites. Then the ranks of official rescuers parted, and a small man stepped into the room. He was old, and fat, and faintly ridiculous, dressed up in a Stetson hat and a khaki shirt. He could have been a Halloween reveler costumed as a good old boy Texas sheriff—except that he had a real Colt .45 in the holster on his hip, and there was something about his eyes that made Gregor think he wouldn't be afraid to use it.

The crowd paid no more attention to the man in the Stetson hat than they had to anyone else since the ruckus started. The man in the Stetson hat looked them over, walked to the edge of Katherine Branch's prostrate circle, and drew his gun. Then he pointed it at the ceiling and fired.

Well, Gregor thought, in the dead silence that followed, *that got their attention*.

The man in the Stetson hat looked pleased.

"Now what the hell," he bellowed, "is going on around here?"

Part Two

Wednesday, October 30

Eagerly I wished the morrow;
    vainly I had sought to borrow
From my books surcease of sorrow—
    sorrow for the lost Lenore—

—E. A. Poe

One

1

The chief paramedic was a young man, neither as experienced or as self-controlled as he should have been, and when he got to Miss Maryanne Veer's body he was held up for seconds by the sight of Bennis Hannaford's face. Then the spell was broken, and Gregor saw an older man come forward and take the latest of the milk cartons out of Bennis's hand. The older man was older only in a relative sense. He might have been somewhere between thirty-five and forty. From the way he held himself and the way he moved, in quick economical chops that were like controlled spasms, Gregor was sure he had gotten his medical training in Vietnam. Bennis moved back, and Jack Carroll moved back in the other direction. Even the chief paramedic showed a little deference to this older one, who was the only person anywhere near the body who seemed to know what he was doing.

On Gregor's side of the room, near the cash register and the cafeteria line, the man with the gun was getting organized. He had put the gun back in his holster—his shot hadn't made a hole in the ceiling or left a mark of any kind on it, so Gregor assumed he was using blanks—and then gone to each of the women lying on the floor and tapped them on the shoulders. The women had sat up and then stood. Now they were milling around in a group near the wall, looking ridiculous—which is the only way they could look, given the way they were dressed. It was funny, Gregor thought, but while all the craziness had been going on, he had imagined the room to be dark, even though it couldn't have been. Bright sunlight streamed through the dining room windows. It was a fine fall day at the end of October, bright and hard and cold, perfect weather for a bonfire. If it stayed this fine until midnight tomorrow, Independence College would have one of the most spectacular effigy burnings in its history.

The man with the gun was going down the line of women in black, asking their names and writing them down in a stenographer's notebook. Some of his men were doing the same thing with the rest of the crowd. Gregor noted with approval that the man with the gun was not as much of a rube as he appeared. He had left the foyer door bottled up by a large, complaisant-looking young man in a makeshift deputy's uniform. Unless someone wanted to take the risk of jumping out of one of the broad windows into the quad, nobody was going to go home without having his vital statistics put down on paper.

The man with the gun finished with the women, shook his head slightly—Gregor didn't blame him for that; those women must have been hell to talk to. Now that they were trying to behave like normal people, it was easy to see they were all high as kites—and then turned, almost knocking into the center of Gregor's chest. The man with the gun was barely five feet eight and Gregor was tall, the way a certain segment of the male Armenian population gets tall, with a few layers of fat and muscle, but mostly fat, to mitigate the height. The man with the gun tilted his head back, stared straight into Gregor's eyes, and said, in that hillbilly twang,

"All right. Who are you?"

"Gregor Demarkian," Gregor Demarkian said.

The man with the gun started to write the name in his notebook and stopped. "Gregor Demarkian? That Gregor Demarkian?"

"I suppose so," Gregor said. He hated it when people put it like that. It made him feel like—like God only knew what.

The man with the gun whacked his notebook against the side of his hip and looked pensive. "Gregor Demarkian," he repeated. "That's very interesting, under the circumstances. What are you doing here?"

"I'm visiting him." Gregor tapped Tibor on the shoulder.

"Who's him?"

"Father Tibor Kasparian," Tibor said. He put out his hand, got a look on his face that said he had no idea at all why he'd thought he ought to do that, and put the hand back in his pocket.

If the man with the gun had noticed Tibor's embarrassment, or anything about him at all, he gave no sign. He was still whacking his notebook against his hip and staring into the middle distance, as if he were concentrating furiously on the Halloween carnival in the quad, easily seen through any of the windows.

"You know," he said, "here I am, with half the service personnel of this county, or what seems like it, and what I think I'm here for is either a terrorist bombing or a woman's hysteria, and I get here, and not only is everything stranger than shit, but I've got you. Now, what I want to know is, why do I have you?"

"You've lost your twang," Gregor told him.

"I don't have a twang, except when I'm up here at the college. They like to think of us locals as unspoiled primitives in a state of grace. I'm David Markham. Swarthmore '47. Stanford Law School '51."

"Krekor is here to give a speech," Tibor cut in. "On the methods of the Federal Bureau of Investigation in apprehending serial murderers." He turned anxiously to Gregor. "Apprehending is the right word, isn't it, Krekor? In this case?"

"Yes," Gregor said.

"I'd heard you were with the FBI," David Markham said. "You're not still with the FBI, are you?"

"No."

"Well, thank God for small favors."

The medics had done what they had come to do. They had treated the most obvious of Miss Maryanne Veer's burns, and, with what must have been the advice of a doctor—every once in a while Gregor had been able to hear them talking through two-way radios, the sharp static cutting into the fuzzy confusion of the room like bolt lightning cutting through a cloud-clogged sky—put a tube down her throat and started administering a more chemically calculated antidote than milk. Now they were pushing back the crowd and making way for the stretcher men. They had the body wrapped in a blanket, as if they were protecting it against shock—although, Gregor thought, it wasn't right to call it a body. The woman was still living. If she hadn't been, they would have covered her face and not gone to all the trouble of tubes and medicines.

Like Gregor and Tibor, David Markham had turned to watch them take the stretcher out. He kept rubbing his thumb against the side of his nose in a way that was both nervous and inquiring, but his face was merely reflective.

"You know," he said, "I heard one of my boys say that was Maryanne Veer."

"That's right," Gregor said. "That's what everyone's been calling her. Miss Maryanne Veer."

"You don't know her?"

"I'd never met her before we started with the milk," Gregor said. "I just got here this morning."

"Mmm, yes," David Markham said. "Did I also hear right about the lye? That she swallowed lye?"

"Technically, we ought to wait for a medical report before we say we're sure, but it had all the indications. Lye, or something based on lye. Toilet bowl cleaner. One of those drain uncloggers. Something like that."

"You're supposed to know about poisons," David Markham said. "Let me tell you what I know about Maryanne Veer. She's local, in case nobody told you. Born and brought up in Belleville. She's about ten years older than I am and from the other side of town, so I never met her family—Belleville is the kind of place where it matters, which side of town your family lives on—but I've heard about them. Her father was a right righteous bastard. They had a house out on Deegan Road, right at the edge before the hills get going for real, and you know what that house had? An outhouse."

"An outhouse?" Tibor was confused.

"An outhouse," David Markham repeated firmly. "It's against sixteen different building codes, and that doesn't matter a damn, not in Belleville and not in anyplace south of here. Hillbillies. That's what Maryanne's family was. A pack of hillbillies who'd come down into town and bought shoes. Most of the people south of here are pretty decent. Ignorant and uneducated but decent. But Maryanne's father. Well, Maryanne's father was what the academic snobs around here really mean when they use the word *hillbilly*. Do you know what I'm trying to get at?"

"Of course," Gregor said. "Whatever else went on here today, Miss Maryanne Veer did not try to commit suicide."

"Exactly," David Markham said.

"I don't understand," Tibor said. "Why does it mean she would not have tried to commit suicide? From this description, Krekor, I would think she would have had great cause for depression."

"True," Gregor told him, "but she would never have used lye. Don't you remember what that girl was saying when we were pouring milk? Maybe you weren't there. There was a girl, Chessey something—"

"Chessey Flint."

"Whatever. She was talking about some cabin some club has up in the woods somewhere—"

"The Climbing Club. On Hillman's Rock."

"It doesn't matter, Tibor. The point is, the cabin has outhouses behind it, and next to the outhouses she says there's a tub of lye. Marked as lye, at any rate. The point is, what you clean outhouses with is lye."

"Maryanne Veer grew up with outhouses," David Markham said. "She knew too much about lye to think of using it on herself. That leaves two alternatives. Accident and attempted murder."

"Maybe not," Gregor said.

"What do you mean?"

"Let's dispense with accident, in the first place," Gregor said. He explained about the broken teacup, about the foaming action of lye in water—which would have been superfluous, because David Markham obviously knew all about lye, except that Gregor had no idea where Tibor had been during his original explanation—and about the absence of any sign of any other food anywhere near the body.

"Of course, I could be wrong," he said. "I had to do my looking around while I was administering an antidote to a woman with third-degree burns in her throat. Those are hardly the best of conditions for making an eyeball search. But before we started administering the antidote, there was a period, maybe a full minute and maybe less, when everyone was frozen. And I didn't see anything else on the floor then, either. She ingested lye. It had to have been something she ate immediately before she began to gag, because lye works that quickly. It couldn't have been in her tea. It had to have been in something else. The something else is now missing."

"Whoosh," David Markham said.

"There's also the obvious," Gregor told him. "I could write you a scenario to show you how lye could get into the tea water, accidentally. I couldn't write you one to show you how lye got into, say, a sandwich, accidentally."

"Then it does have to have been murder," David Markham said, "or attempted murder. Please God, attempted murder. With any luck, they'll get her up to County Receiving and straighten her out in time."

Gregor nodded. "We got to her early. It shouldn't be impossible. But as for murder or attempted murder—look, have you ever heard of anyone who was actually murdered with lye?"

"I've heard of plenty of people who have died from it," David Markham said. "Kids, especially. Every year you get one or two who get into the Drāno and there they go."

"Accidents." Gregor waved that away. "I've read about those things myself. But you're right, Mr. Markham, it's almost always children, who are smaller and have less resistance, and the accidents are almost always bizarre. I remember a case a few years ago where a zookeeper fell off a ledge into a vat of the stuff that had been mixed with water to clean a bears' cage. The results were predictably nasty. But murder—no. I've never heard of a single person who was murdered with lye. I'm not entirely sure it could be done."

"But Krekor," Tibor said, "why not? The substance is lethal."

"Yes, the substance is lethal, but look at the facts in the present situation. Miss Maryanne Veer is not dead. There's a good chance she will not be dead, not from this, although she may be severely damaged. Lye is an extremely corrosive alkali. As soon as it touches the skin, it burns and it burns badly. Anyone ingesting it with food would do just what Miss Maryanne Veer did. One sip—or one bite. Instant pain. Excruciating pain. Then she'd drop whatever she was holding and try to spit out whatever was in her mouth. She might swallow a little because swallowing is a reflex, and she wouldn't have to swallow much to do herself severe damage, but it's highly unlikely she'd swallow enough to die unless she was prevented from reaching medical help. And even then it would take two or three days."

"Maybe," David Markham said, "but you're making an assumption. You're assuming that whoever fed her that stuff knew what there was to know about lye."

"You think the people at this college wouldn't?"

"I think some of them would and some of them wouldn't." Markham nodded across the room. The body was gone, but the small space where it had lain was still empty. It was as if the people who had witnessed Miss Maryanne Veer's pain were afraid to step into the circle, afraid of a hex. Even Bennis was sitting on one of the tables near the window, smoking a cigarette and looking anywhere but at the place where she had so recently been. Jack Carroll and Chessey Flint were farther away, back all the way to the wall, in deep conversation. Gregor thought Chessey was crying.

"Ken Crockett," Markham said, "is local, too, from the richest family in the county. I used to be impressed by the Crocketts before I went out to California and saw what rich was really like. Never mind. Rich or not, Ken would know all about lye. He'd have picked it up somewhere. But the rest of these people?" Markham shrugged. "The rest of these people are like Ken's lady friend, nice little intellectuals from nice little upper-middle-class suburbs, people who have spent all their lives in hermetically sealed, overzoned, planned communities among their own kind."

"The cafeteria workers wouldn't be like that, would they?" Gregor asked. "And they're the most likely suspects, in a case like this."

"No," Markham agreed, "they wouldn't be like that. But I don't agree they're the most likely suspects. They'd have had the best opportunity, but I know most of them. None of them is nuts, as far as I can tell. And none of them had any reason to hurt Maryanne Veer."

"What about Tibor's friend, that boy, Jack Carroll? I don't know anything about his history, but the impression I got is that he's from anything but an upper-middle-class family."

"That's true. He's on scholarship. He works down at the Sunoco to make his pocket money."

"So?" Gregor said.

Markham sighed. "So I think I'm going to go over there and look for a sandwich or a cheese Danish or something, and if I don't find it I'm going to treat this as an attempted murder. You going to be around for a couple of days?"

"I'm supposed to give my speech tomorrow, late. I'll be around until the morning of the first."

"Good. Why don't you meet me tomorrow morning, around seven, right here? I think I'm going to want to pick your brain."

"I'd be glad to."

"*Glad* isn't the word I'd use in connection with any of this," Markham said.

He had stuffed his notebook into the back pocket of his pants while he had been talking to them. Now he took it out, squinted at it, and sighed again. Then he headed across the room toward the open space where the body had been, parting the crowd in front of him as easily as God had parted the Red Sea.

Gregor waited until he had gotten all the way to the other side of the room and gone down on his knees to look under the table Bennis was sitting on. Then he grabbed Tibor by the arm and said,

"Come on. There's something I want to see."

2

What Gregor wanted to see was the floor under the tray-rest just inside the line from the cash register. Talking to Markham, it had hit him all of a sudden that that was where something was likely to be. He couldn't have said what. It wasn't that clear. Like a lot of successful detectives—in police departments across the country, in the FBI, maybe in the CIA (although he doubted it; he'd never had much respect for the professionalism of the CIA)—most of what he knew was buried in his deep memory. It consisted of a collection of rank trivialities that added up to more than the trivial, but if he'd tried to keep either the collection or its sum in the forefront of his consciousness, he wouldn't have had any attention to spare for anything else. Like most men, he wanted to have attention to spare for everything else: for Tibor and Bennis and Donna, for good dinners and enjoyably bad movies; for his memories of his wife. He certainly didn't want to turn into the kind of neurotic law enforcement officer, retired or otherwise, who used the vagaries of his profession as the background music to his life.

The cafeteria line was entirely clear of people. The medical personnel had left campus with Miss Maryanne Veer on her stretcher. David Markham's police deputies were spread out through the students and faculty and food workers who had been at lunch when the poisoning happened. The girl who had been at the cash register and the students who had been tending to the Swedish meatballs and the lime Jell-O had withdrawn into a group of their own in a far corner. They were being comforted by an older woman who was probably the college dietician and their boss. Dr. Katherine Branch and her friends were doing their best to fade into the woodwork, near the place where they had laid themselves out on the floor. Their clothes were spattered with pieces of pumpkin pulp and smudges of face paint.

"It occurred to me," Gregor told Tibor, "that I had no

right to assume that when Miss Veer's tray fell, all its contents scattered in the same general direction. The cup was right next to her left foot. I didn't see her tray—"

"I did, Krekor. It went toward the table closest to her, toward the windows. When it fell, Chessey Flint picked it up."

"What did she do with it?"

"Put it on the table in front of her. It was automatic, I think, Krekor. She is a girl who has been brought up to that kind of politeness."

"Maybe. We'll get back to that later. The tray went toward the windows. Fine. There's nothing to say that whatever else was on it also went toward the windows. Miss Veer was standing very close to the cash register. It makes as much sense to think that something might have fallen in that direction."

"Do you mean you think you were wrong, Krekor? No one has taken the sandwich or whatever it was? It has simply fallen where we have not seen it?"

"If it did, it didn't fall toward the cash register. I could see all the way under the cash register stand, the tray-rest and the food service tables, all the way back to that wall with the canisters on it, from where I was standing when I was talking to David Markham."

"Oh."

They had reached the steel-tube tray-rest and the cash register, the clear plastic-fronted dessert display and the large bucket of crushed ice stuffed with cans of Coke and Dr Pepper and carbonated lemonade. Gregor noticed a few things he hadn't before: little straw baskets full of Halloween spaced out along the top of the plastic shield of the food display; a wart-faced, grey-skinned witch's mask hung on the hot-water canister; a mummy rising up out of the ice next to a can of Vernors ginger ale.

"It's got to be something small," he told Tibor. "It might even be a piece of food, but I'm not expecting to get that lucky. Pick up anything you find."

"I am likely to find a lot of things, Krekor. Lost earrings. Money."

"Leave the money on the edge of the cash register. That's not what we're looking for."

"Krekor." Tibor hesitated, so long and in such an uneasy way that Gregor began to become alarmed. Then he brushed at the front of his cassock and straightened up. "Krekor, do you believe what you said to David Markham, that the people who work in the cafeteria are the most likely suspects?"

"Yes and no."

"What does that mean, Krekor, yes and no?"

"Yes, because they have the best access to the food. You have to take that into consideration, Tibor, whether you like it or not. There's always the chance that what we're dealing with here is a lunatic, like the man who put the cyanide in the Tylenol capsules."

"Did they catch that person and know he was a man, Krekor?"

"I don't remember. It happened when Elizabeth was sick."

"Why the no?"

"A lot of reasons," Gregor said. "In the first place, a lunatic wouldn't have bothered to get rid of the evidence, especially not at the risk of exposing himself. Why should he bother? The frightening thing about incidents of that kind is that they so seldom leave anything that actually points to anybody in particular. In this situation, it would have been easy to set it up in a way that left him completely in the clear. The victim would be random. Our lunatic wouldn't be singled out as a man with a motive. It would be easy to throw suspicion on somebody else. He only had to put the lye in the food in a section of the line where he wasn't working. Why leave the line to pick up what remained of the food, in full view of a hundred or so people, a fair proportion of whom could identify him? If he was par for the course at this sort of thing, he'd be happy to have the rest of us know just what he'd done and how he'd done it. The only thing he'd be trying to protect is the who."

"What else?" Tibor asked.

"What else should be obvious, Tibor. The Tylenol incident and things like it make the papers and cause a lot of fuss, but the reason for that is that they're out of the ordinary. Stranger-to-stranger crime is rising, of course, because of the drug problem, but in ninety-nine percent of the cases, in murder and in attack, the victim and the victimizer not only know each other but know each other well. If the food hadn't disappeared, I would have had to assume a lunatic, on practical grounds. With the food gone, I have to assume something else."

"You are sure the lye was not put into the tea, Krekor?"

"Positive. There was lye mixed with the tea by the time the tea hit the floor. It was hissing away like a snake at her feet just before she keeled over. She would never have drunk it if she heard it doing that."

"Even is she was distracted?"

"It was loud, Tibor. She would have had to be virtually comatose."

"I was afraid of that," Tibor said. "Do you realize, Krekor, that if it was someone who knew her who tried to kill her, it was somebody who is in the Program?"

"Why? David Markham said she was local. She must have known—"

"David Markham also said most of the people on campus are not local, and he is right. Miss Veer knew the staff of the Program and a few of the senior students—Jack Carroll and Chessey Flint, a few else. She knew some of the members of the administration in passing and some of the general staff also in passing. I have talked to her, Krekor. I have made it a point because she was always so lonely. She has a woman she lives with in town. Other than that, her life is in Liberty Hall."

"You can't know that, Tibor, no matter what she said to you. You can never really know anybody well on six weeks' acquaintance."

"I know that I have seen at least one thing on this floor," Tibor said.

Gregor watched him kneel down and stand up again, holding something very small in his hand and frowning at it. When he was standing fully upright, Tibor held it out on his palm for Gregor to see.

"There," he said, "what's that?"

"That" was a solid little cylinder of metal, half an inch in diameter and less than a quarter of an inch thick. Gregor took it out of Tibor's hand and examined it in the light.

"I know what it looks like," Gregor said. "A solder plug."

"A solder plug. I don't know what this is, Krekor, a solder plug. But there is something else."

Tibor went down again, came up again, held out his hand again. What he had this time was a small ragged piece of cotton, dyed black and raveled at the edges, as if it had caught on something and torn.

Two

1

Dr. Katherine Branch did not use real belladonna in the DMSO ointment she put on her wrists to perform the rituals of Wicca, and she didn't consort with the Devil, either. Even if she could have made herself believe in the Devil—she had inherited a stubborn middle-class American resistance to belief in evil of any kind, a resistance that two decades of work in campus rape crisis centers, storefront women's health centers, and studies of intercultural practices of wife-battering had done nothing to weaken— she would not have worshiped him. It bothered her sometimes that her namesake, that Katherine Branch who had lived in Hartford in 1652 and been hanged for a witch on a scaffold hung over the Connecticut River in 1676, had been so thoroughly celebratory of male images of power. For Dr. Katherine Branch, the whole point of Wicca was that it was so woman centered. That was why you called it Wicca instead of witchcraft. You had to take possession of the terms of the debate, wrestle with the differences between male and female vocabularies, insist on your own point of view. That was all anything ever was, point of view. Even gravity was suspect, and possibly illusion. It was always being described in such erectile terms. As for witchcraft, that was the name men had given to the spirituality of women, making it something dark and threatening. The Devil was what men called the Great Goddess of all creation, changing her with all her power into a man.

What Dr. Katherine Branch put into the DMSO ointment she used on her wrists to perform the rituals of Wicca was a little diluted hashish, and she was beginning to think it had been a mistake. What she wanted was a release from the prison of her repressions. What she had gotten was a dry mouth, a headache, and that awful dizziness she always ended up with when she smoked a little grass. When she was dizzy she couldn't analyze and she couldn't organize. She hated not being able to do either. Besides, it might not be as safe as she had thought. The dry mouth was a bad sign. When you got it from antihistamines, you were warned about the effect they were having on your heart.

She stepped back out of the spray of the shower, leaned over and shut the water off. Through the shower stall door, she listened for the sounds of Vivi back in the apartment, and heard them: the clink of metal on glass, the hiss of coffee coming through the Dripmaster. Vivi was in the kitchen. Katherine pushed open the door of the shower stall and stepped out onto the blue terry cloth mat. This was the first time she had taken a shower in Vivi's apartment—or even been in Vivi's apartment for more than five minutes at a time—and all she could say was that the place was claustrophobic. The shower stall was so small it had made her feel as if she was suffocating. The rest of the bathroom was not much bigger. There was not quite room enough for a toilet and a narrow sink with no counter attached. The medicine cabinet looked like it had been left over from World War II. It was the personal touches that bothered Katherine most, however. The blue terry cloth mat with its ribbed rubber backing, the blue terry cloth towels on the rack near the door, the lacquered white wicker utility shelves shoved over the back of the toilet and crammed with extra rolls of toilet paper and white plastic canisters painted over with bluebells and birds: it was all so damn K mart and Sears. Vivi could have chosen better.

Of course, Katherine could have chosen better, too. She could have brought them both back to her own apartment, instead of here. It was just that that hadn't seemed like a very safe choice, after what had happened to Miss Maryanne Veer. Katherine couldn't for the life of her figure out why that had been so. She didn't expect anyone to put lye in her own food, especially not at home. Like most of the rest of the faculty who lived in Constitution

House, she kept almost no food on the premises. She didn't expect Sheriff David Markham and his men to come bursting through her door like a SWAT team, either. She couldn't imagine them doing it and she couldn't imagine what they would do it for. Maybe she was having some kind of reaction to the hashish she had never had before.

She reached for the robe Vivi had laid out for her—wraparound and made for a man; *there* was something to think about—and drew it around her. Then she stepped through the bathroom door into the cramped back hall and said, "Vivi?"

In the kitchen, the sounds of coffee making and domestic neurosis came to a halt. Katherine waited for Vivi's answering call, but it didn't come. Neither did the renewed sounds of coffee making. The silence in the apartment felt as thick and opaque as mayonnaise.

Katherine walked down the hall, through the tiny living room, across the dining ell and into the kitchen. Vivi was standing at the sink, with her back to the rest of the apartment, looking at the plain white stoneware coffee cup she was holding in her hand.

Katherine got to the archway and stopped. "Vivi," she said again. "Are you all right?"

"I'm fine." Vivi let the coffee cup drop into the sink and turned around. In the interests of efficiency, Katherine had let Vivi take her shower first. Vivi now looked "normal," in the sense that she was not in black and had no greasepaint on her face. Beyond that, she was a study in the problems of the hashish solution. Her pupils were dilated. Her face was flushed in places and dead white in others. She was sweating. She pointed across the room to the two-person table shoved into the corner and said, "There it is. I got it. But Katherine, don't ever ask me to do anything like that again."

"It's because of the anointing," Katherine said mildly. "I don't think I mixed the ointment right. I put in too much of everything."

"It has nothing to do with the goddamned anointing, Katherine. It has to to with the police. They were all over Miss Veer's office, in case you haven't guessed."

"What did they do when they saw you there?"

"They didn't see me there."

"How did you get in?"

"I went straight to the chairman's office. Through the window, if you really have to know. With all the rest of the nutsiness going on on campus, nobody even noticed. Then I got that damned file and got out. I wish you'd look at it. I'd like to think I risked my job, my professional reputation, and my neck for something more important than one of your hashish fantasies."

Actually, Katherine thought, she didn't have hashish fantasies. The same drugs that made everyone else see visions only made her feel dull and nervous. Even LSD—which she had tried once in the 1960s, because the man she was sleeping with had tried it, and because she believed in men in those days—had done nothing more than make her light-headed and nauseated. Still, Vivi didn't know that, and Vivi was angry with her—not only because of the file, but because of the hex. Vivi hadn't wanted to have anything to do with that hex, and in retrospect she probably thought she had been right. Katherine couldn't see it that way. You couldn't remain passive in the face of an all-out assault on your integrity. You couldn't remain passive, period. Passivity was what had been turning women into robots for the last 6,000 years.

Katherine sat down at the table, opened the file, and paged through it. There wasn't much in it, and she hadn't expected there to be. It was labeled "Feminist Approaches To," which was short for "Feminist Approaches to the American Idea," and it contained three single-page course proposals she had written herself, two syllabi she had also written herself, and a thin sheaf of faculty after-course effectiveness evaluations. The evaluations were routinely bad. One of them—written, of course, by Ken Crockett—called Katherine's course in the History of Women in Colonial New England "an exercise in the glorification of sexual organs over reason." The one that hurt was by Alice Elkinson. It called Katherine's course in the Feminist Deconstruction of Witchcraft "a concerted effort to indoctrinate students in the moral superiority of a state of permanent victimhood."

Katherine closed the folder, shoved it away from her, and said, "Nothing personal at all. I wonder where they put it."

"How do you know 'it' even exists?" Vivi asked her. "Even if your analysis is picture perfect and right on the nose, what makes you think they would put it down on paper? What makes you think they would leave themselves open to an EOC lawsuit?"

"It's a Republican administration, Vivi. They don't have to worry about an EOC lawsuit. And I know there's at least one personal evaluation, because Donegal Steele wrote it. Marsha Diedermeyer saw him."

The Dripmaster had emptied a full complement of coffee into the glass pitcher at its base. Vivi took the pitcher out, put it down in front of Katherine on the table, and turned around to get cups and spoons. When she turned back, her face was set and mulish, the way it got when someone expected her to help clean up after dinner, just because she was a woman.

"Katherine," she said, sitting down, "listen to me. Get Donegal Steele out of your mind for a minute. Think about Miss Maryanne Veer."

"What about Miss Maryanne Veer?"

"Somebody just tried to kill her."

"Maybe," Katherine said. "Maybe not. It could have been an accident. That's why I sent you to get the file, Vivi. I didn't want to have something lying around that would give them an excuse to incriminate us. You know that's what they want to do. Especially that idiot David Markham."

"I don't happen to think David Markham is such an idiot," Vivi said, "but that's beside the point. What do you think of the other one, the one Father Tibor asked up to lecture?"

"Gregor Demarkian? What am I supposed to think of him? A typical authoritarian male with delusions of genital superiority."

"Well, Katherine, that's all well and good, but delusions or not, Demarkian happens to have a certain reputation."

"A reputation for what?"

"A reputation for catching murderers."

"You mean like Nero Wolfe?" Katherine laughed. "Oh, for God's sake, Vivi, lighten up. The man's a fascist. He was in the CIA."

"FBI."

"Same difference."

"I don't think they think so," Vivi said, "and don't give me a lecture on false consciousness. I couldn't stand it. Katherine, I just went into an office ordinarily protected by a woman someone just tried to murder and stole a file. Under the circumstances, even a raging feminist might start to think that the reason someone tried to kill that woman was to get that file."

"That file?"

"Or some other file sitting in that office, yes. Katherine, that Gregor Demarkian person thinks like a policeman, even if he isn't one officially anymore. And he's no hick like David Markham."

"So?"

"So," Vivi said, taking a deep breath, "what we have to do now is wait till the coast is clear and put the file back."

The coffee in Katherine's cup had a smoky film on top, as if it had been injected with dust. Katherine picked up her spoon and stirred it. Sometimes she found it hard to take, just how much she disliked Vivi Wollman. Sometimes she found it hard to take Vivi, period.

Still, Vivi was waiting for an answer, and Katherine supposed she owed her one. In Katherine's experience, you always ended up owing women something, usually something you didn't have to give.

"Well," she said, still staring into her coffee cup, "here's what I think. I don't think we have to put that file back. I think *you* have to put that file back. And I think you ought to do it soon, Vivi, because if you don't the whole world is going to begin wondering about that guilty look on your face."

2

Jack Carroll had grown up in places that had inspired him only with the determination to get out and go somewhere else, but in spite of the conventional demonology of those places—and there was a demonology; when he had first come to college and encountered it Jack had been shocked—he had never seen anyone killed until he saw Miss Maryanne Veer fall to the Independence College dining room floor. Of course, Miss Maryanne Veer had not been killed, not yet. They had taken her out to County Receiving and were doing their best for her. Jack's private opinion was that their best was not going to be good enough. That raw skin, that strangled gurgling scream she had tried to heave up from deep inside her chest—there had been such pain and finality about it that it had frozen him where he stood, with his hand on Chessey's back and his mind on their private tryst of the morning. Part of him had been watching, unbelieving, unable to move. Part of him had been thinking about sex. There had been something so obscene about the juxtaposition that he had been on the verge of being violently ill. He was still on the verge, now, almost three hours later. It didn't matter at all that he had not been thinking about sex the way he usually thought about sex. He had not been having fantasies about what might happen someday when he and Chessey both went totally out of control. He was no longer sure that Chessey was capable of going totally out of control, or that he was, either. What had been bothering him was the idea that their separate commitments to self-control were coming from opposite directions, working at cross-purposes. In the beginning, Chessey had held back out of principle and he out of fear of losing her. Lately their positions had seemed to be reversed, although Jack didn't think that what Chessey was most afraid of was his own walking out. He wondered what she was afraid of. He had been wondering if her fear was something he ought to do something about, when Miss Maryanne Veer hit the floor.

Now they were sitting halfway up Hillman's Rock, at that point in the climb where they would have had to bring the ropes and the pitons out. It was after four thirty and the world around them was getting dark, and cold. After Miss Maryanne Veer had been taken away there had been formalities to go through, and the formalities had gone on forever. Or seemed to. Jack was just beginning to think it was time to light a fire. Chessey was sitting on a small outcrop of rock, carefully sewing a small black patch of cloth onto the edge of his bat cape, where it had torn. He was lying propped up on one shoulder in a bed of leaves. Chessey had on heavy hiking boots and khaki pants and a reindeer-patterned sweater. She looked impossibly sweet and impossibly childish.

"I don't know," Chessey was saying, "I think it must have been an accident. No matter what that man Mr. Demarkian said. Nobody would actually go out and try to kill a person like that."

"Why not?"

"Because it was so horrible. It makes me sick to think of it even now. Can you imagine doing something like that and then standing around to watch? If someone did it on purpose, they had to have been there to see Miss Veer fall. I was sitting at the table right next to the cash register when it happened. I didn't see anybody leave."

"Maybe whoever did it left a long time before that. Maybe it was somebody who worked in the cafeteria, on the breakfast shift or on setup maybe, and they put the lye into a peanut butter sandwich and then walked away home."

"Not caring who might pick it up or who might eat it? Children eat in that cafeteria sometimes, Jack, when they've got faculty for parents and their parents bring them."

"I know."

"I don't know what's happening to you," Chessey said. "Lately you've gotten so—cynical."

Jack didn't know what was happening to him lately, either. He just knew it was time to start a fire. There was a wind blowing down from the north that was going straight through the sleeves of his flannel shirt and the sleeves of his thermal T-shirt and the skin of his arms. The down vest he was wearing was no help at all. He sat up and reached for his daypack, where he had matches and kerosene and everything else he needed. There were people in the Climbing Club who insisted on rubbing two sticks together and praying to the Great Spirit for fire and rain, but he wasn't one of them. That sort of thing exasperated him to the point of madness.

"You know what?" he said. "I think someday I'd like to be like Mr. Demarkian. I'd like to be that kind of man."

"Fat and old."

"Something tells me we're all going to end up fat and old whether we want to or not. No, that's not what I mean. I mean sure of myself like that, knowing where I'm going. Where I want to be."

"I didn't like Mr. Demarkian," Chessey said. "He made me feel, I don't know, creepy."

"Why?"

"The way he looked at me, I guess. Like he could see right through me and listen to what I was thinking. Like he thought I was stupid or vain or shallow or something."

"You're projecting. You're getting your period and going through one of your insecurity phases."

"Maybe. But I'll tell you who else didn't like him, Jack. Your favorite person on earth, Dr. Kenneth Crockett."

All the sticks he could find were damp. The leaves were sodden. Kerosene or no kerosene, it was going to be a hell of a job to get a fire lit. He made a pile of the best material he could find and dosed it anyway.

"I don't think Dr. Kenneth Crockett is my favorite person on earth," he said carefully, "especially not lately. He seems to be metamorphosing into a self-absorbed jerk. And maybe I'm not surprised that he doesn't like Mr. Demarkian."

"Dr. Elkinson was surprised. He told her he thought Mr. Demarkian was a spy. I heard him."

"What do you think he meant, a spy?"

"I don't have to think anything," Chessey said. "It's like I told you. I heard them. Dr. Crockett said he thought

Father Tibor was asked to get Mr. Demarkian up here, by the police. He said—"

"Chessey, that's ridiculous. The police couldn't possibly know someone was going to try to kill Miss Veer. If they had, they would have stopped it."

"Maybe. But I can see what Dr. Crockett meant, Jack. I mean, the man knows so much about everything. He doesn't even have to ask you things and he should have to. About yourself, I mean."

"He's a friend of Father Tibor's. Tibor probably talks to him."

"Dr. Crockett told Dr. Elkinson she'd better be sure she didn't have anything lying around her life she didn't want found."

"Do you think it was Dr. Elkinson who tried to kill Miss Veer?"

"Jack, for God's sake—"

"Maybe they were in it together. Crockett and Elkinson. They're in everything else together."

"I hate it when you get this way. I really hate it."

"Look," Jack said, "Gregor Demarkian investigates murders. That's what he does with his life. If you'd read the handout for his lecture, you'd know that's what he *has* done with his life. Ken Crockett is just getting all academic liberal intellectual paranoid about it, that's all. Unless he and Dr. Elkinson were the ones who tried to kill Miss Veer."

"*Jack.*"

"Well, somebody tried to kill her, didn't they? How's that cape coming along? When I saw that rip I wanted to kill myself. Forty dollars down the drain."

Chessey had actually stopped sewing several minutes ago, but Jack had had no way of knowing whether she'd stopped because she was finished or because she'd become too involved in their conversation to concentrate on stitches. Now she held the cape up for his inspection, solid and seemingly undamaged, a wall of black against the graying sky of evening.

"It won't look as good in full daylight," she said, "but you've only got to wear it in the daylight for tomorrow and

I figured the point was really the bonfire tomorrow night. Isn't it?"

"Definitely."

"It'll do, then." She folded it, folded it again, and put it down on her lap, a fat black square. "Jack?" she said. "I was thinking. It's so quiet up here, and dark. And we're alone. And this morning was, I don't know, off somehow. So I was thinking . . ."

She let her voice trail into nothingness, a lilting diminuendo that was like music. It struck him that three days ago he would have felt faint to hear that music, and now he felt nothing at all, or almost nothing, just careful, as if the ground were made of broken glass and he was being forced to walk across it on bare feet. He got a wooden match out of his box, lit it, and tossed it onto his pile of sticks and leaves. It caught, sputtered, and caught again. The air smelled full of kerosene.

"No," he said. "Chessey, not right now, all right? I don't think it's a good idea."

He wasn't looking at her, but he heard the music change, and he knew what the change meant.

She was crying.

3

It was five o'clock, and over at Constitution House, Dr. Alice Elkinson had locked herself in her apartment. She had not only turned the switch at the center of the doorknob, but thrown the bolt at the top of the door. Then she had gone to every window in her living room and bedroom and drawn the curtains shut. In the kitchen, she only had shades, and they hardly seemed like enough. Even with all three of them pulled tight, she could see the light streaming in from the porch, making a puddle of dirty yellow in the middle of her kitchen table.

There were people in this world, and especially on this campus, who thought Dr. Alice Elkinson had had an easy life—and mostly the impression was true. She had always been pretty and she had always been smart and she had come from a family with enough money to let her do what she wanted but not so much that it might have made her crazy. Her abilities had always matched her ambitions. The men she had loved had always loved her back.

Still, nobody's life on this earth is an Eden. There had been periods and incidents in Dr. Alice Elkinson's that she would not like to repeat. What stuck out most in her mind now was her one experience of violence before the attack on Miss Maryanne Veer. She had been a third-year doctoral student at Berkeley and still possessed by that adolescent certainty of her own invulnerability, still walking through a world in which bad things happened only to other people. It had been late on a Tuesday night, after eleven o'clock. She was doing what she always did at eleven o'clock on weekday nights, walking home from the library. Usually, she walked only on well-lit streets or streets full of people who never went to bed. On this Tuesday night, she had been too tired for that and had taken a shortcut instead. She had been just behind Sproul Hall when the boy had grabbed her, his arm reaching out of a darkness she could not penetrate, his long fingernails digging into the skin of her wrist and drawing blood. She had jerked away from him, screamed at the top of her lungs, and started running. She had gone all the way home that way, screaming and screaming, until the screaming began to feel like one of those Marine Corps war cries that were supposed to help soldiers charge into battle. Nobody had stopped her. Nobody had followed her. Nobody had asked her what was wrong. Berkeley had been like that then.

Later, what she remembered was sitting in her apartment and wondering if the incident had happened at all. It had been so bizarre, she hadn't been able to keep hold of it. It had not, however, been as bizarre as this.

After she'd locked all the doors and closed all the windows, she had sat down in the best chair in her living room and made herself be still. Now she stood up and made herself walk back the way she had come, back to the kitchen and the back porch door. She had left the back porch door unlocked and slightly open—which said something. Maybe it said she hadn't been able to delude herself into thinking she didn't believe it.

She took a deep breath, opened the porch door wide, and stepped out onto the balcony. There was nothing back here but trees, no other part of the campus to look out on. What sounds she heard were coming from all the way on the other side of the building, where the students were holding another of their pre-Halloween parties on the quad. If the entire faculty of Independence College had been ax-murdered in their beds this afternoon, the students would still be holding a pre-Halloween party on the quad.

The problem with the porch was with those buckets of lye Dr. Steele had left with her.

They were missing.

Three

1

By the time the bells in Declaration Tower rang six o'clock, Gregor Demarkian needed a rest—not a nap, not a mental and physical vacation, but the real rest of being outside the pressurized circle of social restraint. He was not tired. It had been years since he had been part of a real emergency, instead of being called in afterward to lend support and clean up. Even in the three murder investigations he had involved himself in since leaving the Bureau, he had served as a kind of consultant. It amazed him that his body still responded so well to the need to overcompensate for its preferred and natural lethargy. He was adrenalated. His mind was working too fast. Every muscle in his body was twitching and jiggling, as if they had been carbonated. He knew all the rules of official murder investigations, especially the iron one about how, after forty-eight hours, the odds against catching the killer grew more and more remote by the second. In his experience, it was a rule that did more harm than good. It made people rush and occupy themselves with busywork. It was the catalyst for dozens of unnecessary interviews and hundreds of extravagantly examined blind alleys. He did much better when he gave himself the time and distance to calm down, untangle his emotions, and face the problem like a rational man.

The problem, at the moment, was finding the time and distance. They were in Tibor's apartment—he and Bennis and Tibor himself—and the topic on the agenda was dinner. Under the circumstances, it was not a topic Bennis and Tibor were approaching with a great deal of common sense.

Bennis was agitated and distraught. She had seen at least one of her sisters die by violence. She didn't take well to outbreaks of murderousness in her fellow man. Of course, Gregor admitted, nobody did, not even veteran agents of the Federal Bureau of Investigation. With Bennis, though, the reaction was particularly acute, a kind of psychological nuclear implosion. It made Gregor wonder why Bennis was always so eager to become part of his problems—and so obsessed with filling up her spare time in the reading of murder mysteries.

For Tibor, the problem was different, more general, pervasive instead of specific. Most of the violence he had seen in his life—and there had been a lot of it—had been both officially sanctioned and rigorously theologized. He had told Gregor once that the most frightening hour of his life had come one afternoon when he was ten and sitting in his fifth-form Political class. His teacher, a pock-faced woman brought in from the outside the way priests were brought in from the outside to teach religion in some American Catholic schools, had delivered a lecture on "the fundamental lie of Christianity," and that lie had been this: that Christianity demonized violence, illegitimated revolution, and celebrated the weakness of the weak. Change is a garden, she had told them, and that garden could only be properly watered by blood.

Now Tibor sat in his armchair, white and small, and watched Bennis pace back and forth across the living room. Gregor felt sorry for him. He looked so old and defeated, even though he was actually younger than Gregor himself. It had only taken one undeniable instrusion of the reality of the outside world to knock him back into a frame of mind he probably thought he had forgotten.

Bennis had come to rest in the middle of the room, with her foot on one of the picnic baskets the boys—Freddie and Max?—had delivered while they were out. She reached into the pocket of her shirt, took out her cigarettes, and lit up.

"The thing is," she said, waving her wand of smoke in the air, "the one thing I am not going to do tonight is go back to that place to eat. Assuming it's even open. If that

David Markham person has any sense, he'll have sealed it up."

"If he has, he isn't going to leave it sealed for long," Gregor said. "He intends to eat breakfast there tomorrow."

Bennis took a deep drag, tilted her head back, and blew smoke at the ceiling. "Marvelous," she said. "I love macho. I just love it. However, being a girl, I do not have to display it, which is fortunate. I want to go out to dinner."

"Bennis," Tibor said tentatively, "there is so much food here. All these picnic baskets. There is so much food, I should distribute it to the poor. I will never eat it."

"Well, Tibor, distribute it to the poor if you want, but don't distribute it to me tonight. Honey cakes. Doritos nacho-flavored tortilla chips. For God's sake."

"I like Doritos nacho-flavored tortilla chips," Tibor said. "You open the bag, you put it in your lap, you go on reading. Then in a little while you have finished the bag and you are full, and you have not been distracted."

There was a column of ash an inch long on the end of Bennis's cigarette. She tapped it into the saucer Tibor had left on top of the picnic basket for her to use as an ashtray and said, "Tibor, over there on the couch I have a pocketbook. In that pocketbook I have a wallet. In that wallet I have an American Express Gold Card on which I have charged not one single thing this month. I say we get the van, take the Gold Card, and go find the kind of place where a glorified lounge singer interprets Joni Mitchell music all night and you can drop three hundred dollars on a bottle of wine."

"Bennis, please, you are at the edge of what is called Appalachia. There is no such place here."

"Oh, yes, there is. Trust me. With this college sitting here and the tuition at eighteen thousand dollars a year—I saw it in the catalog I was looking through when we were waiting for you to get ready to go to lunch—trust me, there is. Just get me the phone book. I'll find it."

"Bennis, I do not have a phone book."

"Yes, you do."

And, Gregor thought, she was undoubtedly right. In this mess of books and periodicals, pens and pencils and notepaper scribbled over in six languages, there would be a phone book, and probably an entire *Encyclopaedia Britannica* as well. He had been standing near Tibor's chair. Now he moved away and went to the window, to look out on the quad. It got dark so early in Pennsylvania, once the switch from daylight savings time had been made. The only light below him came from the globe lamps spaced out along the quad's sidewalks and the "ghost wands" that so many of the students carried. The ghost wands glowed greenly phosphorescent in the puddles of darkness where the light from the lamps didn't reach, seeming to move on their own.

"What's going on down there?" he asked. "What is it exactly everybody thinks they're doing?"

Bennis had found the phone book and was looking through it, sitting cross-legged on the floor and running her index finger across the large square restaurant ads that crammed the yellow pages. Tibor was sitting shriveled up in his chair, looking more defeated than ever. Gregor's question seemed to give him heart, and he stood up to join his friend at the window.

"You should have read the material I sent you," he said. "It is the thirtieth of October. They are having a Halloween advent."

"Advent?"

"It is not meant as sacrilege, Krekor. It is just students having fun. They have a little later a kind of street fair without a street. Students who juggle. Students who mime. Students who do magic tricks. Then they will have a voice vote and give one of the performers a prize, for talent."

"Well, that seems harmless enough."

"Yes, Krekor, it is harmless enough. It only bothers me that they do it now, with Miss Veer in the hospital and possibly dying. I cannot make it feel right to me."

"You ought to try," Gregor told him. "You were the one who said she didn't know much of anybody on campus but the people in your Program. There are hundreds of students down there. Most of them wouldn't have been in the dining room this afternoon and most of them probably would never have met her."

"Yes, Krekor, I know. But I will tell you who else will

be down there. Jack Carroll and his friend Chessey Flint. And they were in the dining room and they have met her."

"What makes you so sure they'll be there?"

"They will have to be there, Krekor. Jack Carroll is the president of the students. Chessey Flint goes always where Jack Carroll goes."

"Mmm," Gregor said.

"Found it," Bennis said. "Le Petit Chignon. My God, what a name. I don't even think it's grammatical. Anyway, 'Fine Continental Cuisine,' which is always a tip-off. 'Jackets and ties required,' which is also a tip-off. And listen to this, 'live entertainment for discriminating tastes, Wednesday and Thursday nights.' She'll have a piano, a microphone turned up too loud, and an octave and a half in voice range. When she tries to do 'Chelsea Morning,' her voice will crack."

"Wonderful," Gregor said. "Don't you ever like to go to nice restaurants? There probably are a few around here."

"I was brought up on nice restaurants. I want kitsch."

"Bennis," Tibor said, "I do not have a tie, or a jacket, either. I have only my cassocks and what I wear under them."

"They won't object to clerical dress, Father. They never do. It's Gregor I'm worried about. Do you have anything unspotted, unwrinkled, and unshredded you can wear around your neck?"

"I don't have to. I'm not going."

"Why not?" Bennis said.

"Because I'm not hungry, I'm not in the mood for your driving, and I need a little time to walk around, get some air, and think."

"Do you really?" Bennis said.

"Krekor," Tibor said, "I don't think I want to—"

"Oh, yes, you do." Bennis jumped up, looked around the room, found Tibor's coat and grabbed it. Gregor had expected her to drop the whole dinner project as soon as she found he had something else he wanted to do. She was like that about his investigations. She hated the idea of being left out of any part of them, even though she knew being left out was inevitable at least some of the time.

Tonight, apparently, she was no more in the mood for him than he was for Le Petit Chignon.

"We'll call and make a reservation because they'll expect it," she said, "but they won't be full and there won't be any problem. Then I'll go put on my dress and make up my face and put on my pearls. I don't suppose you know how to drive a car?"

"No," Tibor said.

"Well, I'll just have to be the designated driver. Maybe they'll sell me a bottle of wine to bring home. Places will sometimes if you offer them enough money and you don't look like a drunk or a cop."

"Try not to get arrested," Gregor said. "Try to do that."

"I always try to do that, Gregor. Go off walking or whatever it is you want to do. Assuming you know what you want to do. Which I doubt. I'm going to have a little fun."

2

Actually, Gregor thought, walking out of Constitution House into the quad, he knew exactly what he wanted to do. The snag came in getting to do it the way he wanted to do it. For that, he needed a guide. In this carnival of costumes and extremities, he wasn't sure where he would find one. He paused at the bottom of the Constitution House steps and looked around. The real action was taking place far away from him, at the place where the sidewalks came together to make a circular frame of concrete for the statue of the Minuteman. At his edge of the quad, the crowd was sparse. He saw a girl dressed up as Carmen Miranda, with enough wax fruit on her head to provide a legion of baby van Goghs with the material for still-lifes. He saw three boys dressed up as bikers from Hell, huddled together, passing around a little grass. The grass made Gregor feel a little irritated, but not much more. He had made it a point to stay as far out of the Great Drug War as he could get, but he was not naive. Outside the grammar schools, practically everyone, especially college administrations, had given up the fight against grass.

Gregor moved away from the Constitution House steps and into the crowd, picking his way carefully through the increasingly thick clusters of students. He'd had a half-formed idea, upstairs, that it would be easy to find who he was looking for. He had forgotten about the abysmal lack of originality that always seemed to run rampant among the young. There were at least three bats, six Frankensteins, and fourteen mummies in his immediate field of vision. There were no fewer than fifty girls dressed up as identical pumpkins, as if they had each and every one of them given up their chance to play out their fantasies to play it safe in a sorority of timidity. He moved a little closer and caught sight of the boy performing in the center, his back to the Minuteman's chest, a refreshing sight in a plain black eye mask, white tie, and tails. The boy was balancing five Day-Glo–painted polystyrene balls, large to small, top to bottom, on the end of a ghost wand balanced on the tip of his nose. Gregor didn't know if it counted as juggling or not, but whatever it was it was very impressive. He moved a little farther forward to get a better look, and then began to feel silly. This was hardly getting him where he wanted to go.

Exactly what would get him where he wanted to go, he didn't know, so he began to wander aimlessly through the crowd, looking into the blank masks that were presented for his inspection without much hope of recognizing any of the faces behind them. Somewhere near the center where the boy was performing, a tape player was pounding out what Gregor thought of as exercise-disco music. A boy to his left was using an ice pick to punch a hole in the bottom of his can of beer. As Gregor watched, he lifted the can high in the air, tilted his head back so that the bottom of the can was directly over his mouth, and pulled the flip-tab. A stream of beer shot down his throat and disappeared in thirty seconds.

Gregor began moving again. He had worked his way around in a half-circle to the best lighted place in the rectangle when he saw her, sitting alone on the bottom step of a short marble flight that led to the spotlit doors of a dormitory. The torso of her pumpkin costume seemed to have collapsed against her body. Whatever held it up and rounded it out on the girls in the middle of the quad was not operated for her. Her mask was pushed up over her head, flattening down her hair. Her gloves were off and lying in her lap. She looked so small and shriveled, Gregor almost didn't recognize her.

Then she turned her head, directly into the light, and he saw it, through the tears and the chalky deadness of the white makeup plastered over her sickly pale skin: Chessey Flint.

3

Gregor Demarkian had never had the kind of shoulder women liked to cry on. He had never gotten into the habit of offering tea and sympathy to women he didn't know. And yet, walking over to Chessey Flint, he really had no particular intention but to offer sympathy. He was aware that she might know where Jack Carroll was, and that that was important to him. He was aware that she had been in the dining room this afternoon, and that that was important to him, too. He just didn't have any urge to ask her about any of these things while she was sitting all huddled up like that, all small and weak and sad.

He maneuvered his way around a tall boy who seemed to be dressed up as the Straw Man from *The Wizard of Oz*, thought about sitting down beside Miss Flint without a word, and decided against it. He stopped directly in front of her instead, and cleared his throat.

"Miss Flint?" he said.

Chessey Flint looked up, blinked a little at the contrast between the harsh light around her and the shadowed place his face was in, and said, "Oh. Mr. Demarkian. It's you."

"Would you mind if I sat down for a moment? I came out looking for your friend, Mr. Carroll. I haven't found him and I haven't found anything else, either. I seem to be lost."

"It's easy to be lost out here," Chessey Flint said. Then she brushed at the surface of the step beside her, as if she had to clear it off for him, even though it was empty. "I'm sorry," she told him. "Of course you can sit down. I'm just a little—out of it tonight."

"I don't think I blame you."

"You mean because of this afternoon? I don't blame me either. I don't see how Jack can—" She waved a hand feebly in the direction of the crowd and shook her head. "He's out there in the middle of it all, doing what he always does, just as if it didn't matter. I asked him how he could go through with it and all he said was it was his responsibility."

"You don't consider that an explanation?"

"No, Mr. Demarkian, I don't. I suppose you're going to go all male and self-righteous on me and tell me I ought to, but I don't. I don't have much respect for feminists, but at least I'll give them this. All that groaning and bellowing men do about how they have to be responsible even if it means putting their emotions in the deep freeze is just so much stupidity."

"Does your Mr. Carroll have a great deal of responsibility? Is he going to be tied up all night?"

"Jack? No, Mr. Demarkian, not all night. It's, what? About six thirty?"

"About that."

"They judge the talent contest at seven. Then Jack hands out the trophy. After that, he's free and clear for the rest of the night. If he wants to be."

"Well, then," Gregor said, "I hope he wants to be. I want to go up to the parking lot, to that shack where the tools are to fix the cars. Father Tibor said Mr. Carroll knew something about it."

"Oh, he does," Chessey agreed. "He's a licensed mechanic. Jack knows a lot about a lot of things."

"Do you like that?"

Chessey Flint didn't answer. She had lapsed into a private reverie, chin propped up on the palm of her hand, sharp point of her elbow digging into the top of her knee. Gregor didn't feel right about interrupting her, so he lapsed into a private reverie of his own. He couldn't see through the crowd to the Minuteman statue, but he knew that the boy in white tie and tails must have stopped performing. Up until a little while ago, he had been able to see the green glow of the boy's ghost wand poking up above the heads of the people around him. Now the air above that space in the center was occupied by nothing but the light of the lamps shining into it. Instead of cheering and clapping their feet, the watching crowd was laughing.

Suddenly, Chessey Flint sat up straight, stretched out both her arms and legs in a ritual motion of unkinking, and said, "Mr. Demarkian? Can I ask you something?"

"Yes," Gregor told her, "of course."

"Jack said he thought you thought that—that the person who did that to Miss Veer wasn't really looking to do it to Miss Veer. That it was just someone on the cafeteria staff who put that stuff in something it wouldn't be noticed in, like a peanut butter sandwich, and then just left it out for anyone to take and get hurt by it. Is that what you think?"

"No."

"Why not?"

Gregor thought about skirting the whole question. It wasn't his investigation. He hadn't even been asked to help yet. He had no idea what David Markham did or did not want generally known. To tell Chessey Flint only that such an explanation didn't feel right, though, would offend her—and she would have a right to be offended. She was treating him like a human being and she had a right to be treated like one by him.

He wrapped his arms around his knees and gave it to her, the whole thing, from why the lye couldn't have been in Miss Veer's tea to the utter lack of anything else it could have been in anywhere in the premises after Miss Veer had fallen to the floor. Chessey listened to him in silence, her large eyes wide and trained determinedly on his face. When he was done, she stretched again and sat back.

"I see," she said. "I shouldn't have said Jack thought you thought it was one of the cafeteria workers. That wasn't quite what he was getting at. I don't think he knows what to think."

"What do you think?"

"I don't know." Chessey sighed. "I was sitting very close, you know. At one of the tables in the first line beyond the cash register, right on that side of the room. I was even looking straight at her when she started to fall. I just wasn't paying any attention."

"Had a lot on your mind?"

Chessey snorted. "I always seem to have a lot on my mind these days, Mr. Demarkian. I don't think I like being a senior much. It's confusing."

"So is being fifty-five and retired. Life is confusing."

"Maybe. But you know, Mr. Demarkian, I keep thinking about it. I was looking at it and I was not looking at it. I keep thinking I must have seen something. And all I can remember, really all I can remember, is thinking that Dr. Elkinson looks better with her hair back in a scarf."

"Dr. Elkinson?"

"Dr. Elkinson was standing at the cash register with Miss Veer," Chessey said. "They were just standing there talking, right inside the place where you have to pay, near the cans of Coke and Pepsi and that kind of thing. And then Dr. Crockett came up, and I got a little angry."

"Why?"

"Sort of as a matter of principle. He's been taking up a lot of Jack's time lately, with the rock-climbing and the cabin on Hillman's Rock and all that sort of thing. Did you know that Jack was a rock-climber?"

"From what I've heard," Gregor said, "practically everyone around here is a rock-climber."

Chessey nodded. "Practically everyone in the Program is, anyway. Dr. Crockett's always been the adviser for the Climbing Club and he's very popular. Even most of the faculty have gotten sucked into it at one time or another. Dr. Elkinson, Dr. Branch. I think it put Dr. Crockett's nose a little out of joint when Dr. Steele came and it turned out he was a world-class climber too."

"Dr. Steele." Gregor rubbed his chin. "I keep hearing about this Dr. Steele, but I never actually see him. Isn't he new on campus this term? Shouldn't he be around?"

"Oh, he should be around all right, Mr. Demarkian, he just isn't. Nobody's seen him for a couple of days. It's been a little weird, if you want to know the truth. Usually you can't get rid of him. Anyway. About this afternoon.

Dr. Crockett came up, and then Jack came up from the other end of the line. When I was first looking at them—at Dr. Elkinson and Dr. Crockett and Miss Veer—they were all talking together, but when Jack came up he and Dr. Crockett sort of split off by themselves. And I thought, well, if I don't like it I ought to do something about it. I'm supposed to be all grown up. So I did."

"Do something about it?" Gregor asked.

"That's right. I went up, got Jack by the arm, and dragged him back to the table."

"Then what happened?"

Chessey shrugged. "I don't know. That was the point where I really stopped paying attention. To them, anyway. I had a lot to talk about with Jack. The next thing I knew, Miss Veer dropped her tray, the teacup smashed on the floor, and Dr. Elkinson started screaming."

Out in the thickness of the crowd, a roar went up, raucous and hysterical, and people began to stamp their feet. Chessey Flint stood up, climbed a couple of steps to give herself more height, and craned her neck.

"That's the voice vote starting," she said. "I think this time Freddie's going to end up winning it. I hope he does. This is the fourth time he's tried in four years."

She climbed back down to where Gregor was and began doing things to her costume, making it puff out the way it was supposed to. To Gregor, she looked better than she had—much better than when he'd first sat down. He found it a relief. At least she wasn't crying anymore.

She sat down on the step beside him again and said, "It won't be very long now. Then I'll corral Jack for you and you can take him off to the tool shed. I hope you don't mind getting your clothes in a mess."

four

1

One of the things Gregor Demarkian had noticed in his last years at the Bureau—and he hadn't noticed much; he was too caught up in Elizabeth's dying—was how different the new men coming in from Quantico were from the men who had come in before them. It was the men in particular who had worried him. The new women were much more like the women the Bureau had always attracted than they wanted to admit, even if they did have new job titles and new responsibilities. Gregor sometimes thought it must be very difficult to force a woman not to grow up. When the Bureau had first decided to accept women as working agents, Gregor had gone to the library and taken out a pile of books on feminism. He had read his way through not only Friedan and Steinem and de Beauvoir, but Firestone and Dworkin and Carol Gilligan. Some of what he read was outrageous, some of it was tautological, much of it was brilliant—but on one point almost all of it was in agreement, and Gregor was not. In his experience, subculture notwithstanding, women were rarely "infantilized" in any significant way. He had met a few child-women among the rich of Palm Springs and Beverly Hills. Money and a certain kind of flaccid beauty, combined with an utter and determined isolation from real children, had made them into caricatures. The rest of the women he had known, from full-time housewives to Chanel-suited CEOs, had all been determinedly adult. They may or may not have been able to balance their checkbooks. Every last one of them had been able to understand the differences between authority and despotism, responsibility and obsessiveness, commitment and self-enslavement.

With the men it had been something else, and the something else had begun to make Gregor very uncomfortable, at least up to that point where the only thing on his mind had been whether the latest round of radiation treatments would put Elizabeth into remission or into her coffin. It was true that there had always been men in the world who couldn't seem to grow up. The giggling martini-addict golfer and the rabbity suburban hubby with nothing on his mind but the length of the grass in his own front lawn were staple stereotypes of the kind of literature Gregor had been encouraged to consider "serious" in his days at the Harvard Graduate School. Still, there had been a hint of dysfunction about those men, a trace of self-knowledge, a guilt. It was as if they knew they had failed themselves and everyone around them by becoming what they were. The new men Gregor had encountered in the halls of FBI headquarters had no self-knowledge and no guilt, and didn't think they needed either. They blithered endlessly about self-fulfillment and career enhancement and personal growth as if they thought the terms had meaning. They were frozen in self-satisfaction. When one of the women around them complained about their childishness, they just smiled at her, as if they had a secret. They had looked into the future and seen the grave of manhood, marked by marble and covered with a bed of weeds. Resurrecting it would have meant nothing to them but a kind of self-abuse.

What had interested Gregor Demarkian about Jack Carroll, from the beginning, was his seeming immunity from all this. He was still a boy, but he was pulling against himself, struggling in all directions, trying to get out. Watching him come out of the crowd with Chessey Flint under his arm, Gregor thought he was having a little more success than he had been this morning in the quad. He had taken the hood off his head and tucked it into his belt. The faint, sparse streaks of red in his thick black hair were glowing copper in the light from the globe lamps. Behind him, boys were doing headstands and rebel yells and grabbing at girls and being slapped away. They might as well have been another species.

Gregor stood up—it was hard not to feel awkward, old, and fat in the face of Jack Carroll's effortless physical ease and unforgiving muscle tone—and said, "There you are. I hope this won't be an inconvenience."

Jack shook his head. "Not at all. I'll be glad to get out of here for a while. This gets me a little nuts when I have to spend too much time in the middle of it."

Gregor saw Chessey give Jack a sharp, anxious look and then glance away again. Jack had turned slightly to look into the crowd and didn't notice it. He turned back, stroked Chessey gently on the hair, and said, "You want me to walk you up to your door? It'll only take a minute. I don't think Mr. Demarkian will mind waiting."

"You don't have to do that," Chessey said. "Evie's coming up the walk right now."

"You sure?"

"Positive."

"All right. Look, um, after Mr. Demarkian and I are through, I'll come back and throw a rock at your window, all right?"

"Don't throw a rock, Jack. I'll leave the light on."

"Tell Evie if she doesn't stop chewing bubble gum, her teeth will rot."

Chessey turned away, looked up the steps through the open door of Lexington House, and turned back. She was smiling, but to Gregor her smile looked strained and anxious.

"I've got to go," she said. "If I don't get some work done before you start throwing rocks, Dr. Steele will kill me in the morning. It was nice talking to you, Mr. Demarkian."

"It was nice talking to you, too."

Chessey flashed another of her tense little smiles and ran up the steps to the open doors, not looking back.

When she was out of sight, Jack Carroll started walking toward the center of the quad, against the crowd. Gregor started walking with him, even though nothing had been said, because there wasn't anything else to do. It had been obvious since the start of this conversation that Chessey had told Jack what Gregor wanted. It had also been obvious that Jack had agreed to go along with it. Gregor decided to assume that Jack was leading him in the right direction.

They were out on the edge of Minuteman Field, walking silently toward the path that led to the top of King's Scaffold and the parking lot, when Jack began to get restless. He had been walking with his arms at his sides. He lifted them, wrapped them around his chest, unwrapped them, hooked his thumbs through his belt. He looked up at the stars, sharp and bright in the clear cold darkness, and sighed. Finally he said, "Mr. Demarkian? Do you know what all that was about, when I offered to walk Chessey to her door?"

"You wanted to kiss the girl good night in decent privacy," Gregor suggested.

Jack smiled. "That, too, maybe. But it wasn't the main point. The main point was rape."

"*Rape?*"

"You look so surprised. This is a college campus."

"This is the middle of nowhere."

"What's the matter," Jack said. "Do you think rape doesn't happen in the middle of nowhere?"

Gregor brushed this away. "Don't be ridiculous. I read the Uniform Crime Statistics every year. But venue does matter, Mr. Carroll. The middle of nowhere never has as high a crime rate as, say, New York City."

"That's probably true. But I'm president of students. I get this report the Student Security Service puts out— that's a security organization run by students, by the way, no fudging the numbers the way the administration might to pacify the parents. There were twenty rape attempts on this campus last semester and three successful ones. This semester there's been I don't know how many yet, but a lot. Chessey's friend Evie Westerman got jumped right in the foyer of Lexington House at two o'clock in the morning not a month ago. Dick Corbin and I heard her screaming, smashed through one of those big windows on the main floor, made enough noise to wake the dead and still had to drag the guy off her by main force. And in case you think it was some local yokel getting back at the college, it was a sophomore from Concord House. Daddy makes a million and a half a year, Mommy has her own personal art gallery in Rittenhouse Square, and the kid came up to college with a Visa gold card with a twenty-thousand-dollar line of credit just for him. The dean put him on suspension, but I don't think the message got through."

They had reached the path, its wide beaten rut detectable even in the darkness. Jack led the way up and Gregor followed him.

"I take it you don't approve much of the way your fellow students were raised," Gregor said. "You must know they don't all turn out like that, even if they're rich."

"Of course I know," Jack said. "Chessey didn't turn out like that. More to the point, Evie didn't turn out like that, and I think she's got something like fifteen million in her own right. Car money from Detroit. She's still one of the sanest and most honest people I know. But Mr. Demarkian, I come from the kind of background that's supposed to land kids in trouble. Alcohol, dope, sex every night at ten in abandoned cars in vacant lots—I keep thinking of all the guys I grew up with, including the ones who are already in jail. I can't think of one of them who would have pulled the stunt that asshole pulled on Evie Westerman."

"You can't think of one of them who would commit rape?"

"Rape is one thing. Lying in wait for a girl two years older than you are just because she wouldn't go out with you is something else. And I'll tell you what else is something else. The faculty. At least when students pull this kind of crap, it's usually either alcohol or dope."

"Is there a lot of both here?"

"Alcohol right out in the open, to hell with the Pennsylvania sale to minors laws. Dope—you probably couldn't buy any, but if you want an ounce of crack you just let me go stand by the Minuteman for about fifteen minutes."

"What did you mean about the faculty?" Gregor asked him. "Somehow, I can't see Dr. Crockett jumping on some girl in his eight o'clock class. I certainly can't see Tibor doing it."

"Father Tibor is all right," Jack said, smiling, "as for Dr. Crockett—" He shrugged. "I don't know what's going on with old Ken these days. But they weren't who I was thinking of. You ever heard of this guy Donegal Steele?"

"Vaguely." They had reached the steepest part of the path. It was much steeper than Gregor remembered from coming down, and it made him wonder. What did they do about the students in wheelchairs, of whom there were several? What did they do about anybody and everybody, once the ice storms started in the winter? Gregor said, "He seems to have disappeared, this Donegal Steele. At least, I haven't seen him since I got here, and Tibor says he lives right next door."

"I haven't seen him either," Jack Carroll said, "not since the night before last. At the time, he was on his way to pop beers—"

"What's popping beers?"

Jack explained. "When he didn't show up on campus yesterday I figured he'd just gotten totally bombed and passed out at somebody's house in the hills and was too hung over to get back. Now I think maybe he's avoiding us. All this Halloween happiness was making him crazy. He's supposed to have all sorts of standards."

"You don't sound like you think he does."

"It depends on what you're talking about," Jack said. "Chessey's got one of his classes. She says it's pretty rough, a lot of required background knowledge, if you don't have it you're pretty confused. A lot of papers. He's a real terror about grammar and punctuation."

"But?"

"But he's been chasing Chessey's ass since the semester started and telling everyone on earth he got it when he didn't—and I know he didn't, because Chessey spends just about every spare minute of every day with either me or Evie. She's not what you'd call a solitary person. He's been after Dr. Elkinson, too. I heard her tell a friend of hers she nearly threw him off her balcony once, she was so pissed.

She goes out with Dr. Crockett. And then he talks, you know what I mean? He philosophizes."

"I haven't the faintest idea what you mean."

"I ran into him in this place called the Beer Cellar one night, sitting at a table full of guys, all students, giving this lecture on how we've all been pussy-whipped and if we want to get into some woman's pants we ought to let her know who's boss and just do it."

"He sounds like a prince."

"Yeah."

They had reached the top of the path, the flat plain above the plain that was Minuteman Field. When Gregor looked in the direction of the campus, he could see the back of the jack-o'-lantern head of the effigy jutting up above the ridge of the Scaffold. When he looked in the other direction, he could see the shed bathed in the light from a trio of security lamps. It still looked ready to fall over.

"Here we are," Jack said, threading his way through the parked cars, not looking back to see if Gregor was keeping up. "You're sure this is what you want to see, huh?"

"To see and to ask you a few questions about," Gregor said. "I don't know very much about cars. I don't know very much about machinery of any kind."

"Yeah, well, I know all about cars. Where I come from, you learn it as soon as you learn to talk. Before that, I guess you just don't know how to ask your father for the keys."

Jack had reached the shed, a good six yards ahead of Gregor. He opened the door, snaked his hand in, and turned on the light. Then he started to take a step inside, and froze.

"Oh, Christ," he said, "the jerk's been back and on the job again."

2

"The jerk," it turned out, was someone—identity unknown—who came in, used the solderer, and departed without cleaning up after himself. Sitting at the workbench and doing the cleaning himself, Jack told Gregor all about it. In his voice was the outrage of a man who loved and trusted good machinery. In his hands were what looked like thousands of miniature solder eyelashes. They were on his hands, too, and climbing up the sleeves of his black bat suit. As soon as Gregor Demarkian had seen them, scattered thick as dust over every inch of the workbench's surface, he had been sure he had come to the right place at the right time.

Gregor had taken the only regular chair in the room and pulled it up to Jack Carroll's side, so he could look on and talk while Jack was working. He was busy suppressing his fear and distrust of the mechanical—and his crushing sense of inadequacy in the face of machines—so that he could hear himself think.

"The real pisser about all this," Jack Carroll was saying, "is that it's beyond my comprehension how he manages to make all this mess. I mean, for God's sake, Mr. Demarkian. Soldering isn't exactly what I'd call a fine art, not most of the time. It looks like he was sitting here with a toothpick making little pieces of crap to cause me trouble with."

"Mmm," Gregor said. "You said the first time you saw a mess like this was this morning?"

"Not this morning, yesterday morning. I was up here with Ted Barrows, fixing the speedometer cable on my car. I drive a wreck, in case you haven't guessed. Usually if I'm going to mess with my car, I do it down in town where I work. They've got a better setup. But the timing wasn't right yesterday, so I came in here, and I found—this."

"This this? Just like this?"

"Just like. Maybe worse. I don't know how long it took me to clean it up. Look at this solderer—solder gun, some people call it. If you leave it all gunked up like this, you can ruin it. A couple of hundred dollars right down the drain for no good reason at all."

Gregor was still thinking about timing, trying to make it go—but it wouldn't. Maybe it would have if he'd known what he was getting at beyond the concrete, but he didn't. He pushed it aside and took another tack.

"Tell me something," he said, "according to Miss Flint,

this afternoon, just before Miss Veer keeled over, you were standing near her and Dr. Elkinson in the cafeteria line."

"That's right. I'd gone up to get a Coke."

"Dr. Crockett was there, too."

"He came in while Dr. Elkinson and I were talking," Jack said. "I think he was getting a Coke, too. It might have been lemonade."

"You don't remember?"

Jack grinned. "Chessey came hauling up and dragged me out of there practically the minute Ken arrived. I think she's sort of had enough of Ken. I'm not even sure I blame her."

"Now," Gregor said. "Think. You were standing next to Miss Maryanne Veer."

"Right."

"She was holding a cafeteria tray."

"Right, too."

"What was on it?"

"A cup of tea," Jack Carroll said promptly.

"That was all?"

"That was absolutely all. I remember wondering what she needed the tray for. She could have carried the cup in her hands."

Gregor sighed. "It's impossible," he said. "It's just impossible. There has to have been something else on that tray."

"Why?"

This time, Gregor hesitated only a moment. There was no real reason not to let everyone know what he had worked out—what he knew had to be true. There were several reasons why that kind of revelation might be to his advantage. He told Jack what he had told Chessey Flint and David Markham before her, then sat back to see what Jack's reaction would be.

Jack's reaction seemed to be entirely intellectual, as if he'd been handed a logic problem and told that its successful solution would determine his grade in Advanced Psychological Methods for the term.

"You know," he said, "just because there wasn't anything on her tray when I saw it doesn't mean there wasn't anything later. She hadn't reached the cash register yet."

"She had, however, reached the end of the line," Gregor pointed out.

"Well, yes, I know. But she was a little upset. Maybe she forgot and went back for her food after Chessey took me away."

"What was she upset about?"

This time, Jack Carroll's grin was broad and rueful. "Oh, well," he said, "you're not going to believe this, but it was Donegal Steele. I say you're not going to believe it because Miss Veer doesn't like him any better than I do—than any of us do. I think Donegal Steele may be the most disliked man on this campus."

"Because of his views on the sexuality of women?"

"Because of everything," Jack said. "The man is a crud, Mr. Demarkian. You pick a topic, he'll be a crud about it."

"Do you know what kind of, um, crud he is being to Miss Veer?"

"Sure. Miss Veer's been running the administrative side of the Program since forever. Dr. Steele thinks she ought to be forcibly retired and replaced with someone a little easier on his eyes and a little more tractable about his demands. He's always threatening Miss Veer that when he gets to be Head he'll make her—"

"Head?" Gregor said. "I didn't know Dr. Steele was Head."

"He's not. I'm not even sure he's going to be, Mr. Demarkian. He's just always saying he's going to be. He says that's what he was hired for."

"Do you think that's true?"

"I hope not."

"I think I hope not right along with you." Gregor drummed his fingers impatiently against the workbench, now almost clean. Jack had been working while they talked, without a break, not needing to concentrate to accomplish something he had accomplished so many times before. Gregor wished he hadn't explained that a solderer was sometimes called a solder gun. It made the damn thing seem even more lethal than it looked.

"Let's get back to this afternoon," he said. "What was Miss Veer upset about in relation to Dr. Steele?"

"That he was missing, of course." Jack had taken the solderer apart and laid its pieces in a line along the workbench, to clean them individually. "Miss Veer takes care of everybody's schedules and that sort of thing. Classes. Office hours. I guess Dr. Steele missed his whole day Tuesday, and then he wasn't around this morning, either, and she was worried about it."

"How worried?"

"Worried enough to want to call the police and report him missing," Jack said. "That's what she and Dr. Elkinson were talking about when I came up. Dr. Elkinson was trying to talk her out of it."

"On what grounds?"

"On what grounds do you think? Verbally, anyway. Steele isn't the world's most trustworthy character. He doesn't usually skip office hours and classes and things, but still. Personally, I think Dr. Elkinson doesn't care one way or another if the man is dying in a ditch somewhere by the side of the road. I wouldn't either."

"Mmmm." Gregor looked down and saw that he was still drumming his fingers against the workbench. He picked his hand up and put it in his lap. "Let's go back to something else," he said. "Miss Veer didn't have any food on her tray but she wasn't at the cash register yet. If she had gone back to get something to eat, could you speculate on what she might have taken?"

"Sure," Jack said. "I used to work lunch in the cafeteria freshman year. That was the worst of it financially and I needed the two jobs. I've seen her once or twice since then, too. She always ate the same things."

"Which were?"

"A chef's salad with blue cheese dressing. A Belleville Lemon and Lime—that's a regional brand of soda made locally. She drank the soda with the salad. She drank the tea after the salad. She'd put the tea in the bottom of the cup, dump water in on top of it and let the thing steep all through lunch. By the time she was ready to drink it, it was black."

Gregor thought about it. In one way, it was perfect. He couldn't imagine anything more appropriate in which to disguise lye—especially commercially produced lye products, like Drāno or toilet bowl cleaner—than blue cheese dressing. The color was right. The consistency was right. Any small gummed-up wads of lye would look like minuscule pieces of cheese. Still, it wouldn't work.

"It would have been all over everything," he explained. "Pieces of lettuce and turkey and cucumber. Smears of dressing. Nobody could have removed all the traces or even removed a significant portion of them soon enough. It had to be something else. Something more self-contained."

"Maybe she changed her pattern this afternoon because she was so worked up," Jack said. "I'm sorry, Mr. Demarkian. I only saw what I saw. It wasn't much."

"That's all right."

Jack had the solderer put together, lying clean and shining in front of him on the workbench. "I'm done here now," he said. "We could get on to what you wanted to come here for. I'm sorry I held you up."

"That's all right, too," Gregor waved it away. "Are you sure I'm not holding you up? It's not getting too late? What I want you to do may take some time."

"Chessey will wait. If she doesn't, I'll wake her up."

Gregor wanted to tell him not to get too cavalier about that young woman. She might be a little distraught at the moment, but she didn't look like an eternal pushover. It wasn't any of his business.

"That thing," he said, pointing at the solderer. "Is it all cleaned up and ready to go again?"

"Sure."

"Fine. Now I want you to make me something with it, or make this thing out of solder one way or another. A small cylinder, about half an inch across and less than a quarter of an inch thick, absolutely flat or even a little concave at one end, a little bumped out at the other."

Jack Carroll was staring at him in astonishment. "Mr. Demarkian, what are you talking about?"

"I don't know exactly," Gregor said, "but when we've made one right I will know that. Will you do it?"

Jack Carroll would do it, but it was clear he thought Gregor Demarkian was crazy.

five

1

When Dr. Alice Elkinson told Dr. Kenneth Crockett that she wanted to come down to his apartment for the night, rather than having him come up to hers, he found it only a minor inconvenience—usually, he would have found it a major pain in the ass, and protested. Alice had one of the three apartments in this building with full kitchens. Ken only had a cooking alcove, like Father Tibor's and Donegal Steele's. The problems came with breakfast, which Ken always wanted to overeat, and which he didn't like going to the cafeteria for. Alice was remarkably accommodating about breakfast, considering how she operated in the rest of her life. Sometimes, her willingness to cook for him surprised Ken beyond reason. Ken often told himself that that was what he loved about her, her surprises, the fundamental contradictions in her personality—even though some of those contradictions made him nervous. He often told himself that she would be perfect if she would only rid herself of her fickleness. Alice was always hating someone one minute and loving him the next, or vice versa. It made Ken wonder about what was going on between the two of them, and how long it would last. So far, it had lasted five years without a serious break. When he got very, *very* nervous, he told himself he ought to be satisfied with that.

The other problem with having Alice come to him, rather than his coming to her, had to do with the staircases at Constitution House. In order for Alice to get from her apartment on the fourth floor to his on the third, she had to go down the north staircase all the way to the ground floor, wend her way through a series of hallways to the foyer, wend her way through another series of hallways to the south staircase, and come all the way up again. He had to do the same to get to her—but for some reason he always seemed to be able to do it faster. It took him about ten minutes to get to Alice's apartment. It took Alice about forty to get to his. Waiting for her after she'd said she'd be right over sometimes made him crazy.

Now it was ten o'clock on the night of Wednesday, October thirtieth, and Ken Crockett had other things on his mind. Alice coming to his apartment, and the time it would take for her to actually get there, were even useful in the short run. He'd meant to spend his day in reasonable tranquillity. Going up Hillman's Rock this morning, he had imagined himself over the course of the coming afternoon: having lunch with Alice, reading de Tocqueville under the shade of the pine trees behind Constitution House, maybe taking Alice out into the quad after it got dark and getting her to dance. The attack on Miss Maryanne Veer had put an end to that—but the attack wasn't all that had put an end to it. He had come back to his apartment all jangled, not having expected to come back to it at all after that mess in the dining room. Alice had been such a wreck. Ken had been sure she'd want him with her. When she hadn't, he'd been more than put out. He'd been positively angry. It was as if she thought of him as some kind of teenage Good-Time Charlie, desirable for the giggle times but not much use for anything other than that. He'd walked around and around the campus, skirting the Halloween festivities in a mood so sour he thought he was turning into Katherine Branch and Donegal Steele, kicking trees. Then, when he had finally gotten himself calmed down, he went back to Constitution House and found—the package.

At the moment, the package was lying on Ken's coffee table, undone, its papers spread out across the glass surface like used cocktail napkins at the end of an overlong party. When his doorbell rang, he was just picking one of those papers up and turning it over in his hands. He'd been doing that by then for two hours, even though the papers were nothing but lists with various items marked in red. He kept reading the marked items, shaking his head, and reading the marked items again. The whole thing was so damned silly he didn't know what to do with it.

This time, with Alice jabbing and pounding at the bell, he didn't bother to read anything. He put the paper down and got up to let her in. On his way to the door he checked his watch. It had taken her twenty-one minutes to get here. It was a record.

She was leaning against the wall next to his door, dressed as if she were about to go out on a climb—or as if she'd just come back from one.

"Hi," she said. "I've calmed down. Have you?"

"Sort of. I got a surprise when I got back here this afternoon."

"What surprise?"

"A little present from Mrs. Winston Barradyne."

Alice raised her eyebrows, one of her patented Alice-in-a-good-mood expression, except that this time it didn't quite come off. Ken ushered her in, thinking as he did that what he had here was an in-between mood. She may have calmed down—after the way she'd been in the dining room, anything less than outright hysteria would have meant she was calming down—but she wasn't herself again either. Her skin seemed to be twitching and jumping under her sweater, as if it had been stuffed full of Mexican jumping beans. He sat down on the couch and spread his arms over the papers.

"There," he said. "I don't know what you've been doing with yourself all evening, but what I've been doing for most of it is reading through these. Mrs. Winston Barradyne's recollections of just what Donegal Steele took out of the Historical Society library."

"What I've been doing with myself all evening is looking at that goddamned bird." Alice sat down in one of his chairs and put her feet up on his coffee table. The thick sharp cleats on the bottoms of them stuck into the air like a fakir's bed of nails. "It's gone, now. Lenore, I mean. It was up overhead circling and circling until I thought I'd go crazy."

"I think they sleep at night," Ken told her. "I wonder what's wrong with Lenore?"

"Maybe she's been captured by aliens and turned into a flying spying machine." Alice put her feet on the floor again. The cleats cut through his carpet and knicked into the hardwood of his floor with a click. "Are these what Mrs. Barradyne sent you? They look like lists."

"They are lists. Of all the books and all the pamphlets and all the everything else in the Historical Society library."

"The things Steele took out are marked in red?"

"That's right."

"John Cowry—letters from Antietam." Alice frowned. "That's the wrong period."

"I know."

"Are they all from the wrong period?"

Ken grinned. "Every last one of them. Every last damn one of them, Alice. I'm not kidding. Christ, I could take Mrs. Barradyne and wring her neck. You have no idea how paralyzed she made me."

"Yes I do."

"Maybe you do," Ken admitted. "I know you thought this was all silly, Alice, but it really wasn't. I can't imagine what would have happened to me in this place if it had gotten around that four members of the great and illustrious Crockett family, benefactors of the college and outstanding patriotic blowhards for two hundred years, were hung for British spies in New England during the Revolutionary War."

"Why do you think he was asking Mrs. Barradyne all those questions about you? He was asking them, wasn't he?"

"Sure. He's nosy."

"I think the proper word is probably *intrusive*," Alice said. Then she sighed. "Listen to me. I'm talking like an academic. I promised myself I was never going to do that."

"At Berkeley?"

"At Berkeley, I promised myself I'd never talk like a revolutionary. Speaking of which, what do you think our Katherine is doing?"

"Chanting petitions to the Great Goddess."

"I ran into Lynn Granger while I was walking around outside a little while ago and she said she'd seen Vivi

Wollman coming out of Liberty Hall this afternoon—
through a window."

Ken laughed. "Katherine probably tried to talk her into filching the evaluation files for the old Women's Studies
program. Just so nobody got the idea they wanted
Miss Veer out of the way because she had access to a lot of
private information that could ruin their careers."

Alice shook her head. "I don't believe even Katherine
could do anything that trite."

"Katherine is always trite," Ken said. Then he took a
deep breath. It was always a risk asking Alice what she was
feeling. You could get an answer, or you could get an
argument. "Alice?" he said. "Are you all right? I know all
this stuff with Miss Veer upset you, and I don't blame you
for being upset, it's just—"

"It's not Miss Veer," Alice said. She got out of the
chair, walked over to the window and drew his curtains.
The window didn't look directly out onto the quad. Some
of the apartments on the south staircase did, just as some of
the ones on the west staircase did, but not the ones on this
side. She was looking across an empty patch of lawn to a
line of darkened windows on the third floor of Madison
House.

"Ken?" she said. "Ken, listen, I had some things, out
on my balcony, some buckets."

"Yes?"

"Well, you know how it is with me during Halloween.
Half the campus has keys to my apartment. And it's not like
the buckets were important, if you know what I mean."

"No."

"No," Alice said. "Well. Never mind. I was just wondering if you'd come up and borrowed them or something."

"Borrowed them? Why would I do that?"

"I don't know."

And that, Ken thought, was the truth—she had no idea
why she'd just asked him what she'd asked him. It was as if
she'd had to ask him, just to make sure, but the making sure
hadn't brought her any kind of relief. This mood she was
sliding into now was one he recognized.

She was tight as a wire.

2

If there was one thing Chessey Flint hated more than any other, it was Jack Carroll in one of his decisive moods—and that was strange, because, in the beginning, she had loved Jack in his decisive moods. When she'd first met him, there had been something scary and secretly thrilling about seeing him that way, like the way it felt when she made herself ride the big roller coaster at Disney World, even though she was terrified of heights. Lately there had been an element to it she didn't like. She kept feeling Jack was going to tell her something she didn't want to hear or force her to do something she didn't want to do. The only thing she could think of that would fit either description would be that he would want to leave. It was all she thought about anymore. She was beginning to be boring even to herself.

It was eleven o'clock at night, and Jack was standing in the tree just outside her dormitory window, bracing himself on a branch and stretching out his arms to help her climb through. This was the method they had devised to avoid having her come down to the foyer when they wanted to get together at night. It was silly in a way, because there were no curfews at Independence College and no parietal hours in the boys' and coed dorms. If Chessey wanted to leave her room and spend the night with Jack in his, she had every right to do it. The problem was with how deserted Lexington House got after dark. Even with all the manic Halloween stuff going on outside, the corridors and common rooms were empty, except for the common rooms just off the foyer itself, which were full. That, Jack had told her, might actually make things worse. With all the confusion, it would be hard to keep security as tight as it ought to be, considering the way things had been going. Chessey hooked her small hands into Jack's big ones and let him draw her to him, slowly, inch by crazy inch. She really was afraid of heights—terrified of them, in fact. The very idea

that she was balancing on a thin branch four stories above
the ground made her physically ill.

The branch was not so thin. Jack pulled her along it
until she reached the place where a whole raft of branches
came together to join the trunk, then wedged her tightly
into the crook there until she felt safe. In the old days, he
used to ask her if she felt safe. Now he didn't seem to need
to. He got her settled and then climbed back up to the
crook where he liked to sit when they weren't going directly
to the ground. There was a mild wind blowing, flapping his
black cape in the air and bringing them snatches of music
from the quad.

"My cape is filthy," he said. "I had Mr. Demarkian in
the shed and he got filthy, too. I'm sorry."

"You don't have to apologize about the cape."

"All the way back to campus I kept thinking you were
going to tear it off my back as soon as you saw it and throw
it in the wash."

"I've never torn anything off your back in my life."

"I know."

"I want to get out of this tree and back onto the ground
and I want to do it right now. You know how I hate to be
high up. You know it. How can you do this to me?"

"Chess—"

"Oh, *don't*."

Suddenly she was crying again, crying and crying, the
way she cried when she was alone in her room and no one
could see her. It made her so angry with herself, so damn
furious, because it made her think she'd turned into one of
her sisters. Emotions always on full alert and out of control,
life always in a mess and headed for failure—what had she
worked so damn hard for all these years if not to escape
that? Jack was reaching out for her, but she didn't want him
to touch her. Chessey pushed herself out on the branch to
get away from him, not really caring that she was sus-
pended above nothing but darkness and air. She even
closed her eyes and tried to imagine herself falling, into a
void, forever, without ever touching ground.

"Look," she said, "I know that everything's gone
wrong. I know you don't want to touch me anymore—"

"That's not true—"

"—and that you can't stand to talk to me anymore—"

"That's also not true—"

"—and that you're going to leave here tonight and not come back—"

"Chess, don't be an idiot—"

"—but the one thing I absolutely refuse to put up with after all this time is listening to you delivering a little speech about how damned adult we're being and how we're both going to grow up and find out what love is really like at last and all the damned rest of it. I won't do it, Jack. I won't co-operate in that kind of charade and I won't hear any crap about that was then and this is now or any of the rest of it."

There was a silence from way up in the branches that went on for so long she began to think: *Well, I've said it all for him, and now he doesn't have anything left to say.* Then Jack began to climb down from his perch, to test the branch she was lying on with his foot. It wouldn't hold them both. They'd discovered that her sophomore year, when she and Evie had first taken this room. When he helped her out of the window he always stayed in the crook near the trunk. Chessey felt the branch spring and bounce back, shaking her. Jack said "damn" under his breath and retreated.

"Chessey?" he said. "Will you listen to what I've got to say?"

"No."

"You're going to have to. I'm not going to help you down out of here until I'm done talking."

"I'll start screaming at the top of my lungs and someone will come."

"Don't."

"Oh, hell," Chessey said. "I don't have the energy for it anyway."

Jack cleared his throat. "Chessey, look, I'm not going to say there hasn't been anything wrong, because there has been. It just hasn't been what you think it has. It isn't that I don't want to touch you anymore."

"Oh, I see," Chessey said, "you've given it up for Lent."

"Lent is at Easter. Chess, it's just gotten to the point where I can't do that and stop in the middle of it. This morning in your room, there was a point where I thought I was going to rip you up. It's not that I want to hurt you. It's just that the whole damn thing—the way I feel and the way I respond—hell, Chess, whether you realize it or not, the way you feel and the way you respond—Christ, Chessey, I don't know how to describe it. There's been some kind of cosmic shift. It's different and you know it."

"Bullshit."

"Not bullshit. And you know that, too."

Chessey swung herself up into a sitting position, forcing herself to move and forcing herself to stop. For a minute it felt as if she'd launched herself into space.

"Listen to *me*," she said. "If this is the great put-up-or-shut-up speech, you can shove it up your own ass. I don't give a flying damn about cosmic shifts. I don't give a flying damn about anything where that subject is concerned. It's my body and my life and I have every damn intention of doing what I want with both of them my way."

"I know. I'll admit I thought of that at first—coming to you and making a fuss about it and seeing what happened. I gave it up because I knew what was going to happen."

"Don't you dare tell me I'm pretty when I'm mad."

"I won't. I couldn't tell you anything about the way you look at the moment. All I can see is that jack-o'-lantern face in Day-Glo on your—backside."

Her—backside—felt as if it were sticking up into a spotlight, making a spectacle of itself. It felt that way even though she was sitting on it. Chessey shifted a little and then wished she hadn't moved. She hadn't come close to calming down since Jack left her room this afternoon, but she was calming down now. That was not such a good thing when she was dangling up here in space. It was one thing to take risks when she felt she didn't care if she lived or died. It was another to take them in cold blood.

She started to inch her way down the branch, toward the trunk, moving slowly. She felt Jack's hand waving in the air near her face and grabbed on to it.

"I can't breathe," she said.

"I was wondering how you were managing to sit out there all by yourself without fainting."

Jack inched farther back up the tree, and Chessey let him pull her farther in toward the trunk. When she was finally in the crook she relaxed a little, because the crook always made her feel safe. She was only half-aware that he had not gone all the way back up to his usual perch, or that her head was resting against his knees. When he began to stroke her hair, she let him. It just felt so nice not to be tense anymore.

"Look," he said, "I've been thinking about this all day. More than all day. For days. It seems to me we have two problems, not one."

"What two problems?"

"Sex and Donegal Steele."

"For God's sake," Chessey said, "don't put it that way."

"I'm not putting it any way, Chess, I'm just stating fact. We've got to do something about the physical thing between us that will work, and we've got to get Steele off your case. Right?"

"Dr. Steele isn't on my case at the moment. He isn't on anybody's. He hasn't been around."

"He'll be around again soon enough if we let him. The trick is to cut him off at the pass."

"How?"

"The same way we solve the physical thing between us."

"Jack, for God's sake, what do you want to do? Relieve me of my virginity at high noon on Minuteman Field? What do you think will get through to him?"

"Chess, please, please, will you trust me?"

"I don't know."

"Sure you will."

He had managed to slide down farther against the trunk of the tree, to somehow seem to be sitting on his haunches—although how that was possible, stuck in the branches the way they were, Chessey didn't know. He took her face between his hands and lifted her chin until he was looking into her eyes, so much like the way he had the first time he had kissed her that Chessey found herself unable to breathe again, for reasons that had nothing to do with her fear of heights.

"What we've got to do right now," he said, "is we've got to get into your room and get you out of that pumpkin thing."

"Men aren't allowed in the rooms at Lexington House after ten o'clock on weekdays."

"So who's to notice? Evie? When we tell her what we're going to do, she'll pin a medal on us."

"Only if it's bloody murder," Chessey said.

"It's better than that. Please?"

Chessey looked away. "What about you? You're still in your bat suit."

"We'll take care of me later. I'm all right for now just the way I am."

Chessey thought he was all right with her just the way he was—he was always all right, no matter what he did—but it was too stupid a thing to admit in public and besides, he was pushing her out on the branch again, toward the window. She went without thinking about it, the space between her body and the ground eliminated from her imagination. She could feel his hands on her shoulders and his laughter in her ear. She wondered if he realized they'd never tried going in this way before.

The window was still open. She barreled for it, head first, anything to get her hands onto the sill. At the same time she thought: *This time he's going to want to do something* really *crazy*.

3

Out at County Receiving it was midnight and Miss Maryanne Veer was lying in a bed on the intensive care ward, neither conscious nor unconscious, neither dreaming nor not dreaming, thinking about lemons. She had been thinking about lemons at least since she first remembered waking up. She had even thought about them while Margaret was here to visit. Margaret had been Margaret the whole time—weepy and hysterical when a doctor or nurse was in the room, fiery and hard when the two of them were alone. Maryanne and Margaret shared their secret lives only with each other.

Now the ward was dark and quiet. The only other patient was three doors down, suffering the aftereffects of having a heart attack in the middle of a fire. Miss Maryanne Veer closed her eyes and let her mind drift, over the lemons and onto the hand.

This is how it happened, over and over again, no matter what she tried to do to stop it: The lemons were piled in a pyramid on somebody else's table in somebody else's house, each and every one of them perfectly round, each and every one of them marked in ink like those Sunkist oranges but with a line that said: "full of sugar." Miss Maryanne Veer was standing next to them and wishing they were hers. The hand came out of nowhere and handed one to her, taking it off the top. When Miss Maryanne Veer got it into her own hand, she saw there was a straw sticking out of one end.

Lemons, hand, straw: that was it. There was nothing sensible. It wasn't even a hand she recognized, although she kept thinking she should.

Lemons, hand, straw: there was something there that was sensible, maybe even important, but she couldn't pin it down. She ought to tell somebody about it, but she couldn't do that either. She'd already heard them say it was doubtful if she would ever again be able to talk.

They had given her seventy-five milligrams of Demerol to deaden the pain and sent her into outer space instead.

Lemons, hand, straw.

She'd never gotten around to telling the people who mattered that Donegal Steele was missing.

Six

At three o'clock in the morning, Gregor Demarkian, unable to sleep, got off the couch he had been lying on in the suite he was not supposed to be sharing with Bennis but was and went to look out the window. Bennis was behind the closed door of the bedroom, dead to the world. Even the acid smell of her cigarette smoke had faded hours ago. Gregor's back felt as if it had been worked over by a curling iron for days. This was the guest suite in Constitution House, the best apartment in the building according to Tibor. It was on the fourth floor and looked out over Minuteman Field to King's Scaffold.

At this hour of the morning, the campus was dead. There were no students wandering back from late study in the bowels of the library, no stray drunks reeling in from roadhouses out of town. Gregor had never seen a college campus so peaceful in the dark. He kept thinking that one good look at the Halloween decorations ought to change the atmosphere for him, but he couldn't see any Halloween decorations. There were only the ominous lumps of logs rising up against the Scaffold and the straw man pumpkin head at the top.

He didn't know how long he had been standing there at the window before he realized what he was looking at. Five minutes, ten minutes, a minute and a half: he found it hard to keep track of things when he was this tired. His gaze swept back and forth across the top of the Scaffold, back and forth, and finally it stopped.

There was somebody up there, prancing back and forth, doing God only knew what in the harsh light of a moon that looked like it ought to belong to another planet.

A bat.

Part Three

Thursday, October 31

Deep into that darkness peering,
    long I stood there, wondering, fearing,
Doubting, dreaming dreams no mortal
    ever dared to dream before.

—E. A. Poe

One

1

Gregor Demarkian had never given any thought to the differences between large city police departments and small-town cop shops in the sealing and securing of crime scenes. If he had given it any thought, he would have said there wasn't any. Crime scenes weren't something he had been either trained or conditioned to consider. In his early years at the Bureau, he had mostly dealt with crimes without scenes. Kidnappers tended to snatch their victims off sidewalks or in department stores or out of playgrounds, and to do it where they couldn't be observed. In his later years at the Bureau, Gregor was called in mostly as an afterthought. First there would be a series of killings in one state, then a similar series in a second state, then another similar series in a third. At that point, the local police from all three states would start talking to each other, and somebody would say: *Doesn't the FBI have a department that deals with this kind of crap?* By the time Gregor or his agents got into it, there would be no scenes left, just bodies in drawers and evidence in bags. If something new came up while they were trying to get the "crap" coordinated and ultimately straightened out, it was the local police who handled the details of sealing, securing, and gathering evidence.

Still, walking up to the dining hall from Constitution House at five minutes to seven on Halloween morning, Gregor had fully expected to find the cafeteria closed. He thought he'd be meeting David Markham surrounded by empty tables and a nonfunctioning kitchen. It only made sense. Instead, he came into the dining hall foyer to find the wide double doors to the cafeteria line open and stuffed with bleary-eyed students balancing more in the way of books than of food on their trays. The kitchen was, indeed, nonfunctioning—there was a neat little hand-lettered sign near the stacks of trays and pockets of tableware that said, "SORRY FOR THE INCONVENIENCE, BUT THE CAFETERIA WILL BE UNABLE TO OFFER HOT FOOD UNTIL 4 NOVEMBER"—but otherwise business was proceeding as usual. The Halloween decorations had not only been left up, but increased. A jack-o'-lantern cut out of a pumpkin so large it looked like it had grown in a dump for nuclear waste was sitting on the top of the plastic display cover where the hot food should have been, glowing evilly with the interior light of a dozen votive candles.

Gregor passed by the little individual boxes of Kellogg's Corn Flakes and Count Chocula cereal—he hoped the Count Chocula was a special just for Halloween—and by the little sealed containers of milk and orange juice until he came to the coffee. Then he took three coffee cups, filled them, and pushed the tray along to the cash register. From there, he could see David Markham, sitting alone at one of those tables by the window, surrounded by papers. It was remarkable about those tables near the windows. No matter how crammed the dining room got, there was always at least one of them left open. It was as if the students had mentally consigned a certain number of the best places to eat to the faculty, and neither common sense nor self-esteem could talk them into violating them.

The girl at the cash register was tense—understandably, Gregor thought—so he gave her his best reassuring smile as he stuffed his change into his pants pocket. Then he picked up his tray and, not looking at it, headed for David Markham. Linda Melajian back on Cavanaugh Street had taught him that about not looking at coffee while you were carrying it. For some reason—Linda had talked a great deal about natural balance and the inner ear—it helped you not to spill.

"This is something of a surprise," Gregor said, as he put his tray down in one of the few spaces left by Markham's paper blizzard, "I expected to find the place shut and in possession of the authorities."

The sheriff looked at the glowing tip of his cigar and said, "It would be wonderful if we could do things like that, but we can't. Not here. This is the only place on campus to eat. We had enough trouble keeping it shut last night."

"You *did* keep it shut last night?"

"Oh, yes, until about nine o'clock. That was about how long it took for us to get done what we had to get done. You should have heard the screams from the President's office, though. The nearest town to this is fifteen miles away and the nearest mall, meaning the nearest Burger King, is forty. Most of the kids don't have cars. Whoosh."

"What did they do about dinner last night?"

Markham grinned. "Some Dean or other got hold of a pickup truck and went fifty miles to the nearest serious pizza joint. By serious he meant run by actual Italians. Anyway, the pizzas showed up in the dorms around five o'clock and everybody had a party. Like they needed to have another one."

"I'm surprised I missed all that," Gregor said. "I was here."

"You were outside," David Markham said. "I saw you." He began to pick up the papers he'd been working on, stacking them in ragged-edged piles without really looking at them. At Gregor's quizzical look, he shrugged. "My notes. What do I need notes for? I could recite you chapter and verse what we've got so far."

"What have you got so far?" Gregor asked him.

"Not damned much. You know what we were doing here until nine o'clock last night? Taking the food out. All of it. Also looking for available cleaning materials that contain lye—sodium . . ."

"Sodium hydroxide," Gregor said. "Did you find anything?"

Markham sighed. "No. The last word on the food's going to have to come from the lab, of course, and that's going to take a couple of days. The lab's up in the county seat. But we did what you sort of suggested yesterday. We opened all the sandwiches. We checked all the pies and cakes for tampering. We did stuff I couldn't believe. Nothing."

"What about the cleaning materials?"

Markham threw up his hands. "That was worse. Turns out, this campus is something called a central inventory ordering system. You know what that is?"

"No."

"It's this deal where everything the college needs is ordered by one department at one time, to take advantage of bulk rate discounts. The cleaning materials are ordered from there and then sent to Janitorial, and Janitorial keeps them. They had a little problem here a few years ago with a student who tried to unclog a drain by nuclear explosion or something. Anyway, he mixed a couple of different drain cleaners, poured them down the sink and blew up the plumbing. He caused a lot of expensive damage and he could have gotten himself and a lot of other people killed. You mix that stuff, you release fumes that are absolutely lethal. Point is, since then Janitorial doesn't let the buildings have their own stuff. Something goes wrong, no matter how small, you have to call a college plumber."

"I take it nobody called a college plumber yesterday," Gregor said.

"You take it right. There was no lye, and no product containing lye, anywhere on these premises when Maryanne Veer keeled over. At least, not officially."

Gregor had finished his first cup of coffee. He reached for his second and thought this over.

"You know," he said, "this is actually a good sign. It means the lye was brought here deliberately. It makes it unlikely to the point of ridiculousness that what we're dealing with is a Tylenol-poisoning type nut. Unless you found whatever the lye was in when Maryanne Veer ate it, I'd say someone came here yesterday to put Maryanne Veer in particular out of commission in a hurry. And went to a great deal of trouble to do it."

"We didn't find anything that came off that tray except the tea," Markham said. Then he scratched his nose and looked speculatively up at the ceiling. "But you know, Mr. Demarkian, I've been working with this now for quite a few hours. And like I said, I've known Maryanne Veer all my life. You may not have noticed, you haven't been talking to as many people as I have, but we're a little stuck on motive."

"Ah," Gregor said. Actually, he had noticed. He might not have been talking to as many people as he should have been talking to, but he had been talking to Tibor. Tibor always knew more than he thought he did. He had also been talking to Jack Carroll and Chessey Flint.

"The impression I got," he told Markham, "is that the only thing out of the ordinary in Maryanne Veer's life yesterday was her—concern—over the disappearance of a man named Dr. Donegal Steele."

"The Great Doctor Donegal Steele?" David Markham hooted. "Well, Mr. Demarkian, if someone had gone after Dr. Donegal Steele with lye, I wouldn't have been surprised. Hell, I'd go after him with lye myself if I wasn't a law-abiding type. The man is a complete turd."

"So I've heard."

"I don't believe Maryanne was worried about him not being around, either. She hated the bastard's guts. Everybody hated the bastard's guts."

"That may be," Gregor said, "but according to Jack Carroll, Miss Veer was bound and determined to call the police, probably meaning you, as soon as she got back from lunch yesterday to report the man missing. Apparently, he hasn't been around for a couple of days."

"Hasn't he?" Markham shrugged. "He was always blithering about how all this Halloween stuff was 'infantile' and 'anti-intellectual.' That's Steele's kick, intellectual standards. They're the only kind of standards he's got, far as I can see. He'd been here about two weeks, he walked into the IGA down in Belleville, walked right up to Ed Leaver's sixteen-year-old daughter and gave her an ass rub. Girl he'd never laid eyes on in his life, no joke. I had to stop Ed from breaking the asshole's arm and I was sorry to have to do it. But if you think somebody killed Steele and tried to bump off Maryanne Veer because she'd figured it out—"

"No," Gregor said. "I don't like explanations like that. When they come up in mystery stories, they drive me crazy. Besides, I saw Miss Veer for a few moments before she fell over. From the reading I took, if that woman thought Donegal Steele had been murdered, she would have said he'd been murdered. And if she thought she knew who killed him, she would have said that, too."

"Exactly."

"I keep trying to think of some reason why someone would want to stop her from calling you and filing a missing persons report," Gregor said. "If the man is missing because he has been murdered, it can't be the fact that he was murdered, or even the fact that he was missing, that would account for what happened to Miss Veer. It wouldn't make sense. This isn't some tramp we're talking about. This is a senior professor with a national reputation and a book on the best-seller lists. If he stays missing long enough, somebody's going to file a missing persons report sometime. If he's buried out in the back garden, somebody's going to end up digging that up sometime, too."

"I think I like the Tylenol-poisoning theory better than this," Markham said. "Are you really going to drink that third cup of coffee?"

"I may drink two more than that. I've got something I want to show you."

Gregor reached into his pocket and rummaged around carefully for the small square of paper he had folded into an envelope to contain the solder cylinder Jack Carroll had made for him last night. This, after all, was what he had been most excited about on his way to the dining hall. He probably should have brought it up first thing, even though he knew Markham was not as impressed by the original cylinder as he was himself. It was Gregor Demarkian's opinion that a complete oddity found at a crime scene had to be important one way or another. It at least had to be explained. Now that he knew just how hard one of these things was to make, he was determined to find out what it had been made for. He threw the folded paper envelope, secured with a piece of electrical tape, down on the table in front of him and opened his mouth to make one of those pronouncements he secretly prided himself on as being "oracular."

He never got the chance. Just as he looked up, David Markham stood. It was like watching one of those sea changes Bennis went through when she decided to be "sophisticated." Sitting down, Markham had been the Markham that Gregor had come to know, intelligent, traveled, down-to-earth, and a little cynical. Standing up, he was transformed into the worst kind of local yokel, complete with glazed eyes, bad posture, and insincere grin.

"Well, well," he said. "This is really a pleasure. The little lady has showed up early."

Gregor winced.

The twang was back.

2

The little lady this morning was Dr. Katherine Branch, looking considerably more normal this morning than she had on the only other occasion on which Gregor had seen her. Gone was the black and white greasepaint. Gone were the leotards and tights—if that, in fact, was what they had been. To Gregor, Dr. Katherine Branch was recognizable mostly from her hair, which had been blazing red yesterday afternoon and was blazing red now. The rest of her was barely recognizable as female. That, Gregor thought, was surprising. He'd had a good look at Katherine Branch yesterday, and she was most definitely female. In his experience, women with bodies that good—and bodies that good took work, especially in women over thirty; nobody got handed one free by the grace of genetics alone—didn't hide their light under bushels. Or, in this case, sweaters. That was what Dr. Katherine Branch was wearing, sweaters, in the plural, over a pair of baggy pants. She had a turtleneck. She also had something that looked like a cross between a tent and a tunic. The effect was not entirely unattractive, but it was totally asexual.

David Markham was holding out a chair in his best gallant local yokel manner. Katherine Branch ignored it, walked around to the chair next to Gregor and slammed her tray on the table. There wasn't much on it—orange juice in a little waxed cardboard carton, coffee, and an apple that had been sealed in plastic wrap—but it hit its target with a bang as loud as any sound a jackhammer could have made. She pulled a chair out from under the table, banged it into the floor, and sat down in it.

"If you two white male fascists think you're going to intimidate me," she said, "you better get rid of that idea right now."

"Ahhh," David Markham said.

Gregor took another sip of coffee. The interesting thing about that little speech was what hadn't been in it: any real passion or conviction. Gregor wondered briefly what exactly was going on inside Katherine Branch. The signals were mixed.

David Markham had retreated to his own chair and his own coffee. Now he plastered a shit-eating grin across his face and said to Gregor, "I figgered, instead of us runnin' all over the place gettin' statements from ever'body in sight, I'd see if they weren't willin' to do us the courtesy of comin' to us."

"I'm not doing you a courtesy of any kind," Katherine Branch said. "If you couldn't throw me in jail, I wouldn't be here."

Markham's twang had been so thick, Gregor was sure Katherine Branch would twig it. She didn't. She accepted it as perfectly normal. Gregor wondered if she really believed that David Markham could throw her in jail for refusing to talk to him. She was an educated woman. She couldn't be that naive.

She opened her orange juice, looked deeply inside it—to see if it were fizzing?—and drank. Then she turned to Gregor.

"I don't have to talk to you at all," she said. "You aren't anybody. Unless you pull out a card and prove you're still with the FBI, you can't ask me any questions at all."

"I can always ask," Gregor said pleasantly. "You don't have to answer."

"Damn right I don't."

"Of course, I've only got one question," Gregor told

her. "And I could get the answer from a dozen places. Dr. Elkinson, for example."

Katherine Branch made a face. "Oh, Alice," she said. "Alice will be cooperative. Alice makes a goddamned career out of cooperating in her own oppression."

"Mizz Elkinson is a very gracious lady," David Markham said fatuously.

Katherine Branch corrected him. "*Dr*. Elkinson," she said. "Believe it or not—and I find it very hard to believe, under the circumstances—Alice has the best degree on this campus with the exception of that shit Donegal Steele. Who, by the way, is who I think did in Miss Maryanne Veer. Not that he had anything to worry about from her, even if he thought he did. She wasn't going to go out kicking. Not Miss 'if-you-can't-behave-like-a-lady,-you-shouldn't-be-out-in-good-company' Veer. I think he just got so damned tired of having his papers copied by someone he couldn't feel up, he offed her."

"Nobody's offed her yet," Gregor said. "The last I heard, she was in the hospital and doing quite well, considering."

"Doing very well, considering," David Markham said. His drawl was nearly gone, but Katherine Branch didn't notice that either.

She took a long sip of her coffee. "I just hope this wakes her up," she said. "I just hate it when women worship men. Alice, Miss Veer. It's so damned stupid. We're supposed to be smarter than that."

"How can you think Miss Veer was—attacked—by Donegal Steele?" Gregor asked her. "I thought Dr. Steele was away from campus for some reason."

"Well, he hasn't been around, if that's what you mean," Katherine said. "It's been a blessing to all of us, let me tell you. But he's the one with the lye, isn't he?"

"What?" David Markham sat straight up in his chair. "What do you mean, he's the one with the lye?"

Katherine Branch was practically purring—and Gregor finally twigged something himself. Of course, she wasn't so naive as to believe that David Markham could arrest her for not talking to him. That was beyond the silly.

She was here because she had something to say, and this was it.

Sea changes, Gregor decided a minute later, were a matter of psychological aura. The way they happened could almost make him believe in the paranormal. Markham was too shocked to go on with his local yokel pose with any consistency. Looking at him was like looking at one of the reflections in a fun house mirror. Every time he moved, his image changed. But Katherine Branch was the real shock. Her defensiveness had vanished. So had her air of petty complaint, that strange body-language suggestion that she was about to attack from a position of weakness. There wasn't a damned thing weak about her now. All she needed to turn herself into the Spirit of the Age was Helen Reddy music playing in the background.

She leaned across the table, pushed her face straight into David Markham's, and said, "Lye. Donegal Steele is really big in the Climbing Club, really big on ruggedness, really big on a lot of macho bullshit. And don't wince every time I say 'shit,' Markham. It's a good old Anglo-Saxon word."

"It's not very ladylike," Markham said, but the twang was faint and the words were automatic.

"I am not ladylike," Katherine Branch told him.

"What does all this have to do with Dr. Donegal Steele having lye?" Gregor demanded.

Katherine Branch pulled away from Markham and turned to him. "Macho bullshit," she repeated. "Steele is always going on and on about how the college boys need to toughen up and be men and God only knows what. You'd think it all went out with the Neanderthals. In the old days the Climbing Club cabin up on Hillman's Rock used to have outhouses instead of plumbing. The outhouses are still there, but nobody's used them in years. Steele wants to open them up again."

"You mean Chessey Flint was right yesterday?" Gregor asked. "She did see buckets of lye up at that cabin?"

Katherine Branch shrugged. "How the hell do I know? I know that's not where they were four days ago, though, if they were Steele's buckets of lye."

"Where were Steele's buckets of lye?" That was Markham, in a croak.

Katherine Branch stood up and shoved the tray away from her, across the table, into Markham's stacks of papers. Maybe she had done it on purpose. The stacks shuddered and some of the papers fell. She didn't seem to notice.

"The buckets," she said, smiling fully now, completely enjoying herself, "were at least until last Saturday on Alice Elkinson's back porch. I saw them there. Dear Alice just can't say no to a man, even if it's a man she hates. She just has to be a perfect little lady."

"Dr. Branch—" Gregor started.

Katherine Branch gave her tray one more shove. "Here," she said. "If you two big strong powerful men absolutely insist, I suppose I'm going to have to let you take that up for me."

She started to turn away, changed her mind, turned back and gave the tray one last vicious shove. It had all the force of muscles made hard by regular exercise and training in self-defense. The stacks of papers shuddered, slid and fell—first into David Markham's lap, and then off that onto the floor. Katherine stalked out.

"Damn," David Markham said. "Here we go again. Academia nuts."

"She's not nuts," Gregor told him. "She's been rehearsing. That was guerrilla theater we just witnessed."

Markham was on the floor, gathering up papers. He stuck his head up over the table, threw some rescued sheets onto the surface, and sighed. "Dr. Elkinson. Dr. Steele. God knows who. Why didn't she tell us any of this yesterday?"

"She didn't want to."

"Well, we're going to have to go find them now. All of them. Including the Great Doctor Donegal Steele. Lord God Almighty."

Gregor took the papers Markham had been throwing onto the table and started piling them neatly in stacks. Because Markham hadn't bothered to sort them before, he didn't bother to sort them now. He was staring out the great windows at his side into the quad, and through the quad at the faint suggestion of the rise of King George's Scaffold.

He had just had a funny idea, one of the funniest ideas of his life—and yet it was so perfect, he couldn't see how it could fail to be true. Of course, he couldn't see how he was going to go about proving it, either, and that was a problem, but proving it was always a problem. It was what all real police work came down to. Gregor had to trust in the possibility that if he didn't worry about that part of it, if he just followed his funny idea to its conclusion and made sure it worked out as well in practice as it did in theory, the proving would take care of itself.

David Markham's head appeared over the top of the table again. The lines looked too deeply edged on his face. The worry looked too deeply buried in his eyes.

"We've got to get moving," he muttered as he threw more papers in the general direction of Gregor's tray.

"Stop," Gregor told him. "Before we get moving, there are some things I want to tell you. About what I saw and did last night."

From the look of exasperation on David Markham's face, Gregor was certain the man was going to take the gun out of his holster and shoot him.

Two

1

Gregor Demarkian had not had an effortless, smoothly crescendoing career. He had faced his share of disbelief on the part of superiors and resistance on the part of local law enforcement officials. He knew that with the way he worked, that sort of thing was sometimes inevitable. It was all well and good for magazines and true crime books and novels to praise what they called "intuition," and what Gregor knew to be merely a rigorously adhered to commitment to inductive reasoning. It was something else again for people to swallow that reasoning, no matter how meticulously it was explained to them. Even so, he had never been laughed at before, and it rankled. It did more than rankle. It made him feel ready to explode.

Sitting on the other side of the table, David Markham looked ready to explode himself, possibly from an excess of disbelief. Gregor had never thought of disbelief as gaseous before, but apparently it was. Markham looked filled full of it, puffed out at the cheeks and chest and belly. Every once in a while, giggles would escape through his mouth like little bubbles. Sometimes the sheriff held hard to the table, as if he were preventing himself from taking off, like a punctured balloon.

"Look," Markham said, after Gregor had explained the whole thing for about the fifteenth time. It was nine thirty by now, and the cafeteria was filling up. Most of the faculty seemed to have decided there were more interesting places to eat in Belleville, but most of the students obviously had nowhere else to go. Gregor watched them walking past with trays underfilled by tightly sealed packages of cereal and even more tightly sealed cartons of milk and orange juice, poking at everything as if they could tell by touch if it were poisoned. "Look," Markham said yet again. "What you're telling me here is that this boogeyman, the Great Doctor Donegal Steele, is dead."

"That's right. Or close enough as to make no difference. After almost three days, there'd be no way to save him if he fell across this table right now."

"But why?" Markham demanded. "Just because he's missing? For God's sake, Demarkian, the man is a nut."

"I don't care what kind of a nut he may have been," Gregor said. "It's the only thing that makes any sense. Or even could make any sense, unless Miss Veer was poisoned by a random psychopath, and we've—"

"Yeah, yeah," Markham said, "we've decided that wasn't it. Nothing from her tray found anywhere on the floor except the tea and it couldn't have been the tea. Yeah, yeah, yeah. But—"

"But nothing. Markham, think, will you please? Yesterday Miss Maryanne Veer had a perfectly ordinary day except for one thing, and that was that she decided she had to call the police and report Donegal Steele missing. The only reason anyone could possibly have wanted to hurt her was to stop her from doing that."

"You know, we've been through all of this a little while ago. Never mind the simple fact that it would be insane to try to murder somebody with lye just to keep them from making a phone call—"

"Remember me?" Gregor said. "I was the one who told you yesterday that I didn't think the point was to murder Maryanne Veer."

"Well, for God's sake, if whoever it was didn't want to murder her, all he had to do was cosh her, right? Why go through this complicated and very nasty rigmarole with lye?"

"I don't know," Gregor said, "but I do have a theory—"

"Oh. Another *theory*."

"Will you please stop that? I think there's some kind of time limit. It's not that our murderer wants to stop any search for Donegal Steele permanently. It couldn't be done. It's that he, or she, wants to stop it for a certain period of time—"

"What period of time?"

"I don't know. But something is going to happen. Something our murderer can't make happen by himself—"

"Or herself."

"Right. The trick was to take our minds off Donegal Steele until the time came. And what happened to Maryanne Veer was perfect."

"Except that it wasn't," Markham pointed out. "Here you are, talking about the death of Donegal Steele and wanting me to pull men off a major investigation to go look for him, when I haven't got that many men to begin with—and when you still haven't given me one good reason—"

Gregor held up a finger. "I'll give you several. One, Donegal Steele has been missing since sometime on the evening of the twenty-eighth. He missed both his classes and his office hours on the twenty-ninth, without notifying anybody of his intent to be absent, which, according to what we've been hearing, was not like him. The last person to see him as far as we know was Jack Carroll, who told me Steele was on his way to pop beers. That's—"

"I know what popping beers is, Demarkian. I've done enough of it in my time. That's a reason to assume the man's been hung over someplace or involved in a traffic accident."

"Have you had any reports of a traffic accident?"

"Demarkian—"

"Two"—Gregor held another finger up—"there is no other reason for anyone to have attacked Miss Veer in the way and at the time she was attacked." Markham started to protest. Gregor held up another finger. "Three, half the people on this campus hated the man with a passion. Four, Steele's just the type to get himself murdered—and don't snort, Markham, there are types—from all reports, he's abrasive, arrogant, aggressive, and psychologically ugly. Five, that bird has been circling over Constitution House, acting entirely out of character since Steele disappeared."

"Fine," Markham said, "now you want me to take into account the psychological functioning of a bird."

"Ravens are carnivores, Markham. And they'll spot carrion."

"If Donegal Steele had been dead and stashed for over two days in Constitution House, somebody would have noticed the stink by now."

"I didn't say he'd been dead for two days. You know how hard it is to kill somebody with lye. It's practically impossible to get them to ingest enough under any circumstances. Lye burns."

"You think somebody spiked his food with lye—"

"Beer," Gregor corrected. "Beer would be a good thing to spike with lye, especially if the victim was going to drink it from a can, because it fizzes anyway."

"Except that when you pop beers, you start with an unopened can. Then you punch a hole in the bottom, hold the can over your mouth, and pull the tab. How's the lye supposed to have gotten into the can?"

"I don't know."

"There are a lot of things you don't know," Markham said.

Gregor sighed. "I realize that. I realize a lot of things. I know this is going to be impossible to prove until we find not only a body, but the way the lye was delivered. I know it's going to be impossible to prosecute even after we find all of that unless we come up with a motive that fits in with the rest of this. I can think of three possible people with motive, opportunity, and the interior disposition to kill Steele and maim Miss Maryanne Veer. The problem is—"

On the other side of the table, Markham's eyes were widening. Amusement seemed to be passing over entirely into shock. "*Three* people," he said. "You've got suspects for this crazy idea of yours?"

"Of course I do. Jack Carroll. Ken Crockett. Alice Elkinson."

"Why those three? Why not Katherine Branch? She's the one who was just here trying to implicate a man you think is dead, which seems to me a very good ploy for somebody who's just—"

"Katherine Branch couldn't have both poisoned Mary-anne Veer and picked up the evidence afterward. She wasn't in the dining room when Miss Veer fell. Later, after she did get to the dining room, she spent all her time lying on the floor in a corner all the way on the other side from where Miss Veer's tray fell, dressed up as a witch."

Markham pounded his fist against the table, scattering his papers again. "All right then, what about Chessey Flint? She was right where she'd have to be. According to what you say Jack Carroll told you, Steele's been telling lies on her for two months."

"True. And if Miss Veer had been coshed, as you put it, I'd be with you. But lye, while Chessey was sitting right there looking at her, after she'd already seen its effects on Donegal Steele. Not Chessey Flint. Chessey Flint is one of those girls who will always have somebody else to do their heavy work for them."

"You mean Jack Carroll," Markham said.

"That I do. It fits with Steele's body being in Consti-tution House, too. Jack Carroll and Ken Crockett were fast friends. Carroll would have been in Constitution House plenty of times. I'd guess the situation with Chessey was heating up, too. I can see Carroll marching up to Steele's apartment and insisting on having it out. I can't see Chessey doing that."

Markham cocked his head. "What about the other two? Ken and Alice. Jesus Christ. I sound like I'm talking in movie titles."

Gregor smiled slightly. He thought Markham was going to be accusing him of worse than movie titles in a minute. "For Alice Elkinson," he said slowly, "I'd guess rape."

"*What?*"

"It fits, too," Gregor said blandly. "Katherine Branch told us Steele was bothering Alice Elkinson. Jack Carroll told me about Steele's attitude to women and sex, which, quite frankly, sounded to me like the excuses of half the rapists I've ever come in contact with. The other half think all the women on earth are asking for it, specifically from them. Then you've got that business Katherine Branch told us about the lye. If Steele brought lye to Alice Elkinson's apartment, then Alice Elkinson had easy access to lye, and Steele had private access to Alice Elkinson."

Markham sighed. "All right," he said, "let's hear it for Ken Crockett. And if you're going to say he was protecting Alice Elkinson—"

"I wasn't." Gregor looked down at the tray in front of him. He had gone back up for coffee more than once since he had begun to explain his theory to David Markham, but now the cups spread out across the pale blue plastic were all empty again, and he thought he might have drunk too much. He didn't usually have problems with caffeine, but he was feeling twitchy.

"You know," he said, "to my mind, Ken Crockett is the most interesting of the three. I've been told he's local."

"Very local," Markham said. "I was the one who told you. His family is about the biggest thing in Belleville."

"Am I right in assuming that until the arrival of Donegal Steele, he had every reason to assume he'd be the next Head of the Interdisciplinary Program in the American Idea?"

"You'd have to ask some of the academia nuts about that," Markham said. "I'd say in town, though, we wouldn't have been surprised. But, Mr. Demarkian, you can't possibly be suggesting that Ken Crockett would kill one person with lye and maim another just to end up Head of the Program. Especially not now. If Steele had been named Head of that Program, or anything else, I'd have heard."

"No, Steele hadn't been named Head of the Program. But I was talking to Bennis Hannaford yesterday, and this came up, as a side issue to something else. And she pointed out, rightly I think, that there wasn't much of any other reason for Steele to be here. His ideas on education weren't popular, but they were famous. He could probably have his pick of campuses with one or two exceptions. And they paid him a lot of money to get him to come here. Why else would they do that if they weren't expecting to put him in the Head's seat?"

"Maybe none," Markham admitted, "but still—"

"But still, it's a weak motive," Gregor agreed. "That's why I'm so interested in the local connection. What might not have mattered so much to someone from out of town might have mattered a great deal to Ken Crockett. What might have been a major career embarrassment and a reason for taking off for parts unknown to someone else, might have been the worst-case scenario to someone who had his whole life and his whole reputation built around this town."

Markham leaned back, closed his eyes, and let out a long, low raspberry. "Oh, Lord," he said. "You're a very plausible man, do you know that, Mr. Demarkian? You're the most plausible man I've ever met. You do realize this is still all pie-in-the-sky, don't you?"

"No," Gregor said.

"Well, it is."

Markham stood up. The shirt he was wearing was made out of some kind of cheap synthetic fabric, shiny and stiff, and it caught on the crest of his beer gut. Standing there like that, he looked more local yokel than ever, and more phony. Gregor wanted to tell him to sit down and behave like a human being.

Since Gregor didn't say anything, Markham got his hat off the table, jammed it onto his head, and began gathering his papers into one final pile. Gregor doubted he would ever look at them again, or, if he did, that he would ever find anything he wanted in them. Markham stuffed the papers into the inside pocket of his jacket—they didn't exactly fit—and stretched.

"If you're not going to be sensible and come along with me," the sheriff said, "I'm going to go by myself. You're sure you want to spend your time hacking around on this wild-goose chase of yours?"

"It's not a wild-goose chase," Gregor said.

Markham tipped his hat, spun around, and marched away toward the cafeteria's doors.

2

Fifteen minutes later, Gregor Demarkian headed for the cafeteria doors himself. He should have left immediately after Markham, and he knew it, but he hadn't been able to bring himself to. Maybe it was that his head was still caught up in motives, and especially Ken Crockett's motive. He kept feeling there was something missing in the picture he had gotten of the man, and it irked him. Maybe it was just that so many students stopped beside his table once he was alone, mostly to ask about the lecture he'd be giving that night and to probe into his credentials. It surprised him a little, how rigid these young people were about background and training. It was as if they didn't believe anyone could know anything about everything if they hadn't learned it in school.

It was after ten when he finally got up and got moving. The cafeteria was in the middle of its switch from breakfast to lunch. Students dressed in white coats like medical students were bringing large trays of sandwiches into the main cafeteria room from the back and laying them out where the Swedish meatballs and roast beef au jus had been the day before. The sandwiches were hermetically sealed in plastic and looked terrible. Gregor thought the cheese ones looked made out of cellulose and possibly more lethal than lye. As he was passing down the line, he heard one of the working students refer to the sandwiches labeled "meatball" as "mystery meat," and he didn't blame her.

He walked through the foyer, out the doors, down the front steps, and came to rest at the edge of the quad. It was a late Thursday morning and presumably a time when the campus was occupied with lectures and seminars, but he didn't think any of that was actually getting done. The quad was jammed with students and pounding with music. The crowd extended, unbroken like a sea, all the way past the Minuteman statue and out the other side, presumably into Minuteman Field. Gregor couldn't see that far because his vision was blocked by both buildings and people. No matter how tall he was—and he was tall—there always seemed to be someone taller in his line of sight. He walked down to the path and pushed his way gently through clutches of giggling boys and girls. They had never seemed physically bigger to him. They had also never seemed so childish.

He was winding his way in and out of people, in and out of groups so firmly packed they would have been harder to break up than a hydrogen atom, when he felt a tug on his sleeve and turned to see an immensely tall boy in a Dracula suit leaning over him. The makeup the boy was wearing was too realistic to be comfortable. The fangs that grew out from under his upper lip and down across his mouth and chin seemed to be tipped with real blood. Gregor wanted to tell him to get the hell out of here until he'd washed his face. Then the boy leaned forward, smiled a little, and said, "Mr. Demarkian?" in a voice so tentative, it could have come from a six year old, and Gregor found himself sighing once again.

"Yes," he said, "I'm Gregor Demarkian. If you want to know what my talk is going to be about, you're going to have to come to it."

The boy looked confused. "Your talk," he said. "I'm coming to your talk. We all are."

"I hope you don't mean the whole college," Gregor told him. "From what I've seen so far, there isn't anyplace the whole college would fit."

"I mean all of us—us," the boy said, and shrugged. He obviously thought *us—us* ought to explain it all, which it didn't. He turned away and looked off into the crowd for a moment and then turned back, an hiatus he seemed to need just to get the subject changed. "Listen," he said. "I'm Freddie? Freddie Murchison?"

"Yes?" Gregor said.

"I'm a friend of Jack Carroll's. We haven't met, but I brought some things up to Father Tibor's room for you yesterday afternoon. Me and Max. Picnic baskets."

"Oh," Gregor said. That didn't sound very gracious. He added, "Thank you."

"You don't have to say thank you," Freddie told him.

"It's like Jack says. I'm six five. I've got responsibilities. No. The thing is, I was wondering, have you seen Jack?"

"Do you mean Mr. Carroll?"

"Mr.—yeah, I guess I do."

"Do you mean today?"

"Of course today." Now the boy looked worse than confused. He was not, Gregor thought, a very smart boy. He wasn't a very mature one, either. Gregor began to feel a little guilty. He was preoccupied, but that wasn't any reason for putting this boy through what one of his nieces called The Grown-Up Rag. This particular niece of his had just turned seventeen.

"I'm sorry," he said. "I'm afraid my mind is on something else. You're looking for Jack Carroll? Why? Is he missing?"

"Yeah," Freddie said, "he's missing. I've been looking for him all day. And you know what's weird? Chessey's missing, too."

"Chessey Flint?"

"Right." Freddie obviously thought that everybody, even the President of the United States, must know who "Chessey" was and that she was the girlfriend of Jack Carroll. It was information in the atmosphere, like the fact that the Pope was Polish and Ozzie Osbourne was being persecuted by the middle-class mothers of America. He turned around and stared into the crowd for a moment, as if he expected one or the other of the reigning deities of Independence College to materialize in front of his eyes. Then he turned back again.

"The thing is," he said, "it's really important for me to find Jack. It's really important for all of us. Nothing is getting done."

"Is there a lot to get done?"

"Oh, yeah," Freddie said. "The bonfire's tonight. Do you know about the bonfire?"

"Of course I do."

"Yeah, I guess everybody knows about it. Jack's president of students. He's supposed to be running things. And he's not here."

"I could see where that would be a problem."

"It's not like we don't know what to do," Freddie said. "I mean, Jack's a good organizer, if you get the picture. We've got it all set up. But he's supposed to be here."

"Have you tried—"

"I've tried everything," Freddie said. "I went to his room. I went to Chessey's room. I couldn't even find Evie Westerman. Hell, Mr. Demarkian, I went all the way up to that Climbing Club cabin and all I got was zip."

"Zip," Gregor repeated dubiously. And then he began to smile.

And smile.

And smile.

Jack Carroll.

Chessey Flint.

Evie Westerman.

All missing.

Oh, Lord. There was only one explanation for his having missed this one, and that was that he had to be getting old.

He thought of that figure up on King George's Scaffold in the early hours of the morning, capering around in its bat suit, and nearly laughed out loud.

Then he saw Freddie Murchison staring at him in alarm—the boy had to think he was crazy—and made himself calm down. He clasped Freddie on the back in just the hearty way he had hated adults for when he was in college and said, "Don't worry about it. I'm sure Jack will be back in time for the bonfire. He struck me as a very responsible young man."

"Well, yes," Freddie said, "that's the point, isn't it? I mean, Jack never misses out, not on anything, so what I want to know is, where the Hell has he gotten to? I mean, Mr. Demarkian, with the stuff that's been happening around here, I think—"

"Don't think," Gregor said. "Go play. Mr. Carroll will be back."

"Mr. Demarkian—"

Gregor didn't hear the rest of it. He didn't want to hear the rest of it. He was bopping along the path, working his way back to Constitution House, in the best mood he'd been in since he first stepped onto this campus the day before. It was remarkable how much easier it was to make his way through the crowd once he was in a good and hopeful mood.

As for the rest of it, in his private—and soon to be not so private—opinion, David Markham was a goddamned fool.

Three

1

Dr. Alice Elkinson's senior seminar in the Foundations of the American Industrial Revolution ended at twelve o'clock, and by the time the noon bells rang out across campus, she had decided she was having a bad day. Alice often had a bad day on Halloween. It was trying enough that so many students cut class. With all the fuss going on on the quad and on Minuteman Field, she almost couldn't blame them for that. It was worse with the ones who did come, because they only seemed to drive her wild. Was it really necessary for Ted Barrows to deliver his paper on the evolution of patent law with a Freddie Kreuger mask over his face and a sack of ketchup around his neck that squirted every time he hit a high note? What exactly possessed someone like Shelley Linnington—whose ordinary modus operandi was mousy timidity and whining complaint—to let out a piercing scream in the middle of Carl Dorfman's presentation on the technology of mass production and pretend to faint? Alice had scheduled the papers because she'd thought they'd help. She'd had Halloweens when no one showed up for her classes at all. Now she realized she'd done something she'd been warned against, but never listened to the warnings about. Her whole life had been like that. *Don't get your doctorate—you'll make yourself so overqualified, you'll never get a real job. Don't wear your blouses with three buttons undone—nobody will take you seriously as a scholar. Don't fall in love with a man in your own department—you'll ruin both your careers. Don't—*

A breeze began to blow as the bells began to ring outside, and on it came Lenore, slipping slyly through the

one open window like the prophecy of doom Shelley
Linnington was always complaining about during office
hours. Steve Jacoby saw her, shrieked, dropped to the floor
and cried out, "It is she! It is she! Her shade hounds me to
the grave and calls me murderer!"

It might have been a quotation. Alice Elkinson didn't
know. She also didn't care. On top of the fact that this was
Halloween, there was also the fact that she'd had a bad and
restless night. She was not a woman who reacted well to
less than an optimal amount of sleep, and she was not
reacting well now. Her head ached. She picked up the
papers she had fanned out across the desk when class
began—photocopies of the ones the students had
presented—and slapped them into a stack. They were held
together by paper clips and therefore impossible to discol-
late. She had intended to bring them down the hall and
read them during what she was sure would be a very silent
office hour. She now knew she would bring them, but she
wouldn't read them. She had a copy of Judith Krantz's
Dazzle in the top right-hand drawer of her desk. She would
read that.

"All right, people," she said, "if you wouldn't mind
getting in touch with your fellow members of this seminar,
we will be covering Henry Ford and the five-dollar-a-week
wage next session. If anybody sees Mr. Jack Carroll, please
tell him I would like to present his paper on the effects of
wage spirals on mass consumption then."

"What about Lenore?" Ted Barrows said. "She could
present a paper on the effects of the industrial revolution on
birds."

"No she couldn't," Shelley Linnington smirked. "She
lives out here. Out here hasn't been through the industrial
revolution yet."

Ted Barrows turned sideways, raised his eyebrows,
and smirked back at Shelley Linnington. Alice thought: *Oh,
Lord. Now I'm going to have to spend the rest of the term
watching Shelley Linnington discover one of the great facts
of female life. Self-confidence is everything.*

What had ever given the United States Congress the
idea that college students were old enough to vote?

Lenore had come to rest on the stack of papers. "Croak a doak," she said. Alice brushed her off and picked the papers up.

"Until next week," Alice said, to a classroom that was half-empty. While her mind was somewhere else, half the students had sneaked out the door. She shooed the bird away, got the papers wedged as tightly as she could under her arm and went out herself.

Out in the corridor, it was better, because it was quieter, but it wasn't as good as it could be. Going up the stairs to her office, Alice ran into Katherine Branch. Katherine was bobbing and weaving to some music inside her head. That was always a bad sign, as far as Alice was concerned. Katherine in a self-confident mood was Katherine up to trouble. Usually, Katherine wore her victimization like a crown: revolutionary sainthood on the cheap; martyrdom on tenure and fifty thousand a year.

"Talked to the police," Katherine said. "As a high, I recommend it."

Katherine zipped down the stairs and Alice continued up, wondering what that was all about. It was the kind of question it was never safe to ask about Katherine.

Alice got to the third floor, pushed through the fire doors and turned the corner into the corridor. She saw the man immediately, although she didn't exactly recognize him. He was standing at the far end, near the door to her office, reading notices on the corkboard on the wall. He was too tall, too fat, too slouched, and too formal—where had he gotten that navy blue pin-striped suit?—to be a fellow academic. Anyway, she knew all the older men on the faculty of this college. She studied his face until she placed it: that man, that friend of Tibor Kasparian's who was helping the police, Gregor Demarkian.

She walked up to him, looked at the corkboard from around his back—he seemed to be studying a notice about a meeting of the Federalist Club—and said, "Mr. Demarkian? Can I help you with something?"

"What?" He abandoned the corkboard. "Oh. Dr. Elkinson. No. I was just reading."

Alice tried to take him in but he seemed like—

nothing. He was too round and soft and old for her to take him seriously. "It must seem pitifully provincial after some of the places you've been. Sometimes I wonder what our students think when they get out into the real world and find that none of this matters."

"Their educations matter, surely?"

"I don't know. I don't know how educated they get. Sometimes I think some of them just float through here on their way to their MBAs. Or their masters in social work, what with the changes in fashion."

"Oh, dear."

Alice got her keys out of her pocket and began to unlock the door to her office. It was right across the hall from the corkboard, not a distance that would require stopping the conversation. That was good, because she found she didn't want to stop the conversation. Talking to Gregor Demarkian was oddly soothing. She got the door unlocked and pushed it open.

"Do you want to come inside and sit down? You look done in. If you weren't in that suit, I'd say you'd just got back from one of Ken's climbs up Hillman's Rock."

"Oh, no. Nothing that strenuous. I was just making a fool of myself in Constitution House. Are you sure you want me to come in? I don't want to interfere with your work."

"You won't be interfering with my work," Alice said, "although God only knows I have enough to do. Magnum opus number four due at the University of Chicago Press three weeks ago, and I haven't even finished writing the conclusion. Don't worry about it. I'm supposed to be holding office hours. It's Halloween. No one will come. Come on in. I'll make us some tea."

Gregor Demarkian seemed to hesitate, but it wasn't for long. He followed Alice into her office, using his foot to push the little rock prop she kept on the floor into position. Alice opened her window to let in the cross-breeze and plugged the hot water maker into the socket next to her desk. When she turned around, Demarkian was looking at her degrees in their frames on the wall.

"Very impressive," he said. "In fact, all this is very

impressive. Berkeley for your doctorate. Swarthmore undergraduate."

"Oh," Alice said, amused. "I've always been impressive. That's what I do with my life."

"It seems a little like overkill for a place like Independence College," Gregor said, "unless they're paying you a great deal of money."

Alice laughed. "They don't. They did give me tenure when I was practically an adolescent, though, so I suppose it works out. And they give me the time to write. That's important."

"Mmm," Gregor said.

Alice turned away. "So," she said, "do you want to ask me all kinds of questions? That phony policeman David Markham already has, but in the movies I see the police always ask everything four or five times."

"I'm not the police."

"I know you're not. That doesn't matter, does it?"

Gregor Demarkian shrugged. "Sometimes I think it does, and sometimes I think it doesn't. I suppose there are a few things I could ask you, if you feel like answering questions."

"I don't feel like answering questions, I feel like hearing questions," Alice said. "Then I'll know how the minds of the police are working, and I can go back to Ken and be a fascinating woman. Unfortunately, you aren't going to ask me what I was doing at the time of the crime, because you know what I was doing. Standing right there next to the victim in plain sight of half the college."

"Mmm," Gregor Demarkian said. "What about the victim? Do you happen to remember what she was carrying on her tray?"

"You mean on her cafeteria tray? She had a cup of tea, I remember that. She—" Alice stopped.

Gregor Demarkian cocked his head at her. "What is it?"

Alice shook her head.

She wasn't sure what it was. It was funny how much you forgot about traumatic eruptions into your life. She remembered that from the aftermath of the attack at

Berkeley. For a couple of weeks she had been fine, and then things had begun to surface, details and particulars she had repressed so well she'd actually forgotten all about them. It had made her feel like a fool at the time, and it made her feel a little like a fool now. A scholar was supposed to be a noticing person, in spite of all that nonsense about ivory towers and absentmindedness. She had made it her business to be a noticing person. She shook her head again.

"I don't really know," she said. "It's not something—when she came through the cash register, what she had on her tray was a cup of tea. Nothing else. I'm sure of that."

"But—"

Alice felt herself blushing slightly, giving in to the perennial curse of the fair haired. "It was later," she told him, "after we'd paid up. We were standing in the middle of things, so to speak, and she was—I know it must have looked like I was talking to her the whole time—"

"It did."

"—but I wasn't. There was Ken there and I was talking to him, looking away from her, just before it happened. And when I turned back—this is going to sound very strange—when I turned back I could swear to God she was swallowing something."

"Solid or liquid?"

"Liquid," Alice said positively, and was surprised to realize she was positive.

"The tea," Gregor said gravely. "She could have been drinking the tea."

Alice shook her head. "I wasn't doing an analysis at the time," she said, "right after that Maryanne fell over and I wasn't doing an analysis of anything. But I can swear to you that that tea hadn't been touched."

"Why?"

"Because it was slopping. One of the things I did when I was working summers during high school was wait tables in a diner. You got much better tips if you didn't slop the coffee. I have an eye you wouldn't believe for when a cup is overfull, and that cup was overfull. Trust me."

Trust me. Alice felt herself blushing again. That was

the kind of thing people said when they weren't trustworthy
at all, when they had something to hide. Demarkian would
be a fool if he didn't at least consider the possibility that she
had something to hide, like attempted murder. She had
been the one standing closest to Miss Maryanne Veer when
she fell.

She braced herself for another round of questions
about the cafeteria tray and the swallowing and was surprised again. Instead of pursuing the subject, Demarkian
was going off on a tangent.

"Tell me about the Climbing Club," he said. "Who's in
it? What do they do?"

"The Climbing Club?" She found it a little hard to
switch gears. Why would he want to know about the
Climbing Club? "We're all in it. All the faculty in the
Program, I mean. Ken and me. Katherine Branch. Everyone except Father Tibor."

"I'll admit I can't see Tibor climbing rocks if he doesn't
have to. Isn't that a strange hobby for so many of you to take
up? I wouldn't think you'd all have the talent for it."

Alice laughed. "We don't. Ken's good, but I'm a mess.
Jack Carroll's supposed to be a wonder, according to Ken,
but Chessey Flint—" Alice shrugged. "I think it's like
pajama parties and mixers when we were all in high school.
You do it because everybody else does it. It's part of
belonging. And then, of course, there are the people with
ulterior motives, like Katherine Branch."

"What constitutes an ulterior motive for rock-
climbing?"

"In Katherine's case, there are several. In the first
place, she has to try it, just to prove to herself and
everybody else that she hasn't been turned into a puling
little wimp by the sexist expectations of a patriarchal
society. Relax, Mr. Demarkian. I'm quoting. Anyway, then,
of course, she's got to fail—"

"*Fail.*"

"Certainly. If she succeeds at everything she wants to
do—and Katherine's got the talent for that, Mr. Demarkian,
don't let all that nonsense with the witchcraft fool you—
anyway, if she succeeds, her whole philosophy goes up in

smoke. The patriarchal society hasn't wounded her. She's nobody's victim. Good Lord, she'd have to throw all the scholarship she's done up to this point in the trash can and start over from scratch."

"*Did* she have a talent for rock-climbing?"

"According to Ken she did. About ten times better than she ever let on. It used to drive him crazy."

"Used to?"

"Katherine gave it up at the beginning of this term. Stopped coming to meetings. Stopped going on climbs. She said she refused to join any organization where even the women voted for men for president."

Gregor Demarkian seemed to consider this, shifting back and forth in the chair he had chosen—the most uncomfortable one in the room. Alice wondered why he had done that. There was a perfectly good stuffed armchair in the corner and a wing chair next to the window. The water in her teamaker was boiling away. Alice leaned over, took the pitcher off the burner, and started searching around for her cups.

"Do you really want tea? And if you do, what kind? I've got six."

"Any kind," Gregor Demarkian said. "Can I ask you one more question?"

"Of course. But if it's one more question about Katherine, I think I'll go hide in the closet. The woman gives me migraines."

"It's not about Katherine," Gregor Demarkian said. "I want to know what you know about Donegal Steele."

Outside Alice Elkinson's window, a breeze had kicked up, rustling what was left of the brown and drying leaves in the trees and bringing half-hysterical laughter and Lenore. "Croak a doak," Lenore said, perching on the windowsill. Then she took off again, back out to wherever she went, and Alice threw a pair of tea bags into a pair of teacups. Earl Grey for herself, Darjeeling for Gregor Demarkian. Gregor Demarkian seemed to her like a Darjeeling sort of man.

Gregor Demarkian had just asked her a question about Donegal Steele.

It bothered Alice Elkinson enormously that she hadn't expected it.

2

Dr. Kenneth Crockett had seen Gregor Demarkian go into Liberty Hall. Ken had been coming up the path from Constitution House at the time, intent on getting some work done and dropping in on Alice's office hours, but once he saw that tall broad figure go up the steps he changed his mind. He wasn't in the mood to deal with any of it today—with any of anything. He'd had a long night and an even longer morning. He'd been looking for Jack Carroll for hours and getting nowhere. The boy was supposed to be on campus and on duty. In a social sense, this was the most important night of his college career. He had still managed to vanish so completely, he might as well have been the invisible man. Ken had talked to Freddie and Max and Ted, and the situation was worse than any he could have imagined. Jack hadn't just vanished. He had ceased to exist. Even his best friends didn't know where he had gone.

What Ken had decided to do—once he had decided not to go to Liberty Hall—was to go back to his apartment instead and get some work done. He wasn't sure what work he had to do, but there was always something. That was part of being a teacher in a school that expected scholarship as well—and no matter how gushingly the brochures described Independence College's commitment to teaching, the administration most certainly expected scholarship as well. He had papers to grade and a book to work on and a monograph to edit for presentation to the American Historical Society in June. He had that mess of papers Mrs. Winston Barradyne had sent him to clear up, too. Ken thought of those papers and frowned slightly, irritated. It had all been nothing, really, nothing, and he had been so frightened. Walking through the middle of the quad with the sun beating down on his head and the students all looking so ludicrous in streamers and makeup, he found it hard to credit how terrified he had been. That was how he had started to make mistakes. He had never been someone who worked well under pressure. Under pressure, he didn't work at all. It had been paralyzing, wondering what Donegal Steele had found out about his family. It had been killing, wondering what Donegal Steele had found out about him. Ken wondered why Alice had never noticed any of it. She was an observant woman. Her talent for observation seemed to stop before it reached him.

He was on one of the radial paths that led to the Minuteman statue, the wrong one for where he wanted to go. He hadn't been paying attention and he had wandered off course. He changed direction and started cutting across the grass. It felt awful to him not to think about Miss Maryanne Veer. He was sure he had a moral obligation to think about her, the way he had once been taught he had a moral obligation to pray for the sick, to ask God to make them better. His religious training had been sporadic and determinedly Congregationalist, which was like saying it had been determinedly amorphous. Only God knew what the Congregational Church now believed in. Ken Crockett hadn't a clue. He just couldn't help feeling—under the circumstances—that he ought to be thinking of Miss Maryanne Veer and nothing else at all.

He saw her from halfway across the quad, sitting on the Constitution House steps, stretched out, her hand wrapped around a sandwich. With most people he wouldn't have known who it was from that far away. His eyesight was good, but he didn't have X-ray vision. With Katherine Branch it was a different matter. There was nobody else on earth with that hair.

She saw him, too, and sat up, and wrapped her arms around her knees, waiting for him. He walked up to her because he couldn't think of anything else to do.

"Katherine," he said. "Good morning."

She made a face at him. "For God's sake," she said, "stop doing that. It isn't even morning."

"I was just trying to be polite."

"You're always trying to be polite. Do you know what I did with my morning? I talked to that policeman and Gregor Demarkian."

"Oh," Ken said. He looked around. No one was going in and out of Constitution House. No one he could see was actually going anywhere. They were all just milling around, aimless and hyperactive. He sat down on the steps as far from Katherine as he could get. "Well," he said, "that must have been interesting. Did they grill you?"

"Of course they didn't. What kind of an idiot do you take me for?"

"I've never taken you for an idiot."

"No? Well, God knows, I was an idiot once. I was the idiot who slept with you for six months before I figured out—"

"*Katherine.*"

"Does Alice know yet?"

"There isn't anything to know," Ken said. "You're making all this up."

Katherine's sandwich was ham. She finished the last corner of it, licked the tips of her fingers, and stood up. Above their heads, Lenore was cawing and circling, cawing and circling, making enough noise to be heard even above the music in the quad. It was "Monster Mash" again. The entire student body was obsessed with it.

"Listen," Katherine said, "I didn't tell Demarkian about—all that—but I did tell him about the lye on Alice's porch—"

"You're a bitch, Katherine."

"Of course I am. I make a point of it. You should have heard Vivi Wollman on the subject just last night. Kenneth, for once in your life pay attention, will you, please? I think you ought to take that bat suit of yours and burn it."

"What bat suit?" Ken said, and thought: *It's cold. Oh, Christ, it's so damned cold.*

Katherine was off the steps and onto the path, walking backward, not noticing where she was going. That was always true, Ken thought irrelevantly. Katherine never noticed where she was going.

"Burn it," she called back to him. "It's right there on the floor of your closet. If I could find it, so could they. It's got mud all over the hem of the cape."

"Monster Mash" had changed into something else,

something new, heavy metal, full of blood and sex and suicide. Ken Crockett got up, went through the doors of Constitution House, and stopped in the foyer. He was shaking so hard, he could barely stay on his feet.

All these years, all these last few days and everything that had happened in them, all the maneuvers and all the mistakes—

and it was all going to come to nothing.

3

At the only McDonald's off any exit anywhere on the Parkway, Evie Westerman was standing at a counter, checking the contents of a pair of overstuffed paper bags with the list in her hand. The list had been hastily written out and was hard to read. It was also long. Evie kept going back to the part marked "Jack," which called for three Big Macs, two fish sandwiches, and large fries, among other things. She was fairly sure she had counted them all out right the first time. She was also sure she was never going to get herself to believe it.

The girl behind the counter might not have been a girl. She was skinny and dyed blond and chewing gum. She might have been fifteen or forty. She couldn't have been anything in between. Evie was giving her the benefit of the doubt.

"Hey," the girl said through her gum. "Tell me somethin'. You got a boy back there in that car?"

"Yes," Evie said.

"Thought so. Teenage?"

"I think he's twenty-two."

The girl shrugged. "Same difference. I can always tell. Girls come in here with orders like that one, I know they got a boy in the car. Teenage."

"Right," Evie said. She folded the sacks into her arms like grocery bags. They were as heavy as grocery bags. They smelled like grease.

Outside, she looked across the parking lot at Jack's Volkswagen wreck and sighed. She had left Jack and Chess sitting up in the front seats, and now there was no sign of them. The only thing to be said for it was that the parking lot at McDonald's had to be a safer place to disappear than the last place they'd done it, which was stopped for a red light out on the commercial section of Route 92. She marched over to the car, tried to look through the driver's side window—it was steamed up; she'd never believed they did that when she read about it in books—and grabbed the door handle. She yanked the door open and found them as she expected to find them, doing what came naturally.

Except that, before last night, Evie would never have thought that this was what came naturally to Chessey Flint.

Evie threw the McDonald's bags on top of them both and said, "Oh, crap. Why don't the two of you just screw right here in the car and I'll go hide in the trunk?"

Four

1

When Gregor Demarkian left Freddie Murchison on the quad, he first went directly to Constitution House, springing along happily in what he later decided was a state of utter delusion. He hadn't paid much attention to Constitution House before, or to any of the other buildings he had been in, except to make mental notes of the routes he had to take to get where he wanted to go. What he found out about Constitution House when he finally decided to pay attention to it was disheartening. It had both a cellar and an attic, both locked, and probably both vast. He had no idea what the arrangements with the keys were. Both places might be being used for resident storage, with keys passed out to everyone who lived in the house. Both could have been off-limits and as hard to get into as the Pentagon subbasement. Or one or the other. Or either or both. Or—. It didn't take him long to decide that he was engaged in an exercise in futility. In spite of the exploits of Bennis Hannaford's favorite private detectives, in the real world the police were necessary for more than comic relief or political counterexample. They were necessary to search large areas, for instance. If Constitution House was as big as it seemed to Gregor after his prowl through the ground floor, it was going to take a dozen men to go over the attic and the basement with any degree of attention in anything less than a millennium.

Actually, the ground floor hadn't made Gregor feel much better and neither had the staircases. He had no idea when Constitution House had been built, but he thought it must have been a hundred years ago or more. Much more

Modern architects didn't go in for all these nooks and crannies, all these hidey-holes and sliding panels. The place was like some Victorian lady's dream of a haunted mansion, except that it was built in the Federalist style. Gregor imagined little cells of fevered adolescent patriots, cut off from the fighting of the Revolutionary War, wallowing in paranoia and secret passwords, burying themselves away against imagined harm in the walls of their own college buildings. It was a nonsensical image—from everything Gregor had heard, the American people in 1776 had been extraordinarily commonsensical—but it brought home the point with force. Under no circumstances was he going to be able to search any part of Constitution House without the help of David Markham and his men.

It was after that that Gregor had gone to Liberty Hall, haphazardly in search of Father Tibor Kasparian, and run into Alice Elkinson instead. What he had got out of that conversation was a vague feeling that he was overlooking the obvious, but he didn't know why. From the beginning, he had felt he was overlooking the obvious, stumbling over large boulders in the dark, skinning himself on sharp protrusions he should have been able to see. The necessity of the murder of Donegal Steele was only part of it. Now it was half past one and he was wandering through the crowd on the quad again, going back to Constitution House. He knew by analysis that he had been wandering for some time—it had been half past twelve when he left Alice Elkinson in her office; it was now an hour later; he must have been wandering—and he felt like a pinball played by an expert on a machine that refused to go tilt. The only hope he could see lay in questioning the one person he had yet to question and the one person most likely to give him accurate answers. Father Tibor.

Gregor let himself into Constitution House, looked with something like despair at its multitude of closed doors leading to a multitude of closed rooms, and went down the short hall in the corner to the west staircase. Besides the door that led to the hall that led to the foyer, the west staircase—like all the other staircases—had a door to the outside. If one of Gregor's suspects had had a dying

Donegal Steele squirreled away in the upper reaches of Constitution House, it would have been no problem at all to get the finally dead body out and onto the grounds without being seen. Professors weren't students. They had work to do and classes to teach. Do your dirty work late enough at night, and you could be fairly sure that anyone who might have seen you would be safely tucked in bed. Going up the winding stair, Gregor automatically checked for traces of blood—but he had done that before. There was nothing he could see without the aid of a mobile crime unit. That was true even though he knew there must be something somewhere. If Donegal Steele had been dying in Constitution House since late on the twenty-eighth, he was no longer dying—or dead—there now. Anyone who was keeping an eye on Lenore could have figured that out. Lenore had been circling Constitution House since Gregor got to Independence College and, according to Tibor, well before. Today, the bird had lost all interest in the place.

Gregor stopped on the landing that led to Tibor's floor, pressed his face against the staircase window there, and checked. Lenore was out over the campus, circling so widely she looked like she was taking off for outer space. Gregor turned around, pushed his way through the fire door, and headed for Tibor's apartment. For once on this godforsaken day, he was in luck. He hadn't got halfway down the hall to Tibor's door before he heard the low, rich, explosive staccato burst of Bennis Hannaford's laughter.

2

"The problem with you," Bennis was telling Tibor as Gregor let himself in the door, "is that the men you pick for me are always so gay."

"Gay?" Tibor said. "Dr. Crockett? Dr. Crockett is no gay. Dr. Crockett is in love with Dr. Elkinson."

"I don't care what he does for a front, Tibor, the man is gay as a green goose. Trust me. I can tell."

Gregor shut the door behind him, walking into the living room, and looked down at the scene: Tibor stiff and proper in one of the wing chairs, with books on his lap; Bennis on the floor next to an open picnic basket, eating her way through some kind of pastry that dripped. There were streaks of honey running down her chin, and every once in a while she swiped at them with a finger and licked the finger clean. When she saw Gregor, she grinned happily and took another bite.

"Tibor's arranging my love life for me again," she said, through a mouthful of honey. "He means well, but he's just so bad at it."

It was Gregor Demarkian's opinion that Bennis was so bad at arranging her own love life, almost nothing could be worse. So far in their relationship, he had suffered through an avant-garde artist in a black leather jacket and a spiked nose ring, a science fiction writer who believed that computers could be taught to procreate, a Philadelphia lawyer who spoke in what Gregor could only assume to be code, and two rock stars. The rock stars had almost given poor old George Tekemanian a heart attack. All these people had had only one thing in common. They were all extraordinarily beautiful men.

Gregor cleared a place for himself on the love seat, pushing a pile of Mickey Spillane novels to the floor. Tibor watched him do it without protest. Tibor spent a lot of his time pushing piles of books to the floor.

"Perhaps," Tibor said, "this is the answer to what happened to Miss Maryanne Veer. You say Dr. Crockett is gay and—and using a cover. Yes. So, Miss Veer finds out, and threatens to tell, and Dr. Crockett, worried about his career, decides to—"

Gregor choked. "This is the 1990s, Tibor. And this is a college campus. No one would care."

"According to Bennis, Dr. Crockett would care."

"Actually," Bennis said, "he might even have reason to care. It's like that Katherine Branch person."

"We ran into Dr. Branch in the quad, Krekor."

"Strange woman," Bennis shrugged. "Anyway, the thing is, there's a position open here for Head of the Program all these people teach in, right?"

"Right," Gregor said. Cautiously.

"Well, it's one thing to grant tenure to someone who's a little ridiculous, like Katherine Branch. I mean, why not? If they're politically correct about being ridiculous, it even makes the administration look good. So tolerant, you know the gig." Bennis had finished her pastry. She reached for another one. "With an important administrative post, though—and that's what Head of this Program or Chairman or whatever is, from what I can tell, it's the most important Program on campus—anyway, for that sort of thing, you want dignity. I hate to apprise you of this, Gregor, but 1990s or not, homosexuality has yet to acquire the odor of sanctity most college administrations are looking for in their officially visible members. Neither has being a witch. Neither has being a sex bomb."

"*Sex* bomb?"

"It is silliness, Krekor. It is Bennis's personal theory of what makes a professional image."

"Well, Alice Elkinson is a very ambitious woman. You don't put out all those publications everybody's talking about if you're not. Under those circumstances, if I'd had a randy old goat chasing me all over campus right before a promotion decision, I would be furious."

Tibor sighed. "We have been all over campus today, Krekor. We have been talking with students. Bennis has been flirting. I have been serving as bodyguard. If it is necessary to a professional image not to be perceived as a sex bomb, I think it is a good thing Bennis did not become a scholar."

"I would have choked on the dust." Bennis had finished the second pastry. She licked her fingers and stood up. "I'm going to go find myself something to drink," she said, "you people want anything?"

Gregor and Tibor both shook their heads, and she wandered off. The alcove kitchen was neither hidden nor very far away. They could both see her opening the refrigerator door, leaning down to get a good look at what was inside (it was really only half a refrigerator), rummaging through the contents. Gregor couldn't imagine anyone looking less like a sex bomb than Bennis did on an ordinary day: the knee socks, the baggy jeans, the turtleneck, the oversize flannel shirt, the hair either falling or rising cloudlike into the air around her face or pinned precariously to the top of her head. And yet, he knew what Tibor was getting at. There was just something *about* Bennis Hannaford.

Gregor looked up to find Father Tibor staring at him in concern, and shrugged slightly, feeling embarrassed. He had come up the west staircase determined to lay his theory on the line and proceed from there, but now he didn't want to do it that way. He had been made a little gun-shy by David Markham's laughter. He and Father Tibor had discussed the little solder cylinder thoroughly last night, after Tibor and Bennis had come home from the restaurant. Gregor pulled the copy Jack Carroll had made for him out of his pocket and put it down on one of the books on the coffee table. Tibor raised eloquent eyebrows. Gregor shrugged. Bennis had taken to sitting cross-legged on the floor in front of the refrigerator and swearing under her breath.

"So," Tibor said, with an air of being responsible for getting the conversation going, "you are still worried about that."

"Tibor, you remember yesterday when we first arrived here, when we were up in the parking lot? You were being tickled that the professors, and I think I quote, 'all fix their own cars.' "

Tibor nodded. "Yes, yes," he said. "It's very democratic, Krekor, except that I am not one of them. Of course, I do not have a car."

"What about the rest of the professors in the Program? Do they?"

"As far as I know they do, Krekor, yes."

"Do they all fix them by themselves?"

Tibor considered the question gravely, as if he'd been asked to give an account of the reasons for the Greek Schism. "Dr. Steele," he said, casting a surreptitious glance at the wall he shared with the college's least-liked professor, "does nothing for himself or by himself that he considers menial. Dr. Steele even has a woman who comes in to clean his bathroom. It is very unusual. Also, Krekor, it is one of the reasons he always gives for why he thinks Miss Flint will—will—"

"Leave Jack Carroll and end up in his bed in time?"

"Or has ended up in his bed already, Krekor, yes. He says she will prefer a scholar over a grease monkey. But Mr. Carroll, Krekor, is—"

"I know," Gregor said. "He's hardly your everyday grease monkey. What about the rest of them? Alice Elkinson? Ken Crockett? Katherine Branch? Even Chessey Flint."

"Chessey Flint is not a professor, Krekor. I do not think she has a car, but I don't know. If it needed to be fixed, I think Mr. Carroll would do it for her, yes?"

"Yes."

"Dr. Branch fusses around in the shed and under the hood and pretends," Tibor said, "and often in the shed she leaves a mess. Then I think she takes the car into town and has it fixed by a mechanic in secret. Dr. Crockett and Dr. Elkinson fix their own. I have seen them."

"In the shed?"

"Yes, yes, Krekor, in the shed."

Gregor drummed his fingers against a pile of books, *The Sociopolitical Consequences of Unilateral Peace*, Augustine's *City of God*, unabridged and in Latin. Then he reached into his pocket and came up with a folded sheet of paper. It was unlined, flimsy, and cheap, and had been torn off the sort of typing paper pad that could be bought in any small-town pharmacy. The surface interior to the folds had been covered with David Markham's incongruously small, neat, precise handwriting, in ballpoint pen.

"This," Gregor told Tibor as he flattened the paper on yet another pile of books, wondering all the time how the damned things had migrated to the coffee table. Yesterday, the surface of that table had been clear. "This," he said again, "is David Markham's timetable for yesterday morning and early afternoon, up to the point where Miss Veer was poisoned. David Markham likes timetables. He likes lists. He likes notes. He sheds paper wherever he goes."

"I like timetables, too," Bennis said, coming back to them. She had a can of something to drink in her hand.

"Those are my favorite kinds of mysteries. You know. The ones with the train schedules and things."

"This is not a mystery with a train schedule in it." Gregor looked at her drink again, tried to figure out what was wrong with the can, and dismissed the whole subject as irrelevant. "Now," he said, "let's flesh this out a little bit. We arrived here yesterday at eleven o'clock—"

"Quarter to," Bennis said sheepishly.

"Quarter to?"

"I fudged the time a little," Bennis was defensive. "Gregor, I know how you are about speed—"

"Never mind how I am about speed," Gregor told her, exasperated. "I'll give you my last word on speed when we have this done. Let's just get it straight. We arrived here at quarter to eleven. We walked down from the parking lot. We got to the quad in, what, ten minutes?"

"Not so long as that, Krekor," Tibor said. "Five at the most."

"Fine. Five. That puts us at ten of. That means we talked to Jack Carroll at no later than five of. Now, according to what he told Markham, right after Jack Carroll talked to us he went straight to—"

"Chessey Flint's room at Lexington House," Bennis put in. "We talked to this guy named Max this morning, Gregor. This thing between eleven and twelve with Jack and Chessey is famous on campus. Everybody knows. Jack Carroll's been missing all day and—"

"I know about Jack Carroll being missing," Gregor said. "I even have a fair idea of where he is. Never mind. He'll be back. Now, we got to Constitution House no later than a minute or two after eleven, and we saw Alice Elkinson coming out, looking for Ken Crockett. Then we came up here and talked for a while before going to lunch. In the meantime, again according to what Dr. Elkinson told David Markham, Dr. Elkinson went to her office, checked Dr. Crockett's office, and then came back here. She says she got back here at about quarter to twelve. At ten to twelve, she says she got a call from Ken Crockett, supposedly from the Climbing Club cabin on Hillman's Rock. Where exactly is Hillman's Rock?"

"Over there," Tibor said ingenuously, pointing to one of the walls. Then, seeing the look on Gregor's face, he got up, went to the desk he had shoved into one of the corners, and came back with a piece of paper of his own. This was a far more expensive example of the art of papermaking than Gregor's, a thick textured thing stained to look like parchment. Tibor flattened it out on the one clear space on the coffee table, and Gregor read the legend that was written across the bottom in sweeping, embossed calligraphic script: A Visitor's Guide to Independence College.

Tibor patted his pockets, found a pen and took it out. It was made of clear plastic and filled with hot pink ink.

"Now," he said, "here is where we are." He drew a circle around the pen-and-ink drawing of a square building with drawings of shrubs around the edges of it. "This is Constitution House. We are almost at the center of this side of the quad. The—"

"West side," Gregor said.

"Yes, Krekor. Exactly. Here is Hillman's Rock." He drew another circle, this time around what looked like a Girl Scout Handbook rendition of a mountain, far to the east.

"Where is the parking lot?" Gregor asked him.

Tibor moved his hand across the paper and drew another circle, this one to the west, but not so far. The sweep of the circle he drew took in a drawing even Gregor could recognize as King George's Scaffold. Gregor's gaze moved around and around among the three circles, taking in the entire campus.

"What about Liberty Hall?" he asked.

Tibor drew a circle not quite midway between the parking lot circle and the Constitution House circle. Gregor sat back.

"Is there something wrong?" Tibor asked him. "It is a very good map of the campus, Krekor, even if it is artistic. Very accurate."

"That's good to know."

"Then what is it?" Bennis asked.

Gregor leaned forward again. "Let's say you were going to climb Hillman's Rock," he told them. "What would you do? How would you get from Constitution House," he tapped that circle, "to where you were going to start?" He tapped Hillman's Rock.

"Well," Tibor said, "I think it would matter, Krekor, who you were. You could drive there, yes, if that is what you are asking."

"If you were Ken Crockett, would you drive there?"

"No, Krekor, I would not. I would go on foot. All the very serious climbers in the club hike there on foot. It is not as far as it seems." Tibor hesitated. "And Krekor there is something else. If we are speaking now of yesterday, Dr. Crockett did not take his car to Hillman's Rock, at least not until we had been in the parking lot and gone. And after that, the times—" He shrugged. "I saw his car in the parking lot when you were getting out of the van, Krekor. I remarked on it—"

"I remember now." Gregor finished.

Bennis took another swig of her soda. "This is weird enough. Maybe Ken Crockett wasn't rock-climbing at all yesterday. Maybe he was somewhere else. I wonder where."

"Maybe he just did what he always did and hiked out there on foot." Gregor turned to Tibor. "Are the times right for that? Could he have called Alice Elkinson at ten of twelve and still been in the dining room at twenty after?"

"Yes, Krekor, if he started almost right away. He is a very fast walker. I know. I have walked with him."

"All right." The edge of the map was lying a little over the edge of the timetable David Markham had given him. Gregor pushed the map away.

Gregor picked the timetable up and squinted at it. Bennis might love mysteries with timetables in them, but he didn't. "All right," he said again. "Now. Katherine Branch. When David Markham asked her, she said she'd spent the entire time between around eleven thirty and twelve thirty with her coven—I'm not making this up; coven is what she said—preparing, as she put it, for the ceremony of black exorcism they were going to perform in the dining room. The coven got into their makeup in her apartment in Constitution House and then formed a procession, which proceeded to the cafeteria, getting there at—"

"Bullshit," Bennis said.

Gregor looked up. "What do you mean, bull—"

"Well, she's lying, isn't she?" Bennis waved her can in the air. "We got there after twelve sometime, right? And *she* was there, in the open space just outside the cafeteria doors, and she had to have been in the cafeteria first because—"

"Bennis, what are you talking about?"

Bennis sighed. "I'd have said something if anybody asked me, but it wasn't the right time and you were the one who said that whoever had handed Miss Veer the poison had to be standing right next to her practically, and she wasn't in the cafeteria then. Dr. Branch, I mean. But she was outside it just as we were going in to lunch. I didn't recognize her or anything. We'd just got here, for God's sake. But I really couldn't mistake that hair. And she wasn't in makeup, either. Her hair was tied back in this bandanna thing and she was wearing a raincoat."

Gregor was counting to ten. He always ended up counting to ten when Bennis had information to give him. It was practically mandatory.

"Back up," he demanded. "If you say you saw her there then, I believe you. Why do you think she was in the cafeteria first?"

"Because of this," Bennis waved her can of soda in the air. "That was what she was doing. Opening a can of Belleville Lemon and Lime soda. She must have just gotten it, too. It was cold, sweating like crazy."

Bennis was waving the can in the air like a flag. Gregor stopped her hand and took the can out of it. He'd never been so startled in his life.

"Belleville Lemon and Lime," he said slowly. "This is a local brand."

"Yes, of course it is. It's been pointed out to you more than once."

"It's in a *tin* can," Gregor said.

"Yes, Gregor, it's in a tin can." Bennis was looking at him as if he were crazy.

"Not an *aluminum* can," he insisted.

"It's some ecological thing," Bennis said. "You can read about it on the side if you want to. It was in that greener-than-green language that makes me want to nuke the whales, so I never got past the friends of the earth business. All the products of the Belleville Natural Soft Drink Company and the Belleville Organic Beer and Wine Company are—"

"Beer," Gregor said, throwing up his hands. "Oh, my God."

"He is having a stroke," Tibor burst out in agitation. "Bennis, we must get him to a doctor, he is going red in the face—"

"Tin cans have seams," Gregor said, and then saw they had no idea what he was talking about. But he did. Oh, Lord, yes he did. He got up off the love seat.

"Tin cans have seams," he said, as calmly as he could. "Aluminum cans do not have seams. Also, they're soft. I know how it was done."

"How what was done?"

"How Miss Veer was poisoned with lye even though there was nothing on her tray but tea and the lye couldn't have been in the tea. Hell, I know more than that. I know who poisoned her. I even know where the body is hidden."

"What body?" Bennis asked wildly. "Tibor, I don't think the man is having a stroke, I think he's already had it. Gregor, have you any idea how nuts you sound?"

Gregor had a fair idea just how nuts he did sound, but that didn't seem to be important at the moment, and there were things he had to do. It was a relief to realize that for once he wasn't worried about stopping another murder, about getting to the site of a fresh execution and getting there in time. He didn't think there was going to be another murder. He did think there was a fair chance, if he didn't get to the people he had to get to and convince them to do what needed to be done, of the evidence just vanishing into thin air.

He was on his feet, pushing his arms into the sleeve of his coat. They were still sitting where he had left them, gaping at him.

"Come on," he said. "We've got to find David Markham. We've got work to do."

Five

1

The call came in at five o'clock, while Dr. Alice Elkinson was still sitting at the desk in her office, pretending to correct papers under the light of a flex-stemmed reading lamp. The papers were spread out across the gouged and battered oak surface in neat little paper-clipped piles. The stem of the lamp had been pulled all the way over and pointed down, as if it were an examination light in a mad doctor movie of the 1940s. Alice was wasting her time either staring out the window at Minuteman Field or looking up to the wall beside her, where her degrees hung in thin-edged dark wood frames, protected by glass that had been recently polished. Usually when she worked she pinned her hair up, or tied it back with a scarf. Now it was hanging down over her shoulders like a curtain of blond threads. Every once in a while she picked up her red marking pencil, turned it over in her hands, and put it down again.

It got dark early here in October, but not this early. Through the window, Alice could see figures moving back and forth through a half-grey light that looked like ash. She could hear them, too: laughing, giggling, faking sounds of menace and surprise. It was all so different from Berkeley—or even from Swarthmore, where she had started. It was all so different from what she had imagined it to be. For some reason, thinking through to the rest of her life when she was still an adolescent, she had imagined herself in tweed skirts and cashmere sweaters and pearls, under Gothic arches. It hadn't occurred to her that she would have to read through papers with titles like "The

Effects of Capitalist Structural Paranoia on the Work of
Benjamin Franklin."

Idiot.

She started to pick the papers up and put them in a
single pile again—that was beginning to feel like all she had
done with this day, stacking papers and unstacking them—
and as she did she felt the phone next to her arm begin to
hum. The phone system was new and didn't work very well.
Even the most rudimentary of the equipment seemed to
come on line with an anticipatory growl, like a malicious
computer. Alice raised her hand over the receiver and
waited. Somewhere at the back of her head, she was
counting mentally to three without really knowing she was
doing it. There was something about the hum of the phone
that was like the ash-gray of the air outside. It boded ill.

Idiot, Alice thought again.

The phone rang and she picked up, saying what she
always said, thinking she must sound tired or out of sorts or
both. God only knew, she felt both.

"Dr. Alice Elkinson here."

There was a pause on the other end of the line and
then a cough and then another pause. The second pause
went on so long, Alice began to wonder if she had caught an
obscene caller in the act. There were boys on campus who
did that sort of thing, phoned at random and hoped to get
a girl's voice. All the phone numbers on campus were on
the same exchange and nothing else in the area was. Alice
had heard the talk at Faculty Senate meetings: the boy,
the voice, the pause, the realization at the other end of the
line that this was a mistake, the faculty was too quick to call
security. Then there would be a click and a dial tone. It was
the sort of thing that made Alice Elkinson's skin crawl.

Idiot, she told herself, yet again, yet again, and the
word echoed through her skull like a Ping-Pong ball in a
cloud chamber.

She was just making up her mind to hang up when
another cough came, and then a gargling sound that was
surely someone clearing his throat, and then a voice,

"Dr. Elkinson? Dr. Elkinson, this is Chessey Flint."

Alice had been so sure that the next thing she was

going to do was slam the receiver into the cradle, she had to make a conscious effort to freeze her arm.

"Chessey?" she said. "Chessey, are you all right?"

Another pause, another cough, another gargle. Something seemed to be going on in the background: cars passing, small animals creeping out to greet the approaching dark. How could she possibly know something like that? Halloween must be getting to her.

"Chessey?" Alice said again.

"Yes," Chessey said. "Yes. Dr. Elkinson. I'm here. I'm sorry."

"What's wrong?"

What's wrong? Alice wasn't sure, but she thought she heard Chessey laugh, not a good laugh, low and bitter.

"Nothing's wrong," Chessey said, "not now."

"Then what is it?"

Pause, cough, gargle. Pause, cough, gargle. Pause, cough, gargle. It was maddening.

"Listen," Chessey said, "Dr. Elkinson? I'm out here on the Boardman Road. On the way to Hillman's Rock. Do you know where that is?"

"Yes, Chessey, of course, I know I—"

"I thought you would, because of the hiking. Dr. Elkinson, something's happened—"

"What?"

"To me."

Halloween, Alice Elkinson thought, closing her eyes. What was Chessey Flint doing out on Boardman Road?

"Chessey, listen to me, are you alone?"

"I am now."

"What does that mean, you are now?"

"I'm bleeding, Dr. Elkinson. I'm sitting in this phone booth and I'm still bleeding and I don't know what to do. I have to get out of here—"

"No," Alice said. "Don't get out of there. I'll come with the car. Where on the Boardman Road?"

"At a gas station."

There were two dozen gas stations on the Boardman Road. The road weaved in and out among the rising hills. Sometimes it seemed to be supported by gas stations. It was the longest and worst possible route to Hillman's Rock. It was ten uninterrupted miles of curves and technological blight.

Alice was already reaching for her coat, bending over nearly backward, stretching until she thought it was going to break. The phone cord was short and the coat was all the way across the room, on the rack next to the door. Alice got hold of the coat and yanked it toward her, not really caring that the rack fell over in the process, hitting the floor with the hard ripping sound of splintering wood.

"Chessey, stay where you are. Don't move. Do you understand me?"

"I have to move," Chessey said. "I'm going to faint."

"Chessey—"

But there was nothing at the other end of the line, nothing at all. Alice thought about running down the hall to one of the other offices and calling 911. With the phone line open like this, somebody might be able to trace the call. In the meantime, she could get in her car and start the search herself. Then she heard the one sound she hadn't wanted to hear, had been afraid to hear ever since Chessey had said that she "had" to get out of there. Somebody hung the phone up.

Alice Elkinson looked down at the coat in her hand and then out the window, at Lenore circling way out over the campus someplace, circling widely and without regard for the darkening evening. Then she plunged her hands into the right-hand pocket of her coat to make sure her keys were there and headed for the door. At the last minute, the part of her she didn't like resisted. There couldn't possibly be a worse time to have to go hauling out to the Boardman Road. The resistance came and went in a flash, drowned by Chessey's voice and a click on the phone.

Dial tone.

Going down the darkened corridors of Liberty Hall, it felt to Alice Elkinson that her life had disintegrated into something uncontrollable, into crises without number.

2

Standing at the window in the living room of her apartment in Constitution House, Dr. Katherine Branch was also watching Lenore circle above campus, but unlike Alice Elkinson she wasn't making a big deal out of it. In spite of her attraction to witchcraft and some of the more esoteric aspects of the women's spirituality movement, Katherine Branch had never been a particularly fearful or even mildly superstitious woman. Halloween had never meant any more to her than a lot of nonsensical, intrinsically sexist fuss on campus. Technically, she was supposed to be out there now, leading the coven in a procession to King's Scaffold. They had planned for weeks to hold an exorcism against light in front of the effigy before the bonfire was lit. Instead, she was standing here, still in jeans and turtleneck and sweater, holding two impossible arguments at once.

One of those arguments was with Vivi Wollman, who was sitting on the couch just as she had the other day, but not as she ought to be. Not only was Vivi not dressed for the coven, she wasn't dressed for anything Katherine could make out. She was wearing a skirt and a pair of stockings not opaque enough to be called tights, but dark enough to look dirty. She had had her hair permed into tight little curls and her face plastered with paint. Katherine couldn't decide if Vivi looked more like she'd done the plastering herself or gone into town to have herself made up by Babs DeMartin at the Belleville Beauty Palace. Whichever it was, the effect was unrelievedly awful. Vivi Wollman trying to look like a woman was worse than ludicrous.

The other argument was with Evie Westerman, who had rung up just about three minutes ago, while Katherine was telling Vivi to come to her senses. In some ways, the call had been a relief. It had at least distracted Katherine from the fact that she was failing miserably with Vivi, and was probably destined to go on failing. Christ only knew what had gotten into the stupid fool. Unfortunately, the call from Evie was not

entirely a relief. Katherine had had Evie in her Principles of
Feminism class Evie's junior year, and Katherine had thought
at the time that the girl had the capacity to turn herself into a
world-class bitch. Well, now she had. Olympic quality.

"I am no longer willing," Vivi Wollman was saying, "to
ruin my career, my present and my future by the blood-
sucking selfishness you've decided to label 'feminism.' "

Vivi Wollman. Evie Westerman. The similarities in the
names made Katherine's head spin.

"Just a minute," she said to Vivi. "I'm on the phone."

"I don't want to keep you on the phone," Evie Westerman said. "I just want to say my piece and get off."

"I wish you would say your piece," Katherine said. "I
haven't got the faintest idea what you're talking about."

Vivi had got up off the couch and started pacing. Her
skirt fit badly. Every time she moved, the seams rode and
twisted against her hips, the button placket at the back
buckled.

"For Christ's sake," Katherine told her, "fix that thing,
will you? You look like you've stuffed your underwear with
mutated worms."

Vivi came to a stop in the middle of the floor, threw her
hair back—it didn't work; that hair was permed stiff—and
said, "I don't know what it is you think you accomplish by
insulting me, Katherine, but I'm telling you right now I've
had it, I quit, and I'm not going to take any more."

"If you weren't going to take it anymore, you wouldn't
be here," Katherine said. "Jesus Christ, Vivi, where do you
think you're going to go?"

"Vivian," Vivi said. "That's my name. Vivian."

"What I'm talking about is you," Evie Westerman said.
"Yesterday. Up in the shed where they keep the tools for
fixing cars. Up in the parking lot."

Lenore had made her circuit and was coming back at
Constitution House, cawing and cawing, screaming really.
Katherine closed her eyes against the sight—it was amazing
how distracting that damn bird could get—and tried to
think. Vivi had gone into a full-force pace, back and forth,
back and forth, practically bumping into the walls. She was
working up a real head of steam. Katherine kept expecting

to see smoke pour out of her ears, the way it did out of Sylvester the Cat's when Tweetie Bird trounced him again.

That was what Vivi looked like. Sylvester the Cat. Same short-legged, pear-bottomed figure, only shorter.

"Look," Katherine said into the phone, "I still don't understand what you think you're—"

"Of course you do," Evie Westerman said. "Gregor Demarkian is looking for someone who was in that shed yesterday, messing around with the soldering equipment."

"I was not messing around—"

"Yes, you were," Evie said. "I saw you. I've been sitting right here for the last hour, thinking about whether or not I ought to tell Demarkian about it."

"Evie," Katherine said, "where are you?"

"In the Finger Lickin' Bar and Grill."

"Where in God's name is that?"

"On the other side of Belleville from campus. Out on Route Fifty. It's a roadhouse."

"I'd guessed that, Evie."

"I think you ought to be here, too," Evie said. "I think you ought to get here right away. Because if you're not here by the time I finish my beer, I'm going to get back into my car, drive back to campus, and go straight to Gregor Demarkian. And you in that shed isn't the only thing I'm going to tell him about."

"Evie—"

"There's also you and a certain bat suit. And you and a certain pair of buckets of lye. And you breaking into Dr. Crockett's apartment and Dr. Elkinson's apartment and—"

"*Evie.*"

"I'm going to hang up now," Evie said. "Then I'm going to go to the bar and order that beer. Don't be late."

The phone was hung up with a smash so hard and so loud, it made Katherine wince.

On the other side of the room, Vivi had stopped pacing and taken up leaning against the windowsill. Her posture was terrible. Her spine was made of spaghetti and everything slumped. Katherine stared at her in exasperation. Anyone else on earth would have had the sense to get out

of here minutes ago. Anyone else would at least have had
the sense to be getting out of here *now*.

"If you think I'm going to let you get away with this,"
Vivi said, "if you think I'm going to let you fob me off with
a lot of pious platitudes and abusive bullshit—"

Katherine walked over to the closet, opened it up, and
grabbed her coat. She didn't have time right now to think
about how many times she had played this scene, or with
how many people. She didn't have time right now to think
about anything. It didn't matter a flying damn that her
entire history seemed to come down to confrontations like
this one, wars fought on worn carpets with women who
didn't have the sense God gave a kangaroo.

Women.

Her coat was a heavy green parka filled with goose
down and stitched to look like puffy waves of soap on
chemically polluted waters. She threw it over her shoulders
and said,

"Vivi, the best advice I can give to you is put your head
in the toilet bowl and flush."

Then she left.

3

For Ken Crockett, the only thing on earth at this
precise moment in time—five thirty on Halloween, sharp
black splinters of clouds against a grey-dusk sky—was fire.
He knew it shouldn't be. He had known ever since five
fifteen, when his phone rang and he'd heard Jack Carroll's
voice, low and threatening, spelling out what he had to do.
He had told Jack he had written the directions down on the
back of an envelope, and that was true. The envelope was
sitting right there in his apartment on the narrow strip of
end table next to his phone. Ken distinctly remembered
covering it with ink. He even remembered holding down
the edge of it with the knuckles of his left hand, while the
fingers of that hand were still wrapped around the hem of
the bat suit he had found on his closet floor, just as
Katherine Branch had said he would.

"We've got to talk," Jack Carroll had said to him. "You do realize that, don't you, Ken? We've got to talk."

"Yes," Ken had told him. "I suppose we do."

"I can't just walk away from something like that and pretend it never happened. Do you understand that?"

Yes, Ken had thought at the time. He did understand that. What he didn't understand was what he was supposed to do about it. Sometimes he didn't understand what he was supposed to do about himself. Was it some kind of psychosis, not wanting to be what you so obviously were, what you couldn't do anything to change? They had been up at the top of Hillman's Rock that day and getting stupid. It was much too late in the afternoon for them to be that high up and still be sure they could get safely down. The sun had been melting into the trees behind them in a flare of red and gold. Even with evening coming on, it had been oddly hot. Jack had taken off his down vest and unbuttoned his flannel shirt. And *he*—

But he couldn't remember what he'd done. That was the problem. He could never remember what he'd done when he got himself into a spot like that, and the spots were coming more and more frequently lately, especially with Jack. Ken walked around these days feeling flayed alive.

"I've been thinking about going to the Dean," Jack had said on the phone today. "I've been thinking about it for over a week. I don't think it makes much sense."

"No," Ken had said. "I don't think it makes much sense, either."

"I couldn't come up with any sane idea of what I'd tell the Dean. But I can't just sit here driving myself crazy with it, Ken. You must know that."

"Yes," Ken had said. "I mean no. Of course not."

"I want you to come out here right now, okay? Neutral territory. Where we can talk."

There were men at Berkeley and Chicago and Yale who walked around with lavender scarves tied around their throats. There were men in Washington and Los Angeles and New York who bought apartments with their lovers and were buried together under linked headstones engraved with the poetry of passion and AIDS. They were on the lip of the third millennium and there was no sense, no sense at all, to the way he was behaving.

Except, of course, that there was. He was not any of those men. He was Dr. Kenneth Crockett. He didn't live in any of those places. He lived here, in Belleville, Pennsylvania, where every member of his family since the year 1692 had made his home and his life and his name—and that name definitely had not been *fag*.

"Ken?" Jack had said. "Look. I'm up at the cabin. I'm going to leave in a few minutes."

"Where to?"

"Not to campus. I don't want to talk on campus. I thought I'd go over to Harrison's in Chelton and have a steak. Can you meet me there?"

"Now?"

"Yes, Ken, of course now. I have to be back in time for Demarkian's lecture. I have to introduce the man."

"Oh."

Ken had looked at his clock automatically, seen the time, seen Jack's point. Harrison's was a good half hour away by car, no matter how hard you pumped the gas pedal. He felt himself start to sweat and closed his eyes against the rain of salt that poured into them.

"Jack? Look, right now—"

"It's got to be now, Ken. It's got to be."

"But—"

"I'm going to leave right now. Meet me at Harrison's."

He had looked down and seen that the bat suit was bunched and knotted in both his hands, trailing across his face, wound around the telephone receiver. He had been pulling and twisting it while he talked and he hadn't even noticed. Then he had heard Jack hang up without saying good-bye and he had let the receiver fall to the end table. It had seemed like much more than he would ever be able to do to put it back in its cradle.

In San Francisco, there were entire neighborhoods full of nothing but men like him. In New Orleans, there was a section of the city with its own place on the tourist maps, celebrating everything he thought he wanted to forget. Even Minneapolis, Minnesota, had a temple of the mascu-

line all its own, where men who were what he was didn't
have to hide.

And he was here.

He looked down at the bat suit now and told himself to
get on with it. He was in the basement of Constitution
House, standing next to the incinerator. He was all ready to
go. All he had to do was throw the damn thing in there and
make sure it caught.

Fire.

At the last minute, he got the tin of kerosene off the
shelf on the west wall and dosed the bat suit thoroughly.
Then he threw it into the black cast-iron tank and watched
it flare.

He knew what came next, what always came next, just
when the pain got so bad he thought he was going to shred
into blood and skin and bone in the blades of it.

He was going to start to get angry, and once he started
he wouldn't be able to stop.

He was going to be ready to kill someone.

4

It was five thirty-five, and up in Chessey Flint and
Evie Westerman's room in Lexington House, Jack Carroll
was trying to open a bottle of Dom Perignon champagne.
Evie Westerman had given him explicit instructions about
what he was and what he wasn't supposed to do. It was
apparently the height of stupidity to pop a cork on a bottle
of anything quite this expensive. Evie had even gone into
just why it was this expensive, but Jack hadn't been
listening to her. The phrase "vintage years" always reminded him of old women who wore white lace gloves to
lunch.

Over on the more neatly made of the two double beds,
Chessey was sitting cross-legged in a pair of jeans and one
of his shirts, looking happily disheveled but a little guilty.

"Do you really think we should have done all that?" she
asked them. "I think that was a really awful thing I did to
Dr. Elkinson."

"I don't," Evie said. "I think you were brilliant. I didn't know you had it in you. That makes two things I didn't know you had it in you for over the last two days."

"Oh; *that,*" Jack said. "I knew she had *that* in her. What did you think the problem was?"

Evie made a face. "In my opinion, it was a case of pathological nostalgia for the fifties. But what do I know?"

"Got it." Jack waved the cork triumphantly in the air and reached for one of the glasses Evie had set out along the desk. They weren't what he thought of as champagne glasses—they were narrow and tall instead of wide and squat—but Evie had assured him that they were what champagne glasses were really supposed to be, and she should know. He poured the glass he was holding full and handed it to Chessey.

"To all the brilliant things only I knew you were going to be," he said.

Chessey frowned at him. "Still—" she began.

Evie snorted. "Look, what we had to do was get them off campus and out of the way for at least an hour and a half each, right? And we did it, right?"

"You bet," Jack said.

"Still," Chessey said.

"Still nothing," Evie said. "I say we ought to be knighted by the Queen. Except that we don't have a Queen. Never mind. I'll think of something."

Jack poured the second glass full and handed it to her. He saw her point. He even believed in it more than he believed in Chessey's. He did have to give Chessey one thing.

It was not only an awful thing she had done to Dr. Elkinson, it was a thoroughly shitty thing he had done to Ken Crockett.

Necessary or not.

Six

1

There had been times in Gregor Demarkian's life when the case he was working on had blotted out everything else. Seasons and sentimentalities, weather meteorological and emotional, even friendships and family had been drowned as surely as words on a page under a sea of spilled ink. In the early days of the Behavioral Science department, that sort of case had been almost routine. Those were the days before he—or anyone else—realized that the man who murdered thirty young women with an ice pick and a cheese board wasn't an anomaly, but the representative of a class. Gregor thought he had been on the job with the new department for five years before it hit him that that class was not only vast, but growing. Somehow or other, this society seemed to be breeding a prolific race of the morally dead. It had taken Elizabeth's dying to pull him out of that one. For a while—even after Elizabeth had been diagnosed; in the calm days before they both knew how bad it was going to be—the phenomenon of the serial killer, cold-sane and self-conscious in the Bundy style, had taken over Gregor's mind and heart and soul, like a demon possession. He hadn't even been able to eat without thinking about it. He would sit at the desk in the ridiculously huge office they had given him, perquisite of a man raised to the rank of senior administrator, with a half-eaten sandwich at his side and a thermos of bad coffee threatening to fall off the desk's edge, trying to write it all down on paper in a way that would make it make sense.

Of course, at Independence College on the thirty-first of October, it was not really possible to ignore Halloween.

The campus was too bizarrely caught up in the holiday for that. It was now seven o'clock in the evening and full dark and very cold. In an hour, Gregor was due to give his lecture on criminological methods and the FBI. In five hours, the great pile of wood shored up against King's Scaffold would be doused with kerosene and lit, sending flames as big as tidal waves against the star-dotted blackness of the sky. The gently glowing globe lights that lit the paths of the quad and the sidewalks that stretched out to the more far-flung technical buildings every other night of the year were all extinguished. What light there was came from the flaming kerosene-soaked torches carried by Jack Carroll's legions of senior boys. Because there were a lot of those boys, there should have been more light rather than less. It didn't work that way. Flames flickered and danced and were pushed about by the wind. They sowed light one minute and shadows the next. Coming across from Liberty Hall to Constitution House for what Gregor thought might be the last time, he had a hard time holding the features of anyone's face.

Next to him, Father Tibor Kasparian trudged along with his hands wrapped into the folds of his cassock, looking infinitely tired. Gregor knew Tibor had been brought up among psychopaths—raised by them, really, except in the tight protective womb of his unshakably religious family—but he hadn't expected Tibor to be taken like this by what had happened here. He thought he might have read Tibor's psychology exactly backward, the way he had once tried to read words in a mirror when he was a boy and pretending to fight crimes with magic superpowers, like Spider Man. After all, what they were dealing with here was not a psychopath, but an ordinary human being who had invested too much in superficialities and too little in inner strength. It hadn't occurred to Gregor that Tibor might find that worse than the prospect of a man who had decided to play out the fantasies of Stalin and Hitler in private life.

He put his hand on the priest's shoulder and said, "Tibor? Are you all right?"

"I am fine, Krekor," Tibor said. "I am thinking. You are very sure you have this set up exactly right?"

"I think so, Tibor, yes. I have it set up the only way I think it will work."

"It seems like a very large chance, Krekor. You are counting on—"

"On guilt," Gregor said simply.

"Yes. On guilt. But Krekor, I am not sure, in this case, if guilt applies. What you have shown me is something that takes much work, much concentration, much coldness to effect. It is not like hacking away at someone with an ax in a fit of rage. It is not—normal."

"No, of course it is not normal."

"Do you read G. K. Chesterton? He said once somewhere that in order for a man to break the fifth commandment he must first break the first. That the murderer's problem is not with 'Thou shalt not kill,' but with 'I am the Lord Thy God. Thou shalt have no other Gods before Me.'"

"I'll have to read Chesterton."

"It seems like a paltry reason, Krekor. A little thing. For all this blood and pain and trouble."

"I know."

He did, too. For the past hour, he and Tibor had been walking, from one end of campus to the other, from one place that needed to be checked out to the other, nailing it down, making sure he hadn't forgotten anything or assumed something he shouldn't have assumed. Markham's men were out doing the important work, gathering the information and making the discoveries that would later have to be presented in court. That was necessary. The rules of evidence were so convoluted by now it didn't do to tamper with them. What Gregor had wanted, and what he and Tibor had set off to get, was confirmation of the fine points. They had gotten them, but at a price. Gregor's feet hurt. He was sure Tibor's feet hurt, too. They would have taken Donna Moradanyan's van, but neither of them was really able to drive. Tibor didn't have a license. Gregor had one, but he was, as Donna and Bennis and everyone else who knew him always put it, "a positive menace on the road."

They had reached the steps of Constitution House and Gregor stopped, letting a Siamese-twinned version of

Tweedledum and Tweedledee pass between them before he spoke.

"The mistake you're making," he told Tibor, "is the same one I made up until a couple of hours ago. People invest their lives in all sorts of things that may seem silly to you or me, but mostly what they invest them in is their own image of themselves. We construct identities like houses and then we live in them. If someone comes along and threatens to burn the house down, we react."

"We do not all react with lye, Krekor."

"I'm not saying we do. Most of us never face the crisis in the first place. Identities are private, and the population at large usually tries to be polite. Sometimes there's a situation where the crisis can't be avoided, but then I think most people would do what most people have done in situations like that. Simply self-destruct."

"Suicide?"

"Sometimes. Also nervous breakdown, psychotic break, chronic clinical depression. In this case what we had was a kind of double whammy. What Donegal Steele was doing not only threatened to burn our murderer's house down, it threatened to destroy our murderer's vision of the world as well. Think about Cavanaugh Street."

"I have been thinking about it all this afternoon, Krekor. I would very much like to get back."

"So would I. But before Bennis and I left there yesterday, Lida and Hannah and all their kind were doing a very stupid thing. They were leaving their doors unlocked. We haven't had a frantic phone call, so I suppose it's been all right, at least so far—but it might not be. You know what the world is like. You know what kind of a chance that is to take. They won't even consider it. They have invested an enormous amount of emotional energy in their belief that Cavanaugh Street is different from the rest of the world. That is—no, that *they* have found a vaccination to make their small corner of the world immune from all the diseases of humanity."

"And that is what our murderer is doing?"

"Oh, everybody does it," Gregor said. "I remember a case once that came up when I was on jury duty in

Washington, D.C. I never had to serve on a jury. I just had to show up one day and explain I was with the FBI. While I was waiting around in the hall with everyone else that day, I heard a number of men talking about a case that had come up for trial. A young man had stabbed another young man twenty-five times with a penknife, because, according to the defendant, the victim had made a pass at him. The defendant was just in from some small town in Idaho. I remember wondering at the time why the prosecuting attorney had bothered to bring the damn thing to court. Things like that happen every day and they're perfectly understandable. I'm sure that defendant was telling the strict truth. He belonged in a mental institution, but he wasn't lying. But the point I'm trying to make, Tibor, is that the men who had been called and rejected for that jury were all vociferous in their insistence that the defendant was lying, that he had to be lying. A little while after that I ran into the first man I had ever met who refused to believe that rape—the rape of women I'm talking about now—actually existed. It hit me then that he and the men who had been rejected from that jury were doing the same thing. They were all reconstructing the universe in the only way they could to make it comfortable for themselves. They were eliminating that part of reality that would have made it difficult or impossible for them to be the kind of people they had to believe they were."

"But Krekor, this is not a case of rape. This is not even a case of attempted rape."

"I know. But look at what Donegal Steele did. In the first place, he posed a concrete threat. His mere existence on this campus posed a concrete threat—to someone's career, to someone's advancement. In the second place, the way he was going about taking control—and that was what he was doing, Tibor, taking control—emotionally and psychologically as well as practically—everything we've heard about the man and what he did in his short tenure at this college says that's the kind of person he was—anyway, the way he did that jeopardized not only someone's self-image, but that same person's future. In the third place, the fact that he could show up here at all, that he could land on our murderer in a way that was totally out of our murderer's control—"

Tibor sighed. "Is this what you did, Krekor, in the Federal Bureau of Investigation? No wonder you were a wreck when you came to Cavanaugh Street. Aristotle and Augustine spent their whole lives thinking about human nature, and if they had thought like you, they would have been wrecks, too."

"Dostoevsky was a wreck. Wasn't that what you told me?"

"Dostoevsky was an epileptic." Tibor shivered.

"Well, Tibor, maybe I just needed to make it make sense to myself after the fact. The hard evidence is incontrovertible. Hard to present in court, maybe, but incontrovertible. The only alternative I can think of is to have you stand here right now and tell me it was you who murdered Donegal Steele."

Up above them, not only in Constitution House but all over the quad, lights in windows were being blocked out, the windows themselves covered tightly with cardboard and construction paper. Gregor found himself thinking irrelevantly that it had to be seven thirty, that he and Tibor had taken a longer time with their talk than he would have expected. Seven thirty was when the blackout was supposed to go into effect, turning the entire open expanse of the college over to the forces of Halloween. In the suddenly deepened darkness, the torches looked brighter and fiercer and much more dangerous. Flames seemed to lick at the air and the black skeletons of trees like the unquenchable fires of Hell. Gregor wanted to get in out of the atmosphere. He wasn't even happy about the idea of having to walk across this benighted lawn on the way to the hall where he would give his speech. He held firmly to his original ambivalence about Halloween: fun was fun, but there was a point beyond which no sane person would go.

He tugged the edge of Tibor's cassock and said, "Come on. Let's go up and see if Markham is back yet. Maybe Bennis is even finished editing my speech."

But Tibor held back. "Krekor," he said slowly, "I think there is something now I should have to tell you."

"Sure. Tell me anything you want."

"Yes, Krekor, I know. I can tell you anything I want. I cannot tell you I killed Donegal Steele, and so upset all your theories. I did not kill Donegal Steele."

"Of course you didn't. Good Lord, Tibor, what made you think I thought you capable of killing anyone?"

Father Tibor Kasparian sighed. "Krekor, Krekor. Before I came to Cavanaugh Street I had another life in another place among another kind of people. In that place, I was not only capable of killing a man, I was guilty of it. In fact, I killed two."

"What?"

But Father Tibor Kasparian was already halfway up the steps to the doors of Constitution House, moving through the flickering light with his spine straight and his head held high up into the wind. The breezes caught at his sparse hair and lifted them in and out of the light. It was so odd to see him like that, not the fumbling little priest with the talent for languages, not a kind of ecclesiastical comic relief, but a grown man who had once lived in hiding in dangerous places among dangerous people and who had managed not only to get out but to make some kind of stand for the things he believed in. Christianity and Constitutional Law, that was Father Tibor Kasparian. Gregor found himself wondering what else was Father Tibor Kasparian, what in God's name could have happened to make what he had just said true.

Out in the middle of the quad, somebody sent up a firecracker. The rocket whistled and burst into a green chrysanthemum in the air. Firecrackers were illegal in the state of Pennsylvania unless licensed and properly supervised, but Gregor didn't think anyone was going to harp on those rules tonight.

Tibor was disappearing through the Constitution House doors, and Gregor decided to follow him.

2

Up in Tibor's apartment, Bennis Hannaford was sitting on the living room floor, the pages of Gregor's new speech spread out before her, her reading glasses sliding down her nose. She had taken the books that had migrated to the coffee table off the coffee table and put them on the floor. She had unearthed a trio of bright red pencils from God only knew where, sharpened them to points, and stuck them into her hair. She had a fourth in her hand. When they came in, she looked up, blinked at them, and sighed. That was when Gregor noticed Lenore, sitting on page six of his magnum opus and looking wise.

"Bastard," Lenore said throatily. "Bastard, bastard, bastard. You're a bastard."

Bennis put the pen she was holding down on page eight. "It's too bad you can't take a bird into court. Lenore and I have been having a very interesting conversation."

"Leonard," Gregor corrected automatically. "Have you seen Markham? We thought he'd be done by now."

"He's in the bedroom making phone calls. I'd be done by now if it wasn't for that damned blackout. I spent ten minutes getting the windows covered up. Oh, by the way. The Merry Pranksters called."

"The Merry Pranksters," Gregor said acidly, "were a drug-soaked band of overgrown adolescents who thought Ken Kesey was God."

Bennis was unperturbed. "Call them what you want. They checked in. Your contact person was someone named Freddie Murchison. That mean anything to you?"

"Yes."

"Good. To me he sounded like a complete flake. At any rate, everything is copacetic. The doors to the hall have been taken care of," Bennis was counting out the points on her thumb, "everybody you want to see will be there, the solderer will be on the shelf under the top of the lectern and you'll have somebody standing by to help you operate it—"

"I can operate a solderer, Bennis."

"You'll burn yourself to a crisp," Bennis said, "you can't operate your own toaster. Hi, Father Tibor. How are you?"

"I am fine, Bennis. How are you? You are not done."

Bennis blew a raspberry. "I don't think it really matters," she said. "He's just going to get up there and say whatever comes into his head anyway. Nobody's going to be able to tell he doesn't know a comma from a banana split."

She bent back over her work, scooting sideways just a little on the floor to give Tibor room to sit beside and behind her on the love seat. Tibor had bent over the speech—which, of course, wasn't a speech at all, but the notes Gregor had made while outlining the situation for Markham in detail this afternoon after he'd realized the importance of the solder. The speech he had intended to give when he first came up here was lying untouched and unread at the bottom of his suitcase. Collation techniques. Requirements for the collection of evidence at the scene of a crime. Guidelines for the federal coordination of state and local police forces. Gregor was sure that all that was much more scholarly, much more in tune with the "spirit of intellectual inquiry" the college brochures were always talking about, than what he was actually going to do. He was also sure that it would have been a good deal less fun.

For the spectators.

Gregor gave Bennis and Tibor a last look—sometimes he thought that what the people on Cavanaugh Street provided him with was an Armenian-American version of a Norman Rockwell world; and that included Bennis, even if she wasn't Armenian-American and even if he knew perfectly well that her life up until the time she had first come to the neighborhood was nothing Rockwell would have recognized—and then went down the short hall to Tibor's bedroom. Markham was indeed in there, sitting on the edge of the neatly made bed, the phone plastered to his right ear and a look of mutiny on his face. When he saw Gregor come in, he pumped his eyebrows frantically and motioned with his left hand to the chair.

"I don't care about your procedure," he said into the phone. "I don't care about the goddamned official lines of goddamned authority in the goddamned state of Pennsylvania, either. All I care about is that you get me five men in storm troopers' outfits and Smokey the Bear hats and you get them for me in *the next half hour*. . . . How the Hell am I supposed to know what's going to happen? Do I sound like the Oracle at Delphi to you? . . . No, no, no. Just get them here. And get me a tech van. And make sure the paramedics have something to counteract lye just in case. . . . No, I do not have a homicidal maniac. . . . No—oh, to Hell with it. Just get here and get here on *time.*"

Markham wrenched the phone away from his ear, held it in the air over the cradle, and slammed it home. Gregor thought the crash must have been loud enough to have been heard all the way to King's Scaffold.

"Staties," Markham said in mock solemnity. "I hate Staties. Have I ever told you I hate Staties?"

"All municipal police officers hate Staties," Gregor said. "With reason, in my experience."

"Yeah, well, in my experience, the goddamned local commander of our goddamned local troop is a neofascist with all the guts of a Puritan spinster. That's sexist. You can tell anybody you want I said. On this campus, they're disappointed when I'm not sexist. Do you want this information we've dug up?"

"I hope you've dug up more than information," Gregor said. Up to that point, he had remained standing, Markham's invitation to the chair notwithstanding. Now he sat down and stretched out his legs. "Let's start with first things first. Did you find any evidence that Steele was kept at Constitution House?"

"That we did. On the roof, if you can believe it. We'd just about given up. There's this little protected shedlike thing up there, I think it used to cover roofing equipment and that kind of thing. You know how that works? In the days before power ladders and things, you'd get your heavy maintenance equipment up when the building was built and leave it there for when you needed it because you needed it a lot. Bad winters. Anyway, it's empty now. The floor of the damned thing was streaked white with the effects of lye. And clawmarks. Oh, Jesus. You were right about that, too. He was alive up there."

"He would have had to be," Gregor said. "Even with popping beers, he wouldn't have swallowed enough of it to kill him outright. They never do. I like the idea of the roof, by the way. I kept thinking it had to be the cellar because that was the only place I could think of where he wouldn't be heard if he thrashed around. And he must have thrashed around."

"Too many people go into the cellar," Markham said. "There's an incinerator down there. What I want to know is how our friend managed to get him up to the roof. The man's enormous."

"He was also probably conscious, in the beginning. Don't forget that. Conscious and in pain and not thinking clearly."

"He wasn't conscious when our friend brought him down."

"Ropes," Gregor said.

Markham nodded. "Yes, Mr. Demarkian, ropes. We did what you suggested. We got ourselves a search warrant before we even started out, back-timed, by the way, just in case—it's amazing what you can do when you were on the high-school football team with the local judge. Anyway, we got the warrant and we searched and we found the ropes, we found the harness thing he was hooked into—there was what looked like lye on that, too—and we found a very interesting article you hadn't managed to anticipate. I'm glad there was something. We found a heavy-duty luggage carrier."

"Very good," Gregor said. "Wheels."

"Right. Get him down to the ground at about two or three o'clock in the morning when nobody else is around, tie him to the wheels, and just pull him up and out of here. Even you or I could have done it with a little work."

"Yes," Gregor said. "Then, once you have him up there, gravity will help. Did you find the body?"

Markham snorted. "Oh, we found it, all right. It was getting it out of there that was the problem. As you can imagine, we had a lot of help."

"How bad was it?"

"You don't want to know. Christ, it was incredible, the kind of mess lye can make, three days down somebody's throat without anything to slow it up. And that isn't all. Our friend didn't just feed the Great Doctor Donegal Steele a lot of lye. Our friend added a little extra no-frills attraction. More lye, all over Steele's face. It ate his skin."

"Dear God."

"It might have been done after death," Markham said. "By the time we got to him, it had eaten through his eyelids and started on his eyes. Dear sweet Lord in heaven. And our friend has been walking around here for the past two or three days, looking perfectly normal as far as anybody can tell." He stood up, stretched, and looked around the room. It was filled with books, as all of Tibor's rooms were always filled with books. Markham paced around among them as if they were so many pieces of furniture.

"You know," he said after a while, "we actually got a piece of luck, with the body. I was going to save it for later and spring it on you, just to have something to look brilliant with."

"What is it?" Gregor asked.

Markham reached into his shirt pocket and pulled out a little solder cylinder, so much like the one Tibor had found on the floor of the dining room, it could have been a clone. He handed it over and said, "It was caught in the collar of Steele's shirt. Just stuck there. I suppose we should have bagged it for evidence. Procedure, like the Staties would say. The prosecutor wouldn't have been allowed to present it anyway."

"Too easy to plant," Gregor agreed. "But we don't have to tell anyone that, David. Not tonight."

"Oh, Hell. Now it's David. Why not? Are you all ready to go on?"

"Of course I am."

Markham shook his head. "I never thought I'd see the day. Me, the world's most pragmatic small-town sheriff, taking part in a scene straight out of Ellery Queen. Gather the suspects! Produce the revelations! The master detective will—"

"David."

Markham's movements had ceased to be random. He was heading for the bedroom door and the hall and the living room, tucking in his shirt as he went. Gregor thought he didn't look all that displaced to be on his way to "a scene straight out of Ellery Queen."

At the bedroom door, Markham stopped, turned around and smiled. "You know that stuff you asked for? The soda and the beer?"

"What about them?" Gregor asked.

"Well, the person you asked to get them for you was Freddie Murchison, and Freddie is Freddie no matter what happens. He got you a can of soda. He also got you a *case* of beer."

Seven

1

From the moment Gregor Demarkian had stepped off the path from the parking lot onto the campus of Independence College proper, he had thought the schedule he'd been given—a lecture to be held at eight o'clock on Halloween night—was self-defeating. The essence of Halloween at Independence was a kind of movable street fair, an all-campus party that dispersed only during the early hours of the morning. Every once in a while, there would be a planned activity of some sort—a snake dance, a parade, a talent contest—but those seemed as superfluous as icing on a marzipan cake. The real action was in the quad, with the milling costumed crowd that swayed and jerked and giggled to the music being blasted through the windows of the dorms. Gregor didn't believe even a few of them would be willing to give that up to hear an overweight, underexercised middle-aged man talk for two hours about "The Technological and Intellectual Investigation of Crime." He wouldn't have had any respect for them if they had. Bennis always said that adolescence was supposed to be about love unconsummated, and early adulthood about sex celebrated. Gregor was a little too old-fashioned to buy into that, but smart enough to see its relevance. He didn't expect more than thirty people to show up at his lecture, at least a dozen of whom he would have arranged to have there himself.

What he did expect, when he walked out of Constitution House with Bennis and Markham and Father Tibor to make his way to the lecture hall, was a torchlit campus full of capering students. He got the torchlights. While he was busy noticing other things, the torches had been fastened to makeshift holders spread out along the edges of the paths and in a circle around the broad expanse of Minuteman Field. The students, however, had disappeared. Between the torches and the blacked-out windows and the emptiness of the quad, Independence College looked like a ghost town, reliably haunted.

"What the Hell is going on here?" Gregor asked the air.

Markham came back, "It's the blackout. No activity until the procession to the bonfire."

"But where is everybody?" Bennis asked.

Markham pointed down the angled path on which they were walking, to a tall oblong building with something that was not quite a steeple and not quite a spire rising from the front of it. It was a building Gregor had noticed before, the first one visible when you came off the parking lot path. He had never been required to go into it, or seen anyone else going into it, and so he hadn't paid it any attention.

"A lot of them are probably in there," Markham said. "That's Concord Hall, the old chapel. It's used as an auditorium now."

"That's where I'm supposed to give my speech?"

"That's where." Markham contemplated the back and side of Concord Hall. "It's got its advantages, considering. They modernized it about ten years ago. Took one whole wall of the auditorium and turned it into windows. The windows look out on King George's Scaffold and Minuteman Field."

"They'll be blacked out," Gregor said.

"They'll be blacked out with a blackout curtain, installed special at the time it was renovated. The bonfire is an annual event around this place." Markham smiled thinly. "All we have to do is haul the curtain up and there we are."

"Where will we be?" Gregor asked. Nobody answered him. There was something about all this silence that was contagious. He pressed on, ahead of the others, until he got to the back door of the hall. It was propped open, and when he got to it he saw that it was guarded, too—by Freddie Murchison, standing just inside it in the dark. Freddie was, as usual, dressed up as Dracula, with a mouth full of fangs. If his face hadn't been so naturally sappy-silly round and childish, he would have been frightening. Gregor pushed past him, made way for the others and said, "Well?"

"Well," Freddie told him, "we couldn't lock the front doors because of the fire regulations, but we've got guys strung out all along the front hall, the whole football team in fact. They're not much of a football team, but they ought to be all right."

"I'm sure they'll be fine," Gregor said. "What about our friends?"

"Take a look for yourself."

Freddie was leering at Bennis, who had declined to come in costume but had put on one of her best black silk shirts. She had a lot of them, all so fine they might as well have been transparent, and she always wore them with the top two buttons undone. Gregor pushed past them both and went up the small flight of stairs that was the only other way to go than out. The flight led to a fire door that led to a short hall that led to another fire door. Gregor pushed this open and stuck his head through.

The "auditorium" was really the entire second floor of the old church, fitted out now with curving rows of cushioned chairs like a movie theater, its east wall an unbroken curtain of black cloth. The room itself was brightly lit and packed full, mostly of students in varying degrees of self-conscious absurdity. Gregor saw a couple made up as Barbie and Ken, a boy dressed up as a beach ball, an entire row of girls dressed up as pumpkins. He scanned the room until he picked out the faces he was looking for, and the costumes: Dr. Ken Crockett and Dr. Alice Elkinson sitting side by side on the third row center aisle; Dr. Katherine Branch, red hair floating in the air like liquid flame, sitting by herself and looking furious in the middle of the front row; Jack Carroll and Chessey Flint, in costume but easily identifiable, surrounded by friends in the back toward the left. When Jack saw Gregor he nodded slightly, reached down into his seat, and came up with his bat hood mask. Then he pulled it over his head.

"Look," Tibor said from somewhere behind Gregor.

"Look what Freddie kept for us." He pushed in on Gregor's left side and held out his hand. Perched there, pecking at a fine dust of honey-sticky crumbs, was Lenore.

"Krekor?" Tibor said.

Gregor was capable of making up his mind in an instant. Sometimes he even wanted to. "Have you got any more of whatever you're feeding it?" he asked Tibor. "Can you put some of that stuff on my hand?"

Tibor reached into the pocket of his cassock, came up with a mangled piece of Lida Arkmanian's honey cake, and held it out. Lenore followed it, pecking as she went.

"Usually they sleep in the nighttime, I think," Tibor said. "But this is a good bird, Krekor. This is a bird who knows how to be an ally."

In Gregor's opinion, this was a bird who knew how to eat, but that was irrelevant. He had just made up his mind about something else. Back at the apartment, he and Markham and Bennis and Tibor had gone over and over the choreography of this scene. First Tibor would introduce him to the Dean, who was waiting patiently in the front row to finally be allowed to participate in this event. Then the Dean would introduce Gregor, reading from a vita supplied by Tibor and containing Gregor didn't want to know what. Then—

But it was all too complicated and it would take too long. Gregor had always been a man more comfortable with formality than chaos, but there was a limit. He smeared his own left hand with honey and cake and watched while Lenore climbed onto it. Then he stepped out onto the stage and crossed to the lectern. Behind him, Tibor was scrambling frantically to catch up. He was not quick enough and he didn't make it. On Gregor's hand, Lenore pecked, hopped, pecked again, and then cawed out "Bastard, bastard, bastard" in a chillingly venomous voice that carried to the back of the hall.

On the floor behind the lectern there was a can of Belleville Lemon and Lime soda and Freddie Murchison's case of Belleville beer. Gregor tapped the mike on the lectern's surface and was relieved to find it live and loud.

By then, Tibor had caught up with him and begun hissing in his ear.

"Krekor," he said, "Krekor, what are you doing? I'm supposed to speak first. You're supposed to meet the Dean."

Because Gregor had never met the Dean, he didn't know which one of the faces in the front row belonged to him, and he thought that was just as well. He leaned into the mike and said, "Ladies and gentlemen, I was supposed to come here tonight and tell you how the Federal Bureau of Investigation, of which I was a part for many years, goes about the tracking and the capture of serial killers. I have decided to talk instead about a topic much more interesting to me at the moment, and probably much more interesting to you. I have decided to discuss the maiming and mutilation of a secretary in this college's Interdisciplinary Program in the American Idea, Miss Maryanne Veer—and the murder of a professor in that same department, Dr. Donegal Steele."

2

Gregor had heard enough about hushed silences in his day, and read enough about them, so that he shouldn't have been surprised to be presented with one. The hall had gone dead quiet and paralytically still. The only person in the place who was even fidgeting was Tibor, standing right behind him. A man in the center of the front row had gone as white as chalk. Gregor assumed he was the dean. He felt sorry for the man even as he turned away to ignore him.

At the last minute, his eyes swept the room, searching for his suspects, but if he had been looking for some special reaction, he would have been disappointed. They were all still in their seats and impassive. They might have been numb. He moved closer to the lectern and leaned out over the crowd.

"Yesterday afternoon," he said, "we were presented here with a very interesting problem, in fact an impossible problem. Not only had a woman, Miss Maryanne Veer, with very few personal ties to the college and only limited professional ones, been fed enough lye to put her in the hospital for several weeks and possibly to cripple her for life, but she had been fed it in full view of the lunch crowd in a packed dining hall, while she was standing up, while she was holding a cafeteria tray on which was nothing but a cup of strong tea. Now I don't know what you people out there know about lye, so I will tell you something about it. The technical name for it is sodium hydroxide, and it always fizzes when it comes in contact with water. Our first thought—mine, and later that of the police—was that what we were looking at was a Tylenol-poisoning type of attack. At first glance, it looked as if we had someone, a cafeteria worker or a student or a faculty member, intent on causing havoc to whoever might get in his line of fire. Given that assumption, first I, and later David Markham and his men, began to look for what the lye might have been in. It could not have been in Miss Veer's tea, because if it had been the tea would have been fizzing, and it was highly unlikely that she would have drunk it. Even if she hadn't expected to be poisoned, she would have, as any of us would have, been suspicious about what she was being fed. Her natural reaction would have been to dump out that cup of tea and pour herself a new one. So we went looking, at that point, for what else she might have had and what else she might have eaten—someone suggested to me over the course of this investigation a peanut butter sandwich. That would have been good. But there was no peanut butter sandwich. In fact, there was nothing of any kind. Everyone we asked told us the same thing: Miss Maryanne Veer had come through that cafeteria line with a cup of tea and only a cup of tea on her tray. We searched the floor for food that might have gone unnoticed and been dropped when Miss Veer fell. Nothing. We searched the tables. Nothing. We searched the cafeteria line. Nothing. We were finally forced to admit to ourselves what seemed so unlikely to be true: that someone had attacked Miss Veer in particular for some personal reason, and then taken away, or disposed of, whatever food the lye had been in.

"Now we had two new problems, equally disturbing. In the first place, although the lab reports haven't come in

yet, it was clear that whatever Miss Veer had eaten that
contained lye was unlikely to have been large and only
theoretically likely to have been solid food at all. Immediately after she fell, I and a number of people in the crowd
applied the antidote for her condition, namely milk forced
into her mouth and down her throat. I saw no residues of
solid food in her teeth or gums. Then there was the larger
problem: Who would want to hurt Miss Maryanne Veer and
why? I say hurt and not kill, because there is something you
must understand about lye. People do die from being
poisoned by it, but I have never yet heard of a murderer
who managed to bring such a thing off deliberately. It is
almost impossible for someone to swallow enough lye to kill
them immediately. Lye burns—actually, it dissolves human
flesh on contact. People have been known to die by
swallowing small amounts of lye, thinking they've cured the
problem with milk or some other agent, and three or four
days or a week later being presented with a perforated
stomach lining that has finally given out in its attempts to
counteract the alkali. With a dose of the strength administered to Miss Veer, however, and with that dose administered in full view of a hundred or so people, the attacker
would have had to realize that it would have been very
unlikely for Miss Veer to die. So we had someone here who
did not care if Miss Veer lived or not. That could not have
been the point.

"But what was the point? The more we looked into
Miss Veer's life, the less likely it was that there was one, at
least of the kind we are used to in murder investigations.
Miss Veer lived with a woman friend of many years
standing, who was not on campus at the time. She did her
work in her department without causing any obvious rancor
among the faculty and students she worked with. We heard
no underground rumbles of unfairness or dislike. In fact,
the only person on campus who seemed to have any
antipathy to Miss Veer at all was a man I had never met but
heard much about, Dr. Donegal Steele.

"At one point in this investigation, someone suggested
to me that it was Dr. Steele who had attacked Miss Veer,
even though he had not been seen in the dining room at the

time and was a figure unlikely to go unnoticed by faculty or
students. I dismissed this suggestion out of hand, considering where it came from, but it got me thinking. Because
you see, there is one way to commit murder successfully
with lye, although I'd never seen or heard of it done. If you
can get enough of the stuff down your victim's throat and
then keep him away from any and all medical attention for
at least three days, he will die. It's a nasty way to kill a man,
but it could be done. Starting from there, I realized I had
two very interesting pieces of information. In the first
place, no one had laid eyes on Dr. Donegal Steele since
sometime late on the night of the twenty-eighth of October.
In the second place, what Miss Maryanne Veer had been
doing on the morning of the day she was attacked was
worrying about Dr. Steele's disappearance, making up her
mind to call the police and report him missing—and telling
at least one person and possibly more about her decision.

"Now, considering Dr. Donegal Steele as a victim was
much more rewarding than considering Miss Maryanne
Veer. In the first place, he was from all accounts a
personally objectionable man. He made passes at women
and refused to take no for an answer. When he got no, he
got nasty—not physically violent, but slanderous. He tried
for a girl named Chessey Flint and failed. In the wake of
that failure, he told everyone he could that he had suc-
ceeded, causing Miss Flint a great deal of anguish and
putting her boyfriend, Mr. Jack Carroll, into an entirely
untenable position."

Gregor looked up at Jack, who had begun to glower
and squirm in his seat. Beside him, Chessey was beginning
to look panicked, as if she feared an explosion. Gregor
didn't blame her. He had always found Jack Carroll a very
controlled young man, but he was convinced that under
that control was enough explosiveness to satisfy anybody.

Gregor looked back at his notes and cleared his throat.
"In the second place," he said, "Dr. Steele was a famous
man with a book on the best-seller list and more money
than he knew what to do with, hired away from his old
university by the administration of this college for what was
rumored to be a great deal of money and a solid bank of

promises. I haven't talked to the administration about any
of this, but I tend to agree with the people I've talked to. It
was perfectly rational for the faculty members of the
Interdisciplinary Program on the American Idea to assume
that Dr. Steele had been promised the Chairmanship. It
was hard to think of any other reason why he would agree
to come to Belleville, Pennsylvania, no matter how illustrious the Program's reputation might be. From what I've
heard of the man, it wasn't the kind of position he could
expect to get on any campus where he'd spent a consider-
able amount of time. He was too abrasive.

"Now, even after I'd figured this out, I was still left
with two problems. Unlike Mr. Markham here behind me,
I didn't count as one of those problems that Dr. Steele's
body had not been found. I didn't think he was necessarily
a body yet. What I did count as problems were the
following. First, we did not know how the lye had been
administered to Maryanne Veer. Second, that we had to
account for this."

Gregor held up one of the little solder cylinders, he
really had no idea which one. He wasn't sure it mattered.

"We found this," he said, "on the floor under the
cafeteria line after Miss Veer had been taken to the
hospital. We found other things, too, but for the moment
they don't matter. The problem with this was that we had
no idea what it was or what it was for, and, therefore, we
had to explain it. It was the only unnecessary and inexpli-
cable thing found anywhere near the scene of the crime.
This cylinder is made out of solder. There are facilities for
soldering in the shed at the edge of the parking lot behind
King's Scaffold. Yesterday, I had Mr. Jack Carroll take me
up there and reproduce one of these. He not only did it, in
the process of doing it he created a mess of solder shards
very much like the one he had found in the shed on the
morning after the last time he had seen Dr. Steele, and
very much like the one we found that night, after Maryanne
Veer had been attacked. My assumption was that the
cylinder had been made in the shed, but I still didn't know
why, or what for.

"Being brought to that impasse, I concentrated instead

on motive. I considered first whose lives could be ruined, or might even be about to be ruined, by Dr. Steele's presence on this campus. I started with Miss Chessey Flint, whose reputation was certainly in a shambles. I went to Mr. Jack Carroll, who loves Miss Flint and wants desperately to protect her. Then I went to the faculty, and I found a curious thing. Whenever I asked anyone who would be Head of the Program if Donegal Steele were not, I was told Dr. Ken Crockett—a good candidate for this murder and this attack, because he was strong, because he was frequently in a place, the Climbing Club cabin, where I was told lye was kept, and because he was known to work on his car in the shed where the cylinder must have been made."

Gregor looked out at Ken Crockett and noticed that, although Crockett was as white as he had been since he first came to the hall, he had now begun to relax. The stiffness of his shoulders had begun to melt. Gregor looked away.

"According to some people," he continued, "Dr. Crockett might even have a secret he was afraid Dr. Steele might expose—but I didn't like that secret. I hadn't been able to verify it. I still haven't been able to. And it was the kind of thing that could possibly be—worked out. If it was true at all. No, what began to dawn on me was what people said when they hadn't been asked directly about who would be the next Head of the Program if not for Donegal Steele. The official version was one thing. The collective gut instinct was another. And here, I saw, I had a person with a much better motive, a person in a much better—or worse—position, a person far more easily ruined by Dr. Donegal Steele. This was also a person who worked on her car and did it well. This was also a person who had been seen heading in the direction of the parking lot in the hour or so before Miss Maryanne Veer was attacked. This was Dr. Alice Emerson Elkinson."

Dr. Elkinson was sitting in the seat one in from the aisle, blocked off from escape by Dr. Crockett sitting beside her. Dr. Crockett, Gregor noticed, had gone into a kind of waking paralysis. All his muscles that had begun to relax only a few moments before had stiffened into mock rigor. Dr. Elkinson was far more poised. She glanced to her right, to her left, at her hands and up. Then she said, "Are you

accusing me of something, Mr. Demarkian? Of a murder
that never even happened?"

Her voice was strong and soprano-clear, but Gregor
ignored it. He reached under the lectern for the can of
Belleville Lemon and Lime soda and brought it up. Then
he nodded to Freddie Murchison, waiting in the wings.

"Let me show you," he said, "how Miss Maryanne
Veer was poisoned with lye, when there wasn't any other
food on her plate but tea."

There was an ice pick under the lectern, too, just as he
had asked. He picked it up, turned the can on its side, and
punched a hole in the seam. A hiss came up he thought he
was probably the only one to hear. He widened the hole a
little, shook some of the soda out onto the floor—he had to
do it over and over again to get enough out; even with a
reasonably wide hole the physics of the process was
difficult—and then reached for the small bag of lye and
poured some in to fill up the space left by the missing
liquid.

"Miss Veer didn't have a can of this on her tray," he
said, "but you did, Dr. Elkinson. Now we have to wait a
little while here, to let the lye fizz and pop its way to
reasonable peace. It'll never calm down completely, but it
doesn't have to. This is a carbonated soda. It's supposed to
fizz. Mr. Murchison?"

Freddie Murchison came forward, took the can, and
picked up the soldering gun.

"Mr. Murchison is going to make a solder plug," he
said. "To anyone not looking for a trick, the can, when he is
finished with it, will look to all intents and purposes
normal, and as if it has never been opened. So will a can of
Belleville's local brand of beer, which is what people on this
campus use when they commit an alcoholic atrocity called
popping. That was what Dr. Steele was on his way to do
when he ran into Jack Carroll on the twenty-eighth. When
someone pops beers, the beer goes down his throat in force
and at a tremendous pace. That would have gotten quite a
bit of lye into Donegal Steele before he'd have had a chance
to react. As for Miss Maryanne Veer, I think what you

intended to do was to hand her that doctored can of soda either sometime at lunch or sometime after it. You knew it was what she liked. Everybody did. You fell into a little luck. She was so upset, she didn't pick up her usual lunch. You stood there beside her right next to the cash register, opened the doctored soda, and handed it to her. When you both got past the cash register and she took a drink, as she started to drop it and the tray and everything else, *you took it back*."

"Why?" Alice Elkinson burst out. "For God's sake, why? Just to end up Head of Program in a small college in Pennsylvania? Whatever for?"

"Just to end up not professionally dead," Gregor said gently. "What Donegal Steele was threatening to do to you was what he had already done to Chessey Flint—to make you look like a tramp, to make you look ridiculous. He kept coming to your apartment. That's why the lye was there in the first place, when Dr. Branch found it. Dr. Steele was going to bring it out to the Climbing Cabin, but he stopped by your place first and he left it there, to give himself an excuse to come back. My guess is that he gave you the same kind of ultimatum he gave Chessey, one you had no intention of buckling under—but if you didn't, the consequences would have been much worse than anything Chessey could have imagined. After all, Chessey's only concern was Jack Carroll, and Jack believed her. Yours was the entire academic community, because you knew that one thing mattered if you were going to have the career you'd spent so much time working for and yet be a woman. You could not afford to be made to look like what he would make you look like. It would have destroyed any claim you had to be a serious scholar, a serious intellect, a woman on the way up and not just another fool sleeping her way into the good graces of her Chairman."

"Donegal Steele is not dead," Alice Elkinson said, but as she said it she turned, backward, toward the blackout curtains. When she turned all the way around she stopped. The blackout curtains were supposed to be closed, but they weren't. Gregor had watched over Alice Elkinson's head while two of Freddie's minions pulled them up, probably prompted by Markham through Freddie himself. Now the view was open to Minuteman Field and King's Scaffold, the huge pile of logs against the outcrop lit by the torches around the field's rim. On top of it all, the effigy sat resplendent in flounces and velvet, a mad old king with a pumpkin for a head.

"Dr. Elkinson," Gregor said, even more gently this time, "it's gone. The body's gone. We took it out of there while you were chasing around looking for a wounded Chessey Flint who was back in her dormitory room safe and sound. The biggest mistake you made was taking it out there at three o'clock this morning, dressed up as a bat."

"It's Jack Carroll who dresses up as a bat," Alice Elkinson said in a strangled voice.

"I know," Gregor said, "but at three o'clock this morning, Jack Carroll was in a motel room in Elgin, Maryland, having just married Miss Chessey Flint."

Alice Elkinson whipped her head back to the front, back to Gregor, and now her eyes were blazing.

"I fed him lye and I put him up on that roof and I would do it again tomorrow if you damn well want to know. That flaming bastard was the prize. He waltzed right in here on nothing but a meretricious piece of right-wing crap and thought he was going to take over. He hadn't done half the work I'd done and he didn't think he had to. He could just manipulate the images. That's what he always said. All you had to do was know how to manipulate the images. Well, after I fed him that beer, I manipulated the images, all right. I went up there with a glass of lye in water and I poured it all over that bastard's face."

Ken Crockett was clutching her arm. Alice shook him off.

"I took him right up onto the roof on Constitution House and put him in that lean-to thing," she said, "and it worked. I left a piece of Jack's suit on the floor next to the cash register and you didn't even find it—"

"We found it," Gregor said, "we didn't believe it."

"Nobody ever believes anything except what isn't true," Alice Elkinson said. "That's the problem with places like this."

On Gregor's left hand, Lenore had finished with the honey cake crumbs and become restless. The bird took off and began to circle in the brightly lit room, churning around and around like it was caught in a cyclone.

"Bastard," it cawed out in that horrible voice. "Bastard, bastard, bastard."

Epilogue

Quoth the raven,
Nevermore—

—E. A. Poe

There was more movement on King's Scaffold and
Minuteman Field that night than there had been on
Halloween at Independence College for many years. When
Dr. Alice Elkinson had gone out at three o'clock in the
morning to exchange the effigy of George III for the body of
Dr. Donegal Steele, she had put her best effort into the
body's concealment. She had scattered the straw down the
waterfall of logs that seemed to cascade from the ridge
down the face of the outcrop. She had exchanged Steele's
clothes for the costume from the drama department and
covered his head with the King's jack-o'-lantern skull. The
police had confiscated all of it. At one point, they had even
threatened to confiscate the bonfire itself. Steele's own
clothes had to be somewhere. In all likelihood, they were
down there among the wood somewhere, thrust out of
sight. At any other time and in any other place, the area
would have been roped off and no one allowed near it until
it had been thoroughly searched.

Gregor Demarkian's position was that the clothes
could hardly matter. The woman had confessed in full view
of two or three hundred people—considering the present
rules of evidence, that could hardly matter, either—and
most of what the prosecution would need to complete their
case could be had from the one person on campus least
likely to protect their murderer: Katherine Branch. Gregor
kept saying it, over and over again. The key to making the
lawyers happy was Katherine Branch. In the end, David
Markham gave in. He didn't want to be the cause of the first
bonfireless Halloween at Independence College in more

than two hundred years, any more than Jack Carroll and
Freddie Murchison and their friends wanted to graduate
with the first class that had not managed to set off a bigger
and better conflagration than the class before it. David
Markham took the list Gregor had written out for him while
he was arresting Alice Elkinson, squinted down at the thick
numbered lines scrawled across a piece of paper Freddie
had torn out of someone's notebook, and scowled. Then he
rounded up the few uniformed men he had left after Alice
Elkinson had been driven off in the direction of the
Belleville jail and got to work. By then, Ken Crockett was
gone, too, chasing the hiccuping sirens and glowing red
taillights of the police cars. Gregor thought Ken Crockett
might be doing what he did best, and what had made
Gregor dislike him so instinctively the first time they met:
taking on a load of guilt and responsibility for something
he'd had no control of at all. In Gregor's mind, the man had
no idea who he was or what he was or what he felt. He
simply made decisions for himself and carried through,
whether or not he was making any sense. His present
decision seemed to be that he was supposed to be in love
with Alice Elkinson, and that his failure to leap to her
defense in the auditorium was the worst kind of cardinal
sin. Now he was chasing around the countryside, trying to
think of some way to atone for it, trying to hurt himself
enough to delude himself into believing he had been
punished.

In the meantime, Gregor and Tibor and Bennis sat
comfortably in the smaller common room on the first floor
of Lexington House, drinking food-colored, brightly orange
mimosas in black plastic glasses. That was what people did
at Independence College while waiting for the bonfire
procession at midnight. They had sprawling, chaotic parties
in their dorms, carefully screened from the silent emptiness
of the quad by all that blackout paper. In Lexington House
the party consisted of dorm sisters in pumpkin costumes
mimosas ladled like punch into hollowed-out pumpkins
(alcoholic to the right, soft to the left), and Lou Reed on a
stereo system loud and sophisticated enough to have served

at a Bruce Springsteen concert. The Lou Reed had been
Bennis Hannaford's idea.

"And hard to find it was, too," Bennis said, coming
back with another full glass of the mimosa version on the
right. "I mean, for God's sake, you'd think any college
student worth the name would at least have a copy of 'Walk
on the Wild Side.' " She sat down in the chair she had
vacated only a few moments before, looked up at Evie
Westerman sitting on the arm, and sighed. Evie had
attached herself to Bennis just after the scene in the
auditorium broke up and had been hanging on, fascinated,
ever since. "Evie," Bennis said, "do you think you could get
just drunk enough to sort of glaze out a little? Every time I
look at you, I think you've got X-ray vision."

"How did you get your hair like that?" Evie asked her.
'Is there a name for that kind of treatment?"

Bennis shook her head. "Evie, my hair is like this
because I was born with my hair like this. Everybody in my
family has hair like this. However, if you must, you can get
the same effect with a cloud crimp at Sassoon's. And a dye
job. Now will you *please*—"

"What I don't understand," Jack Carroll said from his
place stretched out on the floor at Gregor's feet. Chessey
was down there with him, sitting cross-legged on the carpet
near his legs. He had one hand around her ankle. "What
really bothers me is, why Alice Elkinson? I mean, your
whole explanation seemed to center on motive—"

"Not at all," Gregor said. "My whole analysis was
grounded on one incontrovertible point. Miss Veer decided
to call the police about Steele's disappearance late on the
morning of the thirtieth. Before that, no one had any reason
to attack her. Therefore, whoever did attack her had to be
someone who had the time to get to the shed and make that
plug before meeting Miss Veer in the dining room. That
couldn't have been Katherine Branch, because Bennis saw
her in the foyer outside the cafeteria when we came in for
lunch. Granted, those plugs are much easier to make when
you have the can to work them into, instead of doing them
blind the way we did last night. Still, they're not that easy
to make. Then there was Dr. Crockett. In the first place, he

was all the way over on Hillman's Rock just before noon. He'd been there all day. He might still have had time to get down, all the way over to the shed and back, except that he was sitting at a table with me a good fifteen minutes before Miss Veer fell. He wouldn't have had time for that."

"So that left Dr. Elkinson," Chessey Flint said.

"Or the two of you," Gregor said blandly, "but there was that bat up on the Scaffold. I didn't catch on when I saw it—her. It didn't hit me right then what she was doing. But I did know it didn't look like Jack, and that it was suspicious. And later, of course, I talked to Freddie Murchison and figured out where the two of you must have gone—"

"The three of us," Evie said morosely. "I'm never going to do anything like that again. Have you any idea what it's like, spending the night alone in a motel room while the people next door make the walls shake?"

"*Evie.*" Chessey was appalled.

"Back to Dr. Elkinson," Gregor told them. "If you think about it for a minute, you'll see it was very odd. Everybody was always wondering what Donegal Steele was doing at Independence College. His degrees. His book. His reputation. Nobody ever wondered what Alice Elkinson was doing at Independence College. But think about it. She got her degree from Berkeley. She got tenure here so fast and so young, I had to assume that her publications and her professional reputation were exceptional. I don't care what kind of reputation the Program has. Bennis was right. People like that don't end up at places like this. They go to big-name universities."

"Unless they're in a hurry," Bennis said. "That's what it was, wasn't it? Youngest tenured faculty member. Youngest Head of Program. And then—"

"Up and out," Gregor agreed. "And Donegal Steele. The significant point about Donegal Steele wasn't how awful his behavior was. It was that he'd told lies about Ms. Flint—Mrs. Carroll?—*and been believed.* He was a convincing man. He really could have ruined her."

"Well, this will ruin her," Evie said. "What was all that stuff about Dr. Branch? When Markham left Concord Hall he was saying her name over and over again and cursing under his breath."

Gregor laughed. "Oh, that. Well, this morning Dr. Branch talked to David Markham and me at breakfast. She had a lot of information. The only way she could have gotten it was by doing a lot of snooping on her own, which I wouldn't put past her. Your Dr. Branch, I'm afraid, is addicted to various forms of nonmonetary blackmail. There are a couple of buckets of lye missing, and a bat suit. My guess is that Dr. Crockett tried to destroy the bat suit to protect Dr. Elkinson, but my guess is also that he wouldn't have bothered if Dr. Branch hadn't seen it first. As to the lye—" Gregor shrugged. "Either Katherine Branch moved it herself to put the fear of God into Alice Elkinson, or Dr. Crockett moved it after he found out Dr. Branch knew it was there. Markham will work it out. I've told him where to look."

"And Katherine Branch will testify," Bennis said. "Take a look at it, everybody. This is Gregor Demarkian's Great and Inscrutable Detective Act. It makes me nuts."

"What about that sweater," Evie Westerman asked, "is it one hundred percent cashmere, or do you go for Lycra in the neck?"

Out in the foyer, a grandfather clock pealed the first of its four bongs to announce the time as quarter to twelve. A second later, all the pendulum clocks on campus seemed to start in at once and the carillon began to toll. Jack Carroll stood up, pulled his hood out of his belt, and put it on. Chessey stood up after him, searching vaguely for her mask.

"Gotta go," Jack said. "Last real frivolity before law school."

"Law school," Chessey breathed reverently.

Evie Westerman blew a raspberry.

Gregor got up, held a hand out to help Tibor to his feet, and followed the students into the Lexington House foyer. Just as they got there, somebody doused the lights.

"Here we go," Bennis said from somewhere behind them. "I've finally gotten rid of Evie. She has to march."

2

In the quad, there were now so many torches the college looked on fire. Torches and people, costumes and silence: it was eerie to watch, that stream of heads and fire moving east toward the Scaffold. Gregor found himself wondering what it had been like the first time, and sure it had been nothing like this. That would have been a rite of politics. This was a celebration of mortality and sex. Gregor moved Tibor and himself into the crowd, keeping his hand on the priest's shoulder, watching for signs of Jack Carroll's tall, broad figure at the front. Someone had given Jack a torch and he was holding it higher than all the others, waving it in the air like an exploding firework he had mysteriously managed to bring under control.

They moved across the quad and then around the sides of Concord Hall and out onto Minuteman Field. The air was thick with the smell of kerosene and sharp cold with the lateness of the year. Freddie and his friends had managed to replace the effigy in time. In the light from the moving torches, it looked not only more outrageous than the first had been, but more outrageous than the disguised body of Donegal Steele had been. The new costume from the drama department was scarlet red and plush. The new jack-o'-lantern head was a monstrous mutant twice the size of the old.

Gregor stopped at the edge of the field and let the students behind him surge past. He still had his hand on Tibor's shoulder and intended to keep it there. Tibor had been much too quiet, and he had been looking depressed.

"What is it?" he said, while the rest of the crowd began to press toward the mountain of logs. "Are you worrying about all that stuff you told me this evening?"

Father Tibor Kasparian sighed. "No, Krekor. It is something else I have to tell you now. Something closer to home."

"What is it?"

Tibor scuffled his feet in the dirt. "Well, Krekor, do

you remember, when we first went into Lexington House, I disappeared for a while?"

"Of course I do. I thought you went to the bathroom."

"Well, yes, Krekor. I did that, too. I went to the bathroom. But mostly what I did was to call Lida. To make sure everything was all right."

"And?"

"And everything was not all right, Krekor. They have had a robbery. They have had a man in a suit like the Terminator who came in and tried to take Lida's diamond necklace and her engagement ring."

"Those *doors*," Gregor exploded. He grabbed Tibor by both shoulders and turned the little priest around to face him. It didn't do much good. The torches were fine for illuminating the big picture, the bonfire pile and the effigy and the craggy face of the outcrop. They did more to hide Tibor's face than to reveal it. And then Gregor caught it, the only significant word, the truly insane thing. "What do you mean *tried*," he demanded. "Tried?"

Tibor took a deep breath. "Well, Krekor, you see, he did not get away with it. Lida hit him. With Bobby Costikian's magic Jedi sword."

"With—"

"And then when he was down, old George Tekemanian jumped on his chest and kicked him in the—in the—"

"Oh, dear sweet Lord Jesus," Gregor said. "What are those two, crazy? They could have been killed."

"No, Krekor, they could not have been killed. The man was keeping his gun in his pocket. Donna Moradanyan got it after George—"

"*Tibor.*"

"It is all right, Krekor. Lida let me talk to the policeman who came when they called. The man was being taken away and everything was calm again. Lida said the children were all very excited and impressed."

Very excited and impressed. Gregor could just imagine it. In fact, that was the problem. He could imagine it exactly. Lida Arkmanian. Bobby Costikian's magic Jedi sword. He gripped Tibor's shoulders more tightly and started to say what he should have said all the way back on

Cavanaugh Street, to berate and explain, to finally make his point—but he didn't have the chance. There was a shout from the front of the crowd. When Gregor looked up, he saw Jack Carroll in full bat regalia in a cleared space right in front of the log mountain. He looked so tall, he must have been standing on something, but Gregor couldn't see what. The smell of kerosene was now almost overpowering. Jack lifted his torch, swung it around and around his head, and threw it at the wood.

For a second, it seemed like nothing had happened, the maneuver had not worked. Then a thin stream of flame shot up, and another, and another. Torches began to fly through the air, arcing and landing like rockets. It took no time at all for critical mass to be reached and the whole thing to explode.

It wasn't really an explosion, of course. It was only light and heat, so much light and heat, roaring at the sky. Above their heads, Lenore, who had been circling close to the jack-o'-lantern, widened her arc. His, Gregor corrected himself mentally, and then gave it up.

The bonfire was beautiful.

It could have been a star.

It could have been the sun.

"Charming...Ms. Brown writes with wise, disarming wit." --
The New York Times Book Review

WISH YOU WERE HERE

A Mrs. Murphy Mystery
by Rita Mae Brown
and Sneaky Pie Brown

Small towns are like families: Everyone lives very close
together ...and everyone keeps secrets. Crozet, Virginia is
a typical small town -- until its secrets explode into murder.

Crozet's thirty-something postmistress, Mary Minor
"Harry" Haristeen, has a tiger cat (Mrs. Murphy) and a
Welsh corgi (Tee Tucker), a pending divorce, and a bad
habit of reading postcards not addressed to her. When
Crozet's citizens start turning up murdered, Harry remem-
bers that each received a card with a tombstone on the
front and the message "Wish you were here" on the back.

Intent on protecting their human friend, Mrs. Murphy and
Tucker begin to scent out clues. Meanwhile, Harry is
conducting her own investigation, unaware her pets are
one step ahead of her. If only Mrs. Murphy could alert her
somehow, Harry could uncover the culprit before another
murder occurs -- and before Harry finds herself on the
killer's mailing list.

On sale soon wherever Bantam Crime Line Books
are sold.

AN345 -- 10/91

At Annie Laurance's Death on Demand bookstore,
murder is often more than just a reading experience and
the mysteries are just leaping off the shelves.

CAROLYN HART

Carolyn Hart's Annie and Max are two of mystery readers'
best loved characters and in these award-winning books
you'll join them on their adventures of mystery, danger and
several volumes of murder most foul.